Montana summer

Montana summer

a novel

JEANETTE MILLER

Covenant Communications, Inc.

Cover photography by McKenzie Deakins

For photographer information please visit www.photographybymckenzie.com

Published by Covenant Communications, Inc.
American Fork, Utah

Printed in the United States of America
First Printing: July 2011

16 15 14 13 12 11 10 9 8 7 6 5 4 3 2 1

ISBN-13: 978-1-59811-909-1

To Mike,
who is continually dumbfounded by my computer ignorance
and rescues me anyway. It could never have happened without you.

Jeanette Miller extends grateful acknowledgment to…

My parents, Larry and Janine Hutchinson,
for their love and encouragement.
Mom, thank you for all your suggestions
and for joining me on my journey to experience Montana.

My husband, Michael,
for his love and support.
Someday I will learn how to back up a document on my own.

My children Jacob, Kacey, Adam, Haylee, Spencer, and Emma,
for enduring a mom at the computer far too often.

Sally Wyne,
for editing my manuscript and
providing valuable comments and suggestions.

Pauliina Cox,
for endless support, chocolate desserts, and our weekly "girls night out." Your friendship means everything to me.

Kathleen Rugg,
for reading the embryonic manuscript years ago
and still being enthusiastic. Thank you for being a true friend.

My grandmothers, Bernice Hutchinson and Claris Cronkhite,
for blessing me with treasured summer memories.

Thank you, Grandpa and Grandma Cronkhite,
for letting me borrow the idyllic setting of your home.

My mother- and father-in-law,
for venturing with my family to Bozeman,
when you could have stayed longer in Yellowstone, just for me.

My skilled rescuers at Montana Whitewater Raft Company.

My long-lost roommate Heidi, who was my inspiration for Shelby's hair.

Dorothy Keddington, whose novels started it all.

Prologue

Underneath her serene façade, that blasted girl has a heart of ice. She's got the tongue of a viper and the cunning of a weasel . . . Cameron stopped his racing thoughts and chuckled at the beastly image he'd conjured up to describe his ex-fiancée. He was making her sound pretty awful. But then again, she *had* been awful. How on earth could he ever have been attracted to her in the first place?

Blessing the comforts of his new fly-fishing waders, he adjusted his footing on the slippery rocks of Montana's icy Gallatin River. The smell of pine and clean mountain air filled his lungs. Three rhythmic casts whipped overhead, then his well-used salmon fly landed softly on the water's surface, just beyond a riffle near a weed bed. With his upper torso wrapped in the chill of dawn air and his lower half immersed in cold rushing currents, Cameron Thompson brooded over the current havoc in his life created by one miserable female.

Never again! As long as he had breath, he would never fall prey to the unscrupulous schemes of a woman. There probably wasn't a female on earth he would want anything to do with. All the decent ones had been taken, and the rest of the women he knew were either as vain as peacocks or as mean as grizzly bears. Come to think of it, he'd seen grizzlies in the wild that were teddy bears compared to his ex-fiancée. Her claws had sunk deep, and she had dragged him mercilessly into her deceitful trap.

An almost-imperceptible bobble at the end of Cameron's line instantly transported him from pessimism to delight. He set the hook, securing a fat, shimmering rainbow trout. The fish writhed in furious protest, flipping about and slapping the water with a flash of fins before being scooped up by the triumphant swoosh of his net. Now this was living! No cares, no worries. Just the big sky above and glorious fly-fishing below. And he intended to keep things exactly like this for a very long time.

Chapter 1

It had happened! It was almost too good to be true. But the diamond on Shelby Hamlin's ring finger winked repeatedly, confirming that she was engaged. For many girls on campus, this was the crowning glory of their BYU experience. But to Shelby, getting married meant so much more that her head was spinning.

Cornered by two of her roommates in their crowded off-campus apartment, Shelby succumbed with pleasure to their fluttery excitement over her ring.

"Oh my gosh, it's gorgeous!" Sara said, practically drooling as she turned Shelby's hand under the fluorescent hall light to catch the white brilliance in each facet of the solitaire.

"Wow! It's beautiful!" added Amanda wistfully. "You're *so* lucky . . ."

Shelby beamed at both her roommates and draped her arms over their shoulders to envelop them in a hug. *Thank goodness for these two amazing friends*, she thought. She had no one else to share this moment with.

"You're going to marry Brad Thompson! He's like—the most perfect guy on campus!" Sara continued, listing off Brad's virtues in a speech that seemed memorized. "He's smart, mature, tall-dark-and-handsome, a returned missionary getting his MBA—and he's *nice* on top of it all!"

"I know," Shelby said. "Imagine someone like *me* marrying someone like Brad!"

"No negative self-talk, Shelby," said Sara, the psychology major. "You're beautiful, with those hazel eyes and that strawberry blonde hair a lot of girls would give anything to have. You're a brilliant student, a great nurse, and the best friend anyone could ask for."

"And besides," said Amanda, "after all you've been through, you *so* deserve to be happy."

Throughout her young life, disappointments had been fired at Shelby in an endless tirade. She could certainly appreciate all that being married to Bradley Thompson would mean. Her discovery of the gospel a few years ago had provided an anchor in the storm-tossed sea of her life, and now Brad was guiding her to firm ground. He was stalwart in the Church. He was truly the best man she had ever known.

Shelby laughed to herself. If people could have a theme song, Brad's would definitely start off with "Firm as the mountains around us . . ."

"I can't believe you're engaged!" Amanda said rapturously. "You and Brad are like Jane Eyre and Mr. Rochester, connected by an invisible cord attached to your hearts. It's soooo romantic!"

Shelby and Sara laughed. With Amanda, everything was "so" something—"so nice," "so cute," "so much." The youngest roommate, Amanda feasted on every version ever made of *Jane Eyre* and loved to gush over the romance between the characters. She owned three copies of Charlotte Brontë's novel and sometimes quoted whole passages. Definitely a hopeless romantic.

Shelby headed down the hall to the tiny kitchen in their apartment. Sara and Amanda trailed behind her, eager to savor every tidbit of information Shelby would share.

"Shelby, you're *so* lucky!" repeated Amanda.

"I know," she said, spinning around joyfully with her arms outstretched, her wavy hair fanning out behind her. "I'm *so* happy!"

Unfortunately, the space in the kitchen was so confined that, while she was spinning, Shelby's left hand smacked into a mound of butter on a plastic dish. Butter and dish launched off the countertop, their flight ending upon impact with the wall.

"Oh no!" Shelby moaned.

Amanda's laughter turned into a snort. "Look at the wall!" The soft butter was slithering downward, leaving a trail of yellow blobs in its descent.

Sara grabbed a dishrag. "Don't worry, Shelb. We can clean it up."

"But look at my ring!"

They gathered around her outstretched hand to inspect the damage. The diamond was now a greasy lump on her ring finger. The girls looked at each other and burst into laughter.

While they cleaned everything, Shelby couldn't help feeling relieved that Brad hadn't been there. He would have rolled his eyes at her latest blunder. He was so proper. He didn't accidentally spill drinks all over people, drop things, or walk into furniture or walls, as she admittedly had been known to do. She had the bruises to prove it. Maybe that's why they got along so well—they were so different.

Shelby scrubbed her ring with dish soap and warm water in the sink. "What do you think?" she asked, holding up her fingers. "Will he be able tell?"

"No, it's good as new," Sara pronounced. "He'd never know your ring just had a butter bath."

Shelby groaned, opening a cupboard. "I need some chocolate."

Sara opened a few more cupboards. "I have some cookies in here . . . somewhere."

"Perfect."

"I'll make some popcorn," said Amanda, placing a bag in the microwave.

"By the way, Shelby," said Sara, her face in the freezer, "when are you going to get married? Have you set the date?"

Amanda instantly responded for Shelby, "It's got to be this summer! A June wedding would be *so* perfect. You could have an outdoor reception with roses everywhere and twinkling lights and a gazebo and . . ."

"Hold on!" Shelby broke in with amusement, grabbing the ice tray from the freezer and popping a few ice cubes into a tall glass of water. "We haven't decided anything yet!"

Sara opened a bag of cheap cookies, the kind they had all deemed inedible but continued purchasing because it was all they could afford. Amanda emptied a steaming bag of artificial butter–flavored microwave popcorn into a bowl, and they all headed into the living room for their ritual late-night snack.

"Brad thinks that the best time to get married is in August. Right before fall semester begins. He thinks we should start looking now for an apartment and that I should try to get a summer job lined up so fall semester can start up smoothly." Shelby was a graduate nursing student and could probably get hired on again at the hospital. "But if he gets his internship, things could change."

"When are you going to try on wedding gowns?" asked Amanda eagerly.

Shelby swallowed a sip of ice water and reached for a handful of buttery popcorn before she answered with a shrug. "I don't know."

"We should go to the malls this week. I bet there will be some great sales going on." Sara said through her cookie crumbs.

"How did Brad pick out such a perfect ring?" Amanda wondered. "I know he has exceptional taste, but how did he know what you wanted?"

"Well . . ."

Shelby looked down at the traditional solitaire and twisted it on her finger. Maybe it wasn't exactly what she would have picked out, but Brad really did have impeccable taste. He always seemed to know just what was right in so many other areas of his life.

She liked having someone she could trust to make good decisions. She didn't want a repeat of the life she'd had while growing up. Memories forced their way in to remind her of the Bay Area hills she had explored alone when she was seven, the lake in Texas where she had made a new friend when she was twelve, the forests in Virginia she had wandered through at fifteen when she needed solace. Half a dozen other places flashed through her mind—places she hardly remembered from her childhood years. Constantly moving as a child, she'd never been in one place long enough to make close friends. The few friends she did have would often have a hard time writing letters after she'd moved away.

Shelby squeezed the unwanted images away. Today was a day to be happy. She would become Brad's wife, and together they were bound for a well-planned journey through life. Now that her father had died and her mother had all but disowned her when Shelby had joined the Church, it was even more of a blessing to have Brad. It was hard not having anyone else . . .

Suddenly the front door opened with a bang, bringing a welcome interruption to her thoughts. Jessica barged in with a stack of books in her arms and kicked the door closed with her foot. After mumbling irritably, "Can you get out of my way?" She stomped past her three munching roommates and slammed the bedroom door shut. Sara and Amanda looked at each other and rolled their eyes.

"Looks like she's in another one of her moods," whispered Amanda.

"Seriously, when is she ever *not* in one of her moods?" Sara added quietly. "She totally needs counseling."

"Someone had a bad day." Shelby couldn't help feeling bad for Jessica. She was a complete grouch, but there were times when she appeared to be nothing more than a frightened little girl in a big scary world. Shelby had tried to befriend Jessica, knowing what it felt like to have no friends, but Jessica had always returned her kindness with brusque remarks or a flippant comeback.

Having deviated from the important issue at hand, Amanda burst out, "Shelby, we need to get you a bride magazine! Then you can start picking out colors and styles and everything for the wedding."

"Hey Shelby, you should have seen this wedding gown I saw at University Mall. It was exquisite . . ." Sara continued. Her voice went on and on, outlining every detail imaginable from neckline to train until Shelby's mind was so full of lace trim and pearls that her thoughts began to wander elsewhere in search of rest. *They seem even more excited about all this than I am,* she mused. But of course she was just imagining things. Her dreams were coming true. She couldn't imagine anyone happier than she was at that moment.

* * *

Shelby turned the page of *Bride Magazine*. Brad looked over her shoulder at the hideous wedding gown being modeled and snorted.

"Hey, no laughing," she attempted to say sternly, but barely suppressed her own amusement. Winter semester was over and Shelby was determined to start planning for the wedding. Picking out a gown was a major task, and she had hoped to get some ideas from Amanda's stash of bridal magazines. Her overly romantic roommate didn't have a steady boyfriend but made a regular practice of studying the gowns so she would know exactly what to pick when Mr. Right walked through the door.

Brad wanted to set August 20 for their wedding date, but how would they figure out all the wedding details by then? There was so much to think about. At least she wasn't taking classes during spring or summer terms so she could focus on the wedding. Work at the hospital would keep her busy enough as it was.

"Do you actually . . . *like* any of these dresses?" Brad asked, his apprehension undisguised.

Shelby sighed at his dismay over the gaudy white concoctions. "C'mon, they're not all bad."

She flipped forward several pages. "Check this one out. I kind of like the train on the dress."

"Shelby, it's sleeveless! You can't wear anything like that!"

"I know. I'm just saying I like the skirt. Don't you think it's pretty?"

The grimace on Brad's face was answer enough. "Where are the normal dresses in this magazine?"

Shelby made a face and turned the page. She pointed to another gown. "This is nice. I like the way this skirt flares out from the waist."

"But it doesn't have any style. Don't you want it to be more formal?"

"I don't know. I kind of like its simplicity." She turned the page again and rolled her eyes at Brad's sudden intake of breath.

"Now this is more like it," he exclaimed, dramatically pointing to a dress that had so many layers of lace-embellished tulle that it conjured up images of hippos dancing in tutus. Completely exasperated, Shelby tossed the magazine at her grinning fiancé, stood up, and stretched her arms.

"Heard anything about the internship yet?" she asked, ready to talk about something other than wedding gowns. And this was one subject that would distract him for a long time.

"They'll let us know next week if we got accepted." Brad lit up excitedly. "I'm not too worried. I think I'll get it without too much trouble."

"Well, I hope you get it. You've worked hard enough for it."

Brad leaned back with his arms stretched behind his neck. "It would be so great, Shelby."

He looked almost dreamy-eyed when he talked about the internship in Salt Lake City with Baxter&Wells. It would be over three months long, from the end of August through the first part of December. "It would give me the business experience I need, and the pay isn't too bad either. I feel really good about it."

Shelby smiled to herself. She knew how much he wanted the position. Besides their wedding, it was all he talked about. At least she'd get to claim him before his internship did.

"Brad, I was thinking about something . . ." her voice trailed off in hesitation as she checked Brad's posture and the expression on his face. There was something she needed to talk about with him but had constantly put off. It was time to gather the courage to bring it up. "What would you think if we just had a small group of people get together after the wedding instead of having a big reception that night?"

Brad's head shot up. "What? Why don't you want a reception?"

"Well, I just feel . . ." Shelby wasn't sure how to explain, "awkward I guess, since I won't have any family there."

"You don't need to feel awkward—"

"Brad, *no one* will be on my side of the line."

Shelby's lack of family had always been a sensitive subject. In limited conversations, Shelby had explained that her father had died when she was a teenager and that her mother refused to have any contact with Shelby once she joined the Church. She was an only child with no extended family that she really knew.

"Don't worry about that, Shelby. My family is now your family, and there are enough of them to spare!" Brad laughed, describing the endless stream of relatives who would be there hugging everyone, descending on the refreshment table like ravenous wolves. "And my sister Laura's kids will make their ever-present mark with all their running around and boisterous voices. There definitely will be no lack of family!"

"But I'm not sure I really want a reception, Brad," Shelby said quietly.

"Let's just . . . think about it. We can ask around to see what's best."

Shelby clenched her jaw as a knot began to form in her stomach. Then she turned away and rubbed her forehead in frustration.

"Hey, what's wrong?" he asked tenderly as he stood to console her. Shelby lowered her head as moisture filled her eyes. "I don't know . . . It's nothing."

Shelby couldn't explain it even to herself, but there was an ache deep inside that she never allowed to the surface. It came in the shape of loneliness and moaned for lack of belonging. But it was too painful to acknowledge. It was easier to push aside. Yet, for some reason lately, it was begging to be released and validated. She longed for her mother right now. Her heart yearned for a brother or sister. And she would do anything for the simple luxury of having a hometown.

Shelby sniffled and quickly wiped away her tears. "I don't know what's wrong with me. I'm sorry, Brad."

"Shelby, I love you. We'll get everything worked out perfectly. It will be the best wedding anyone could hope for. Don't worry about it anymore, okay?" She felt his arms move around her in a gesture of comfort. But inside she felt the raw pain of loneliness embedding itself deeper into the unhealed wounds of her heart.

* * *

Later that evening, as Shelby was halfheartedly balancing her checkbook, Brad called, the excitement unmistakable in his voice.

"Hi, Brad. What's up?" She said in the most cheerful voice she could muster.

"Shelby, I couldn't wait to talk to you tomorrow. I had to call now."

"What's wrong?"

"Nothing. It's just that I've been praying to know how to help you feel better, and I . . ." he paused to take a breath and continued, "I just feel right about this, like Heavenly Father really wanted me to get this answer."

"What are you talking about?" Shelby asked, puzzled.

"I think that you should stay with my parents in Montana for a few weeks this summer. They are dying to meet you. And it would be so good for you to feel close to them before we got married. I really think it would be great—especially so you could have a family near you. My mom would love to help you pick out bridesmaid dresses and flowers. She's really good with stuff like that. We could even take you to Yellowstone for fun. What do you think?"

Shelby couldn't explain how she could go from a state of exhaustion to feeling enthusiastic simply from a phone call, but she did. Something inside felt so good about Brad's idea that she couldn't hold back.

"I'd really like that, Brad. I think it's a great idea."

Financially, she could probably do it. It would only be for two or three weeks. But then a thought came that shattered her hopeful feelings. Maybe his family wouldn't want her to come yet. Maybe they wouldn't like her. Or maybe they had too much going on this summer. She couldn't expect to throw herself on them and think that everything would turn out great—that perhaps for once in her life she could experience being part of a family and the wonderful feeling of belonging.

Shelby quickly added, "But how would your parents feel about it? They might feel uncomfortable having a total stranger forced on them."

"No way!" exclaimed Brad. "They've been begging me to bring you up. They want you to come, Shelby. Please say yes." He was almost pleading.

"Are you sure?" asked Shelby with returning hope.

"Absolutely."

"Well . . . I really would love getting to know them before we get married."

"You'll come, then?"

Shelby laughed at Brad's eagerness and felt her heart swell with gratitude and excitement.

"Yeah, I'll come. Thanks, Brad."

"You bet. You're going to love it up there, Shelby. Oh, I uh . . . forgot to tell you that my older brother Cameron might be there part of the summer. He's kind of been going through some personal problems and stuff. But you won't run into him much at all. He kind of avoids being around people and puts in long hours with the Forest Service."

"Didn't he get married recently?" Shelby wondered. Come to think of it, she couldn't remember Brad ever saying much about his older brother. In contrast, she'd heard a lot about Scott leaving on his mission to Guatemala and tales of Laura and her three rascally children.

"Yeah. Well . . . he sort of . . ." Brad seemed a little embarrassed to talk about Cameron, but he took a deep breath and answered sourly. "He backed out two days before the wedding and caused a big mess."

"Wow. That must have been tough." Shelby couldn't imagine going through anything so traumatic. For both parties involved, it must have been very painful. It seemed strange that Brad had never mentioned anything about it.

"He's never really been . . . dependable. But let's not talk about him any more. There are far better things to think about!"

Brad seemed relieved to move away from the subject of his brother. He told Shelby some funny things that happened in his math lab that day and updated her on some new information he had learned about the internship before hanging up. But Shelby remained curious about Cameron and why Brad was so reluctant to talk about him.

Chapter 2

The sun was just rising over Y Mountain, and fat black crows were squawking loudly as Shelby tossed her backpack into the trunk of her old, gray Accord. Then she wiped the back of her hand across her forehead. It was already promising to be a hot day. Turning to Brad with disappointment, she sighed. "I don't want to go without you."

Brad gave her a quick hug. "You'll be fine!" he cheered.

"If only your internship hadn't come so early . . . I don't want to meet your family all alone."

"Shelby, we've been through this already." He smiled a little through his frustration. "I know June is sooner than I expected, but I promise I'll come to Montana for a visit as soon as I can get away. If I don't take this internship now, there's no guarantee I'd be able to get another one. And they've already agreed to give me time off for the wedding."

"I know, I know," Shelby interrupted. "I'm sorry. You're right. I'm just disappointed, that's all."

"Hey, I found that picture I told you about." Brad pulled an envelope out of his leather briefcase and handed it to her. "It was taken right before Scott left on his mission to Guatemala."

Brad pointed out each family member in the photo. His parents sat in the center, surrounded by their oldest daughter Laura, her husband Bruce and their three children, Cameron to the left, Brad on the right, and Scott down in front. Each smiling face radiated a happiness that conveyed the obvious love and closeness they shared with each other. Shelby was drawn to the photograph. There was a strong family resemblance among the siblings. Laura was a slender brunette with friendly brown eyes. Scott was a lot like Laura, only younger. Brad looked as stylish and handsome as he always did. But it was a different face that held her captivated for some unexplainable reason. Cameron's sapphire-blue eyes seemed to beckon her with the intensity of his gaze. Not nearly as attractive as Brad, this older brother had an indefinable expression on his face that unsettled her.

Brad's voice seeped into her thoughts and pulled her back to the parking lot. "I want you to keep this photo . . . to remind you that on August 20 you will be part of this family and that they will all welcome you with open arms. And just remember, the next Thompson photo will have you in it."

The quiet sincerity of his words made Shelby feel warm all over. A lump formed in her throat. "Thank you so much, Brad. I'm really glad to have this."

Reaching through the open passenger side window of her car, she set the picture on the seat and then stood up to face him. A sudden flurry of questions inundated her mind, but she couldn't seem to verbalize any of them. As the bell tower tolled its hourly melody in the distance, they both instinctively looked at their watches.

"So, I guess you're all ready to leave. Do you still have the directions?" asked Brad.

"Yep."

"And a road map?"

"Uh huh," she smiled with a hint of exasperation.

"Do you have enough gas to get to Pocatello?"

"Yes, I'm ready!" Shelby laughed.

"Well . . ." He hugged her longer than she expected and even kissed her full on the mouth, something he had never done in public before. Brad's policy on public displays of affection had sometimes left her secretly wishing for more passion in her life. But his other qualities far outweighed such longings. "Good-bye, Shelby. I love you."

There was a tone of finality in his farewell and possessiveness in his touch that surprised her.

"I love you too, Brad." A peculiar feeling washed over Shelby. But unwilling to analyze it or give it any thought, she got into her car, buckled up, and started the engine. Calling out a good-bye through her window, she pulled out of the parking lot of her apartment complex and waved one last time.

As soon as she was out of Provo heading to the freeway, Shelby glanced over to Brad's family photo resting on the passenger seat. Face up, it beckoned enticingly. She couldn't resist the opportunity of studying each face again, so she picked it up and checked to see if the light ahead was turning red. It defiantly stayed green. Releasing the photo, she continued driving restlessly through two more green lights, unable to steal more than a peek.

"Why is there never a red light when you want one?" she asked out loud.

Right before the freeway entrance, when the last traffic light turned red, Shelby quickly shifted into neutral and pulled the parking break up. This was always a long light. Shelby grabbed the photo again and looked at each face. While the faces of Laura and Scott made her smile, there was something about Cameron's expression that was unnerving. It seemed secretive and somewhat defiant. Shelby took note of the slight cleft in his chin, the wave of chestnut brown hair over his forehead. Despite his guarded expression, a few lines creased at the sides of his eyes, betraying a tendency to laughter. What had made him so somber when the picture was taken?

A horn blasted from the hulking black Suburban behind Shelby's car, making her heart lurch and her nerves tremble. The photo was frantically tossed aside. With guilty embarrassment, she pressed the accelerator. The gears ground slightly before she finally composed herself enough shift into first and ease forward. Wishing she could sink through the seat, she looked straight ahead as the angry driver whizzed past her with his arms waving. She vowed not to look at the photo again while she was driving and turned her stereo to the classical station she often listened to while studying. Assuring herself that the Suburban was far ahead, she rolled her windows down all the way and let the wind blow through her long hair.

It was the first time since coming to BYU as a freshman that Shelby would be traveling anywhere beyond Salt Lake City. The thought was a little intimidating. She had come to feel like BYU was "home" over the last five years, and it gave her a sense of security. There had been no reason to venture out, and she liked it that way.

But then came memories of her mother bitterly yelling and crying for Shelby not to join "that cult of Mormons," threatening to disown her daughter if she were to move to Utah. To leave her now that her dad had died would be unforgivable. The ranting had gone on for days. As hard as Shelby tried pleading for understanding, her mother had cemented her threat into an unbreakable reality. Leaving her mother was the most anguishing thing Shelby had ever done in her life. She was separated from the only family she knew, unmistakably unwelcome to return. But she knew she could never deny the sweet and compelling whisperings of the Spirit, which had guided her here. There was no doubt in her mind that she had done the right thing. But it was painful to remember. If only her mother would allow Shelby back into her life.

* * *

After filling up at a gas station in Pocatello, Idaho, and getting a cheap hamburger at a fast food restaurant, Shelby drove for a few hours past miles of sagebrush and farmland dotted with the occasional black and brown patches of fuzzy-nosed cattle grazing peacefully in the sunshine. Continuing on Highway 20, Shelby saw a sign that read ASHTON: GATEWAY TO ADVENTURE and felt a sudden rush of excitement come over her.

With the steady increase in elevation the grassy valleys were transformed to mountainsides densely forested with lodgepole pine. She knew she was getting closer to Montana and sensed a change, not only in the scenery but also within—a feeling that life would be different once she met the Thompson family.

Although she was tired of driving and nervous with the anticipation of meeting Brad's family soon, she wasn't oblivious to the exquisite beauty of the low sun peeping brilliantly through the pine trees and dancing over the rippling lakes.

Shelby drove through the quaint town of West Yellowstone and headed north. She made a mental note to remind Brad to take her to Yellowstone National Park as soon as he could come up. Carefully following Brad's detailed instructions, Shelby followed the signs that led her past the Big Sky area nestled in the Madison Range by the spring-green valleys of the Gallatin River. It had to be the most exquisite place Shelby had ever seen.

Driving into Bozeman gave her a strange, almost familiar feeling. Turning off Main Street, she traveled for several miles on a winding country road, enjoying the expanse of trees and grassy slopes while watching for periodic turnoffs to private residences. On either side of the road, patches of tall, lavender-pink fireweed blossoms decorated the landscape.

When she finally turned into the Thompsons' long gravel driveway, Shelby took in the whole picture this place presented. Pine and aspen trees cradled the brown, wood-sided rambler cast in shadows from the late-afternoon sun. Snow-capped mountains jutted above the tree line while welcoming wildflowers in delicate lavender and bright yellows speckled the expanse of grassy areas. Sloping away from the home to the right was a large green pasture with an old, weatherworn barn. Comfort and serenity enveloped her almost as if she were a long lost traveler being welcomed home from her final journey. A lump formed in her throat. How she wanted to belong here! When she married Brad, she would be a part of this beautiful place.

As she drove up to the house, the crunch and rumble of gravel from the driveway alerted two dogs to her arrival. One was a big gray-and-white husky with a smiling face, the other a smaller dog with an untidy brown coat and lolloping tongue. The dogs barked loudly, and tails wagged furiously as they pranced around her car. Shelby was relieved to see a man of medium build and a smiling woman coming out of the house to greet her. She leaned over to reach for her purse and sweater before getting out of the car but saw the family photo staring up at her. *Yikes!* Grabbing the picture with an embarrassment that puzzled her, she tucked it inside her purse. Then she turned back to open her car door with a tentative smile.

"Hello! You must be Shelby!" Millie Thompson exclaimed as she gave Shelby a big hug. Then Karl Thompson gave her an equally warm embrace.

"Thanks for letting me come."

"Down, Bomber! Down, Wags!" Karl commanded the jumping dogs.

Millie put her arm around Shelby and drew her close to her cuddly side. "We're so glad you're here! We've been giving Brad a hard time about not bringing you up sooner."

Karl said, "We hope you'll stay for a long visit. Why don't you two head into the house, and I'll help bring in your suitcases if you'd like."

"Thank you. I'll unlock the trunk." Warm relief swept over Shelby as she accepted their kindness and hospitality.

Millie was soon guiding Shelby along the walkway in front of the porch and up to the front door, chattering away pleasantly with each step.

"And I'm making plenty for dinner—fried chicken, mashed potatoes and gravy—so I hope you're hungry. I even made apple pie! I bet you're tired after the drive so I'll show you to your room, and you can freshen up a bit."

She opened the heavy wood door and invited Shelby inside. The heavenly aroma of cinnamon and apples wafted through the front room. Crocheted afghans were draped over the backs of the worn sofa and wooden rocking chair. An assortment of carved woods and wildlife sculptures decorated the room, along with western trinkets and cozy throw pillows. There was a wood-burning stove along one wall that looked like an antique. Pictures of family members adorned the walls, end tables, and bookshelves. A feeling of love wrapped Shelby with its warmth and beckoned her in to stay.

"The guest room is this way." Millie led her down a hallway to the left that had more family portraits hanging in rows on the walls. Shelby had never seen so many picture frames on a wall before. She passed a photo of Brad's high school graduation that she remembered seeing once, several of Laura and her children, and a missionary plaque with Scott's photo on it.

But when she came to the photo of Cameron, she stopped as though rooted to the ground. Sister Thompson disappeared into one of the bedrooms, but Shelby didn't notice. Her attention was entirely focused on this man she had never met before. She studied his rugged features, the confident set of his shoulders and an almost arrogant expression that seemed to challenge her from within the frame. What was it that was so disquieting about him? Would he be here this summer as Brad had indicated that he might? The thought of meeting him gave her an unpleasant feeling.

"Oh, there you are," called Millie from the bedroom doorway. "I thought you were right behind me when I realized I was talking to myself!"

Shelby jerked her eyes from Cameron's picture and said apologetically, "I'm sorry, I was . . . just . . . looking at all the family pictures."

"I have plenty of them, don't I?" Millie chuckled and wandered back to the gallery of photos where Shelby stood. "I just love being surrounded by family—even if it's only in pictures. This is Laura and her little family. They live in Idaho Falls. This is Cameron, our oldest, and here's Scott." She chatted a bit about some of the photos and then led Shelby back to the same bedroom she had disappeared into before.

"Now, this will be your room while you're here. I hope it works for you. This used to be Scott's room . . ." Her expression was one of gentle longing for her absent son.

"You must miss him a lot, Sister Thompson."

There was a heavy sigh. "I do. I miss all of my children now that they have left home." Then her face brightened as if just remembering. "Oh, and please call me Millie."

"Okay," Shelby said with a shy smile. It seemed that liking her future mother-in-law was going to be very easy.

Shelby looked around the room and found twin beds made of heavy pine and covered with blue and green patchwork quilts. In the corner was an old-fashioned hutch with an assortment of pictures and childhood mementos on the shelves.

"This is a nice room," Shelby commented. "I like the corner hutch."

"Thanks. It was my mother's. It was passed down to me when she died." Millie touched Shelby's shoulder and said, "Please feel at home here. You can use any of the dresser drawers, and there are hangers in the closet. Here's a stack of extra blankets in case you need them. It can get cold up here at night."

"And here are your things," Karl said as he came in the bedroom with a suitcase in one hand and a small duffel bag in the other. "We hope you'll feel comfortable here."

Then Shelby was shown the hall bathroom next to the bedrooms, where she washed up for dinner. It was a pleasant bathroom with lots of old-fashioned knickknacks and forest-green plaid curtains over the window. There was a plaque hanging on the wall that read GRANDPA'S FISH TALES SOUND FISHY.

Studying her reflection in the mirror, Shelby wondered what the Thompsons thought about her. Did they think she was good enough for their son? Did she make a decent first impression? Realizing she was scowling, she gave her reflection an enormous, toothy grin.

"You can do this," she rallied. "Just be yourself!"

She dried her hands on a dark green hand towel with a moose embroidered on it. Then she opened the bathroom door. Hearing the clanking of pans, Shelby walked down the hall to the kitchen where Millie was putting the finishing touches on a delicious-looking meal.

"Can I do anything to help you, Millie?" Shelby asked.

Millie turned to give her a warm smile. "You just sit down and relax. Everything is about ready." She walked over to the sink and picked up a large bowl filled with carrot peelings, egg shells, and a swimming mass of unidentified objects.

"I'm just going to take this bowl out to the compost pile, and then we can eat."

Shelby eyed the bowl warily, but an idea came to her. "I'll take it for you," she said. It seemed to be a noble attempt to show Millie she wouldn't be taking advantage of the Thompsons' hospitality while she stayed with them.

"Oh," Millie hesitated. "You shouldn't have to do one thing after that long trip."

"But I'd really like to help you."

Millie's smile was full of warmth. "Thank you; that's very thoughtful."

Shelby took the bowl and asked where the compost pile was.

"If you just follow the stone path down the hill, you'll find it next to the garden."

After Millie held the back door open for her, Shelby went outside. The trees overhead were swishing gently, and Shelby stopped for a moment to look up at them. A dark winged bird swooped down from one of the branches and zoomed past her along the backside of the house.

Shelby looked down at the bowl she held and wrinkled her nose as something brown sloshed onto her thumb. *Yuck!* The sooner she dumped this mess, the sooner she could get washed up again.

Concentrating on keeping the bowl level, Shelby hurried along the stone path that curved around the side of the house. Just as she rounded the corner, Shelby collided headlong with a tan shirt. The impact sent her reeling, and the contents of the bowl went flying. Shelby looked up in horror at a stunned man who gaped at her in disbelief, shreds of slop dripping from his shirt and clinging to his hair. It was Cameron.

Chapter 3

"What in the—" His deep voice broke off, but his irritation and dismay had been obvious. He picked a jagged eggshell off his sleeve.

"Oh no! I'm so sorry!" Shelby exclaimed in mortification as she retrieved the bowl. "I can't believe I did that!"

Taking a step toward him, she frantically brushed at a blob of orange mush on his shirt in an effort to help. It only made the stain increase in size. He stopped her hands roughly and moved them aside.

"Don't bother." Utterly aggravated, he glowered at her with displeasure. "Who are *you*?"

Still flustered, she answered apologetically, "Shelby Hamlin."

"My mom said you'd be coming," he frowned. "I'm Cameron."

He grudgingly held out his hand to shake hers, but seeing shreds of some kind of peeling dangling between his long fingers, he quickly pulled his hand back in awkwardness. Dreading that she would laugh and appear to be mocking him, Shelby put a hand over her mouth. But he didn't miss the guilty mirth in her eyes.

"Nice to meet you," he said, the audible sarcasm in his voice painfully obvious.

Shelby met his haughty gaze. She had not mistaken his rudeness. But she most assuredly had misjudged his looks. If Brad was considered handsome, his older brother would have to be drop-dead gorgeous. From the brown muddy hiking boots and faded jeans to the Forest Service shirt stretched by broad shoulders, Cameron Thompson was the embodiment of masculine strength. His thick brown hair looked tousled in front like he had recently run his fingers through it. His blue eyes were like summer lightning, scorching everything in their path.

When she realized she was blatantly staring, Shelby took an awkward step backward in embarrassment and looked down at her feet.

Cameron looked down at the slop on his shirt and wrinkled his nose. "What is this mess anyway?"

The question caught her off guard. "I have no idea," she said in a shaky half-laugh. "I was supposed to take whatever it was to the compost pile."

"It looks like another one of my mother's concoctions," Cameron said resentfully as he bent down to pick up some of the larger food pieces off the ground.

"You don't have to do that! I'll clean it up." She was mortified already, but to have him clean up her own disaster was too much. From his squatting position, Cameron tilted his head up at her at a rakish angle and reached for the bowl. Shelby was momentarily taken aback. He'd just been assaulted by flying debris, yet he was offering to help the assailant clean up the mess, despite his initial rudeness.

"I don't mind," his mouth twisted slightly, suddenly revealing a dimple in his right cheek. Shelby blinked in mesmerized confusion and opened her mouth to speak. All that came out was a muted squeak.

Feeling like she'd been reduced to a bumbling idiot, she bent down across from Cameron and picked up another eggshell. With her eyes averted, she helped him retrieve as much as possible, tossing the pieces into the bowl between them. The rest would just have to ooze into the gravel.

"Thanks." She abruptly seized the bowl from him, avoiding the mocking spark in his eyes. "I'll take this down to the compost pile now."

"Do you even know where it is?"

"Of course," she declared a bit too quickly, willing to admit anything just to get away from him as fast as possible. "You probably want to get inside now to clean up."

He smirked in open amusement as she practically shooed him away. "I guess I do prefer not to *wear* my dinner at the table."

Cringing, Shelby moved aside to let him pass. "I really am sorry I dumped this on you."

"It's all right," he said as he walked toward the house. "Don't worry about it." After Cameron tossed her an indistinct look over his shoulder, he went inside and shut the back door.

Shelby almost let the bowl drop to the ground as she smacked one hand across her eyes. What a disastrous beginning that was! How could she go back in there and face him? She could only imagine what he thought of her. What would the Thompsons think? Maybe she'd be lucky and he'd disappear before dinner was served.

She followed the path down the hill to the garden, passing a boat and several snowmobiles along the way. When she found the fenced-off compost pile, Shelby dumped a half-empty bowl onto the pile.

If only she could push a magical rewind button and end up in this same spot with a full bowl! Then she could gracefully meet Cameron without a hitch and after he left, Shelby, Millie, and Karl would sit down to a cozy dinner together. Brad would find out she was getting along perfectly with his parents, that everything was moving along as smoothly as an eagle glides through the sky. *Yeah, right.* After the last ten minutes she felt more like a stumbling, reckless chicken.

Turning around to look at the house, Shelby wrinkled her brow in sudden irritation. *What's he doing here anyway? He didn't have to be so rude and inhospitable just because of a little—And how was I supposed to know that around every corner of this place was an obstacle course? It just isn't fair that I'm such a klutz at such a bad time!*

Shelby deeply inhaled the clean mountain air, convinced that her nerves were working overtime and that she needed to relax. The Thompsons would like her well enough, just as Brad had said—if she could stop being so nervous! It shouldn't be too hard if she chanted something like "stay calm and collected," should it?

As Shelby hesitantly walked through the back door, she saw Millie bustling around the kitchen talking to Karl. Shelby darted into a bathroom off the family room and shut the door. Once her hands had been scrubbed, she squared her shoulders, lifted her chin courageously, and walked back to the kitchen.

Millie was just placing a brown ceramic container of hot gravy on the table. "I think we're ready," she smiled.

Karl looked up from the magazine he was reading and invited Shelby to sit next to him. She instantly noticed the four place settings and inwardly groaned. *Oh fabulous, he's staying for dinner.* Did that mean Cameron would sit opposite her? How would she remain calm and collected with his disapproving gaze on her? But she certainly didn't want to sit *next* to him.

Millie asked, "Did you meet Cameron outside? He disappeared somewhere, but Karl saw him come in." Shelby darted a look at Karl, wondering just how much he "had seen."

"Yes. I . . . we . . ." Shelby faltered. Just then, Cameron walked into the dining room wearing a clean, red plaid shirt, his damp hair brushed back.

"We sort of bumped into each other a few minutes ago," he said, smirking again when he saw the look on her face. Shelby felt a wave of heat spread across her cheeks and quickly looked away.

"There you are!" Millie exclaimed happily as she walked over to give Cameron a hug. He kissed his mother's cheek and then walked around the table to sit across from Shelby. She glanced up at him but quickly lowered her lashes when she saw him studying her, an arrogant look on his face. Shelby fussed with her napkin until the prayer was said and everyone began to eat.

"I'm glad you made it home in time for dinner, Cam," said Millie as she passed him the platter of chicken.

"Thanks, Mom."

In time to get a bowl of compost dumped on him, Shelby thought ruefully.

"How are things at the station?" Karl asked him.

"Fine. We started the water samples down on the south fork," Cameron said as he took a drumstick and then passed the platter to Karl. "Bob says hi." The men continued talking while Millie carried on her own conversation with Shelby about the wedding and places of interest she wanted Shelby to see during her stay.

When Millie suddenly expressed a wish for Cameron to show Shelby around a few areas of the National Forest Service, he looked up in disbelief. Shelby felt the scrutiny of his eyes, and shrinking from the discomfort it gave her, she nervously blurted out the first thing that popped into her head.

"Are you staying here during the summer?" *That was polite, right?* But Cameron's face became like granite, and a muscle clenched perceptibly along his jaw.

"For a little while, anyway." His voice had instantly turned cold and abrasive.

Uh-oh.

Challenging her with his stare, he picked up his fork and stabbed relentlessly at a piece of chicken. Shelby looked down and studied the rim of her dinner plate.

"Son, you know you can stay as long as you like." Karl reached out to put a firm hand on Cameron's shoulder. "This is your home."

Millie joined in with a lighthearted, "If you don't stay, the youth in the ward will be devastated." She looked over at Shelby to explain, "Cameron offered to take the Young Men on a trip through Yellowstone and a river rafting trip down the Gallatin."

"I got roped into it. And the only reason they want to go river rafting, Mom, is because the Young Women are coming too," he said contemptuously and took another stab at his chicken.

"Sounds like fun." Shelby said, wondering what had made Cameron act so abrasive all of a sudden. She remembered Brad's reluctance to talk about his brother, making it sound like Cameron had a lot of problems. *I'll buy that.* She wondered if there was more to the story than just a broken engagement. Maybe it was embarrassing for him to be staying with his parents when he should have been married. Perhaps he was just psychologically unstable. *Just mind your own business!* came a warning voice in her head.

Millie began chatting again, smoothing over some of the tension with her light conversation while they ate. She proudly spoke about Cameron's job as a biology teacher at Bozeman High School, teaching awards he had received, and some work he had done with Montana State University there in Bozeman. Shelby found herself wondering if all his high school students dreaded his classes.

Millie continued with anecdotes of Laura's three children and inserted the latest news about Scott's transfer to a remote village in Guatemala. There was little doubt that Millie Thompson adored her children and that they were the biggest part of her world.

Shelby glanced at Cameron while Millie talked. He still seemed tense. When Millie began preparing dessert, Shelby got up to help her.

"Thank you for dinner. This is the best meal I've had in a long time, Millie."

Her praise was sincere and brought a touch of sadness to her heart. A flood of painful memories threatened to surface. There hadn't been many good meals at home with her parents. There were plenty of tasteless frozen dinners or meals thrown together with little thought for nutrition. The few times they had eaten together had usually ended in a fight between her parents.

She glanced over at Karl and Cameron talking fondly together. The lamps from the front room cast a warm glow over them. Millie was scooping vanilla ice cream onto the side of each slice of hot apple pie. What a contrast this all was from her own past.

Shelby caught Cameron's questioning glance. Her heart lurched uncomfortably at the realization that he had been watching her. She hoped she hadn't displayed her feelings too obviously. She mentally shook away her thoughts as Millie handed her two plates to pass out to the men. Shelby brought the first to Karl and laughed at his enthusiastic lip smacking over the dessert.

"My Millie can sure make a pie," he said lovingly to his wife and then proceeded to devour his dessert. Millie chuckled.

When Shelby walked over to Cameron and handed him his plate, his fingers inadvertently brushed against the back side of her hand with an undercurrent that jolted her senses. Cameron's eyes met hers as he softly mumbled, "Thanks." They immediately looked away from each other.

Millie brought over a piece of pie for Shelby and one for herself. Sitting down again, Shelby reminded herself to relax, but it was a hard task to accomplish while her hand still burned where Cameron had barely touched her.

Shelby scooped up a bite of flaky crust and plump apples dripping with cinnamon. "Mmm . . . this is delicious. I don't think I've ever had anything that tasted so good." She savored the taste in her mouth and then sighed. "I can see I'm going to have to take some cooking lessons from you, Millie."

"So . . . you can't cook?" Cameron said derisively.

While Shelby felt her jaw drop, Millie gently scolded Cameron about how every young bride had to start somewhere, and Shelby would do just fine.

For the next few minutes, Cameron ignored Shelby while Karl praised his wife between mouthfuls of pie. Millie almost blushed at all the praise and self-consciously expressed her gratitude until she was able to turn the conversation away from herself to talk freely about her family, grandchildren, and all the fun things they could do together this summer as they planned for the wedding.

"We want to take you to Yellowstone when Brad comes," Millie went on. "And we have to take you boating when Laura and Bruce come up from Idaho Falls. Our ward will have a picnic and fun activities too." It warmed Shelby's heart to be included in Karl and Millie's plans, to feel so much a part of everything.

Karl looked over at her and chuckled. "I wouldn't be surprised if you were asked to help out with some of the ward activities."

"Just look out for crazy Sister Brown," Cameron muttered.

Wondering who Sister Brown was, Shelby noticed how the dimple appeared in his cheek in spite of his efforts to appear gruff. When Cameron glanced across the table, Shelby couldn't quite define the expression on his face. After a brief moment of eye contact, Cameron abruptly gathered up his dishes and stood up.

"Thanks for dinner, Mom." He kissed her cheek, put his dishes in the sink and, without a backward glance, disappeared out the front door.

Chapter 4

Birds were twittering their cheerful calls as the early rays of sun welcomed Shelby to her first Montana morning. The smell of pancakes and sausages drifted into her room, tantalizing her senses and coaxing her to leave the warmth of her bed. She stretched lazily and yawned. Glancing at the clock on the dresser, she was surprised to discover that it was only 6:30. She heard voices coming down the hall from the kitchen.

"They sure don't sleep in around here," she said to herself with another yawn. But eager to continue making a good impression on her future in-laws, she dragged herself out of bed and headed for the bathroom.

Panic hit all at once.

What if Cameron's out there? She dreaded barging into him again. Then, looking down at her thin pajamas, she wondered why she hadn't had the sense to buy a robe before driving up here. Shelby bit her lip and tiptoed over to the bedroom door. Daring to take a peek in the hallway, she decided all looked safe. Making a mad dash for the bathroom might not say anything for poise or refinement, but somehow it seemed necessary.

It turned out that her fears were unwarranted. Cameron was nowhere to be found. Shelby got dressed and then called Brad, even though he had already called last night to see how she was doing. It was nice just to hear his voice.

Then she ate a quiet breakfast sitting in the swing on the front porch, basking in the most glorious peach-colored sunrise she had ever seen. She felt so alive out here watching the birds fly from tree to tree, seeing chipmunks scamper about, and enjoying the cool morning breeze drift gently over her face. A row of lilac bushes drooping from the weight of branches in full bloom released their sweet, heady fragrance.

Millie soon came outside with a tall glass of orange juice. As soon as she was sitting comfortably in a chair next to Shelby, Bomber came bounding over with his panting grin, followed by Wags, who hit everything within reach of his wildly wagging tail. They were like wound up balls of energy, moving everywhere all at once and eager to sniff out this new arrival. Shelby laughed and put out a hand to them. They danced around her playfully, vying for her attention. Bomber, being the larger of the two, kept managing to oust his rival, but Wags wiggled his way around legs and chairs to fend for himself.

Millie said, "Wow, you've just managed to win two hearts!"

"Well, they're both really cute." She turned her face down to rub Bomber's ears but Wags pushed in jealously to get his fair share of strokes.

"Okay, you silly rascals, sit! Good dogs." Millie stroked their coats. "By the way, I'd be happy to take you into town this week, if you'd like. Brad said you needed help picking out things for the wedding, and I know Bozeman has a few bridal shops."

Oh. Shelby thought about the day that she had been looking through Amanda's bride magazine and Brad had teased her about the styles of many wedding gowns. She wondered if he had persuaded his mom to help Shelby select a gown that wouldn't make him laugh. He liked taking things into his own hands. It was a perfectly good trait. No reason to feel annoyed.

"I'd love to go into town with you," she said cheerfully while she absently squashed an ant with the heel of her tennis shoe.

If Brad had such good taste, he must have learned from Millie. She could probably give Shelby some great advice. It's just that she kind of wanted to come up with ideas on her own, to have ownership in some part of the "big day." Maybe it was just that she felt there would be such a lack of her family's presence when August 20 rolled around. In just under two months, she would be Mrs. Shelby Thompson.

"I've already reserved the cultural hall for the reception, and there's a florist I'd like to take you to."

"That sounds . . . great."

"Are you nervous about getting married?" asked Millie, looking a bit concerned as she studied Shelby's face. Shelby had to think for a minute as she tried to improve her expression.

"I don't know. . . . Maybe a little," she admitted shyly.

"It's a big step, I know," Millie mused. "I was so nervous when I got married that I bit off all my fingernails!"

"You did?" Shelby asked.

"Yes. But you know, I've never once regretted my decision."

"What a good feeling that must be."

"You'll have that too, Shelby. I'm sure of it."

Shelby smiled her thanks to her future mother-in-law and felt truly grateful she had come to Montana. It would be wonderful to get to know Millie over the next several weeks.

* * *

The next afternoon, Shelby and Millie sat together again on the front porch contemplating the wedding gowns they had seen that day in Bozeman. There certainly hadn't been very much to choose from. Shelby was impressed that Millie had tried to stay in the background and had encouraged Shelby to try on any gown that appealed to her. She had tried on several that she thought Brad would be pleased with and had come up with a few possibilities, but they had been terribly expensive.

"There is a lady in our ward who sews beautifully if you're interested. I'm not as good as she is, unfortunately, and I bet she could make a lovely wedding gown for a good price."

"I wish I knew how to sew." Shelby's mom was definitely not the domestic goddess that some women were, so there weren't many such skills passed on to Shelby. "I just want something simple, although I'm sure Brad would like everything to be quite formal."

Millie looked surprised. "Well, Brad doesn't get to pick out your gown," she said with a wink and conspiratorial grin. "Just do what *you* want!"

"Really?" Shelby sounded incredulous.

"Trust me. It's your chance to be completely autonomous before getting married."

Millie's bubbly laughter was interrupted when the dogs began barking wildly at a beat-up old car laboriously making its way up the drive.

"Oh no," Millie muttered miserably under her breath.

Then with a guilty look on her face, she turned to Shelby. "It's our neighbor, Elvira Brown. She's an elderly lady in our ward and just a bit . . . Well, she's quite a character. I hope she doesn't drive you crazy. She means well."

Millie stood up and walked over to the car. Shelby followed in curiosity. Steam was spewing from the rackety engine as Sister Brown reached out the window to open her car door from the outside. She was short and round with brightly painted wrinkled lips. Juggling a metal cane in one hand and a lopsided loaf of bread in the other, the elderly lady got out of the car, and introductions were made.

"Welcome to Montana, dear. I've brought you a loaf of wheat bread. It's my new recipe."

As Shelby took the bread, she had an instant struggle to keep her composure. It felt like lead, and it had tiny green things embedded on the sides. *Holy cow.*

"It's made with spinach," she said proudly. "It's very healthy, and you'd never know it."

"Uh . . . thank you, Sister Brown. That's nice of—"

"Call me Elvira. Now you must tell me all about the wedding," she interrupted, grabbing Shelby's arm and turning her toward the house.

Millie shook her head and sighed, then followed them up to the front porch. Elvira barged into the house, invited Shelby inside, and almost shut the door before Millie could sneak inside her own home. Millie and Shelby exchanged amused looks over the untamed mass of permed silver hair that resembled a steel wool pad stretched out of shape.

When Shelby set the loaf of bread down on the coffee table, it made such a thud that she had to check to make sure she hadn't dented the wood. Sinking heavily into the sofa, Sister Brown proceeded to squeeze every drop of information she could get out of Shelby, beginning with how she and Brad had met to the color of the reception guest book.

"It must be a white guest book, you know. It simply *must* be white. I cannot abide colored guest books."

"Why do you say that?" Shelby asked incredulously.

"Well . . . because! I went to a civil wedding—what a tragedy they weren't married in the temple, as *you* will be, dear—but they had the most appalling guest book. It was a horrid shade of green, and it had . . ."

On and on she rambled almost without drawing breath until Shelby felt she would suffocate. When Millie left the room for a few minutes, Elvira leaned closer and asked Shelby how she was enjoying her stay so far.

"Is it too far north for you?"

"No, I love it here." Shelby answered honestly.

"Yes, dear, the Thompsons are the best folks you'll find anywhere. The very best." Her voice dropped significantly in volume before she continued. "But I must say that I'm simply taken aback by that older son of theirs and all the problems he has caused. I'm shocked—almost speechless, I'm telling you! Now, if you ever feel uncomfortable with the situation, please feel free to stay with me for a few days. I could cook you some of my specialties and . . ."

Listening to an outline of potentially dangerous meals, Shelby didn't get a word in edgewise—which was just as well since she wouldn't have known what to say to this eccentric old lady in the first place. When Millie returned, much to Shelby's relief, Sister Brown scooted herself out from the cushions and made her way back to her car.

"Thank you for coming, Elvira," called Millie.

"You are most welcome, dear. I love to make my visits and bring a little cheer to people's lives. It's a shame you won't be here more than a couple of weeks, Shelby. But enjoy your stay."

As soon as Sister Brown had started the engine, Millie whispered a recommendation to toss the loaf of bread in the garbage because even the dogs wouldn't eat it.

The old car clanked down the driveway, backfiring once before it was out of sight, leaving Millie and Shelby to stare after it in amusement.

* * *

Dinner was over and the dishes were washed. Millie and Karl were down in the family room watching TV, and Shelby was curled up on the sofa in the front room flipping through the pages of her wedding planner when Cameron came home. She hadn't seen him since dinner the night before last. *Thank heaven!* But she wondered where he had gone. His summer job surely wouldn't have him working such long hours. At least she hadn't had to worry about pretending to be "calm and collected" while he had been away.

As Cameron walked in the front door, Shelby looked up from her planner and saw him juggling several warehouse-sized boxes of food that were all threatening to topple out of his grasp. Shelby jumped off the sofa and hurried over.

"Here, let me help you. What can I take?"

"The box over here. . . . No, on my *other* side," he grumbled as a huge box of cereal escaped and landed on the carpet.

Ignoring his indignant "tchh," she retrieved the box and closed the door behind him. Then they walked into the kitchen, where Cameron heaved the boxes onto the counter.

"Thanks," he said brusquely.

You have got to be kidding me! There was no need for him to act so unfriendly. She hadn't done anything wrong this time! She was a guest in this home, and not just *any* guest either. She was a future relative.

"You're welcome," she almost snarled. "Are there more things to bring in?"

"Just a few more boxes."

"I'll help you . . ." *If you can be civil,* she wanted to add.

A faint masculine scent of pines tantalized her senses as he passed in front of her. His navy blue flannel brushed against her arm, and she leapt back and bumped into the refrigerator. He looked back to see if something had happened.

She blinked up at him with an air of innocence mixed with defiance, not about to reveal that her hip was throbbing. "Uh . . . I'll just follow you . . ."

He gave her one last look, mumbled something that sounded like ". . . if you can handle it," and then headed back to the door.

When his words registered, she called out crossly to his retreating back, "I'm not going to spill anything on you!"

Cameron stopped in his tracks. He turned around and looked her over, eyebrows raised. Suddenly, his mouth broke into a reluctant grin.

"Well, that's good," he almost laughed and then sauntered outside.

Shelby rolled her eyes but followed him out to his red Dodge Ram. *He must think he's really something, driving that obnoxious, huge truck . . . He probably has a rearview mirror twice the normal size just so he can gawk at his criminally handsome face.* Walking behind Cameron, she tried to think of some brilliant comebacks, but her thoughts wandered as he strode in front of her. *Some people sure look good in Levi's . . .*

Guiltily, Shelby swung her gaze back to the truck. Cameron reached in to grab a stack of boxes and then handed them to her.

"Are these too heavy for you?"

"No, of course not," she spat out, instantly regretting her hotheadedness.

She headed back into the house without waiting for him, knowing she had better cool off. That good impression she had wanted so hard to make was going to go right out the window if she let Cameron's surliness get to her.

When Cameron came into the kitchen again, she had unpacked a case of root beer, chips, candy bars, and a host of basic junk food. She turned to face him with her arms crossed in front.

"So, is this what you eat to stay so fit?" she teased sarcastically.

"No," he countered. "I also like to pour a little bacon fat over the top of everything."

As she scrunched up her nose in revulsion, he suddenly threw his head back and laughed. Shelby hadn't counted on such a reaction and felt an unfamiliar sensation go through her.

"What? That doesn't sound good to you?" he mocked, opening a bag of cholesterol-loaded chips and popping a few into his mouth. Then he extended the opened bag and asked, "Want some?"

"No thanks," she said, unable to preserve the frown.

"They're good . . ."

"Even without the bacon grease?"

"Well . . . sometimes I have to eat 'em plain."

The look of disgust she hurled at him was diminished by her insuppressible smile.

When Karl wandered into the kitchen Shelby turned away from Cameron and fussed with the cans of pop in apparent interest. *Okay, this is crazy. Why am I feeling so rattled?* She knew she should be a pleasant houseguest, and hey, she was trying, but she was feeling so awkward that she was finding it difficult to be consistent.

"Hey, Cam. Are you back?"

"Yeah. Those kids won't dare tell me that they're hungry this trip." He explained, "The last time I took the Young Men on a hike they gave me so much grief about 'wasting away' and being 'tortured by starvation' that I vowed I'd be ready for them next time."

Karl chuckled, and Shelby turned back to ask, "Where are you going this time?"

"We're going on another hike."

"When are you leaving?"

"In a month, but I thought I'd get an early start on preparations."

Millie appeared and teasingly poked her son in the ribs. "What are you up to, mister?" Shelby saw quickly that Cameron was extremely ticklish.

"Hey!" he cried and jumped out of his mother's reach. He grabbed her from behind and held her locked in his arms. "I'm bigger than you are, Mom," he whispered in her ear and then smacked a kiss on her cheek.

Shelby observed the interaction between mother and son in awe and admiration. Seeing Cameron playing the part of the loving son also came as a surprise. While he talked to his parents about the upcoming trip she thought about what she'd seen so far of his personality. He apparently was a confusing mix of contrasting emotions: unpleasant one moment and completely likeable the next. *What could Brad have meant when he said Cameron isn't very dependable? What's the story behind this unpredictable guy?*

Shelby suddenly realized that Cameron's deep blue eyes were resting on her, a penetrating expression on his face. She felt her cheeks turn warm.

Millie's voice broke in. "Cam, would you like to make us a fire? We need to roast some marshmallows and make s'mores."

"We 'need to,' huh?" teased Karl, earning a poke in his own side from Millie.

"Sure, Mom." Cameron volunteered. "I'll head out there now."

He started to leave, but Millie called out, "Wait. Maybe Shelby would like to help build the fire?"

He looked back at Shelby skeptically. "Do you?"

"Uh . . ." her voice trailed off. Looking from Karl to Millie for an escape, she found none. "I actually don't know much about building a fire. You'd have to show me what to do."

He conceded by waving an arm. "Come on, I'll show you."

Cameron led her outside to the huge wood pile stacked against the back side of the house and had her take a handful of sticks and small branches while he put on a pair of worn leather gloves. When he had loaded his arms full of split logs, she followed him down the hill. It was a mystery to her how a man could look even more masculine than ever just holding a stack of logs. But she shouldn't be taking notice in the first place.

Shelby saw the ashes and soot in the fire pit and asked if he liked campfires.

"Love 'em. There's nothing like staring into the flames and hearing the popping embers while crickets chirp in the background. It's like heaven—especially when the clouds give you a break so you can see the stars."

"That does sound nice." Shelby knelt down beside him and watched his hands as he deftly stacked logs into a pyramid shape. "How can I help?"

"Put the kindling right in here," Cameron said as he grabbed a few pieces, "like that."

They continued working together, Cameron surprisingly courteous and Shelby eager to learn. His hands guided hers until they were finished. Once the fire was going, he sat back on one of the big logs that circled the fire and invited her to do the same.

"Now that's a perfect fire."

"It is rather impressive," she boasted jokingly. "What talent we have."

Cameron laughed quietly. Shelby wrapped her arms around her legs and felt the intensity of the fire spread over her in undulating gusts of heat. Cameron quietly studied the flames as they curled upward into the blackness. When he suddenly looked over, his words surprised her.

"Shelby . . . I need to apologize for being . . . sort of . . . rude since you came."

"It's okay. I'm sorry too . . . I wasn't exactly the greatest guest."

"No, you've been fine."

"It doesn't help things to get a compost smoothie dumped on you."

Although his head was down, he didn't look angry. But he didn't reply either. There was an awkward moment of quiet. Then he spoke, "It's just me. I haven't been handling life very well lately."

Shelby searched for something to say in response. Not knowing what he was going through, it was impossible to determine what would be appropriate. The seconds that ticked away felt like hours. She was relieved when he suddenly changed the subject.

"So tell me . . . when did you meet Brad?"

"It was during fall semester. We were in the same ward."

"Oh." More silence followed. Shelby fidgeted a little on the log.

"I forget—when are you getting married?" Though slight in change, his tone turned grim.

"August 20."

He grunted. "That's soon."

No kidding. Shelby shifted her weight again.

"Where are you from?" he glanced at her. Uneasiness washed over her, and she turned away and played with a stick.

"I . . . moved around a lot," she shrugged. "Why the interrogation?"

Cameron's head lifted. "I'm sorry. I just . . . wanted to know more about you."

Smooth, Shelby. Way to go, she chided herself. She glanced over at him with remorse. "No, I'm the one who should be sorry. I just hate that question. I've spent five years at BYU answering 'Hi-what's your name-where are you from' everywhere I went. Having to repeat the same story over and over again was awful. I got to the point where I'd just say 'Provo' and change the subject. I've lived in so many places that it's all just . . ."

Cameron briefly waved one hand at her. "It's okay. You don't have to tell me."

"I suppose it's . . . well, it is only fair . . ." her eyes suddenly twinkled impishly, "because *I* was actually going to try to find out more about *you*."

That brought a smile back to his face. But she didn't have a chance to continue or find out more about him because Karl and Millie arrived with marshmallows and the works.

The campfire was circled about with laughter as they munched on their s'mores and talked into the night. It was surprising to Shelby that she was beginning to fit in with them. The best part was the feeling that they truly wanted her there with them.

Shelby was roasting her fourth marshmallow when Karl reluctantly got up to head inside.

"I can't stay out late like I used to," he yawned.

Millie stood up too and said she had some laundry to do before going to bed. The older couple walked back up the hill to the house hand in hand. Cameron watched them go with a remote look in his eyes and then stood up to poke at the fire.

"Oh no!" Shelby yelled. "My marshmallow's on fire!"

Cameron pulled her stick over and blew several times until all that was left was a shriveled black mass dangling in front of her.

Shelby scrunched up her nose. "It's ruined."

Cameron proceeded to slip the gooey mass off her stick and popped it into his mouth with a mischievous grin.

"Hey! That was mine!" Shelby said, mildly indignant. Laughter and a mouthful of marshmallow were the only recompense she received.

"By the way, you've got marshmallow all over your face," he stated ungraciously.

"No I don't."

"Yes you do. It's stuck to your nose."

Shelby made a face at him. "I think you're just teasing me."

"No I'm not," he said gruffly. "Come here . . ."

He looked like he was up to something, so she resisted. When he was suddenly beside her, his fingers softly rubbing at her cheeks and nose, her breath caught in her throat, and she could feel the illogical pounding of her heart. His gentle fingers suddenly stopped beside her lower lip, and he was completely still. Shelby found a tender wistfulness in his deep blue eyes.

An owl hooted noisily overhead, and Cameron moved away from her. But there was still something in the air between them as they sat looking into the crackling flames, and a warmth spread over her that she was sure had nothing to do with the fire.

* * *

Long after Shelby had gone inside, Cameron sat by the fire and tossed wood chips and twigs haphazardly into the dying flames. He watched them snap and crackle as they burned and disintegrated. As small waves of heat moved over his face and through his thick hair in little gusts, he was deep in thought and miles away.

He couldn't explain what he was feeling, nor was he sure he really wanted to face it. His first impression of Shelby was that she was a walking disaster. It had infuriated him that she would be visiting at a time like this, when he had come for solitude.

He didn't want her around. So why had his pulse raced at the mere sight of her? He was decidedly against women in general, so what was wrong with him?

All he knew was that his brother had chosen the most beautiful woman Cameron had ever laid eyes on. Her long, silky hair was a golden mist that radiated amber warmth. Every time he saw her he had to fight the image of his fingers dipping in the waves of her hair. And she had the most expressive eyes he had ever seen. At first he thought they were blue, but tonight they looked almost green. She was certainly spirited, he thought with amusement. Yet there was softness in her face that made her seem gentle and vulnerable.

Brad had definitely triumphed again. Brad always seemed to do everything right.

Sure, Cameron loved his younger brother and admired him very much. It was just so frustrating to be the eldest son and feel like he'd never quite measure up. Being a high school science teacher would never earn him the kind of money Brad would get once he got that doctorate degree. Brad was more outgoing, taller, smarter—he was even in his elders quorum presidency in his BYU ward. And no one would ever let Cameron forget the other major point: *never* had any scandal been linked with Brad's name . . .

Cameron closed his eyes as if to shut out the lashing words that assaulted his memory: *Cameron, why can't you face up to your responsibility? That baby is yours, and you know it. How could you abandon her like this?*

People had been so cruel to him. A few friends had even shunned him. Now they'd probably all be gossiping about how he had run back home to hide like a coward.

"Let them," he growled as he forcefully threw a handful of pine needles in the fire, sending a shower of popping sparks into the air.

Cameron stood quickly and stamped out the sparks that had sailed into the dirt. With hands thrust in the pockets of his jeans, he looked up into the vast twinkling sky. He found the Big Dipper, Orion, and other constellations as a cool breeze wafted over his face. He drew in a deep, cool breath and slowly let it out. But instead of seeing the twinkling stars overhead, an untouchable image teased his mind—one with long, gold hair and beautiful hazel eyes.

Chapter 5

Lipstick and blush were the finishing touches before Shelby smoothed out her lavender skirt and pronounced herself ready for church. She stood back from the mirror to scrutinize her appearance from every possible angle she could maneuver and then frantically plugged her flat iron back into the socket. Glancing at her watch, she knew she'd have to hurry if she expected to fix that one section of hair in the back.

Under normal circumstances back in her apartment, Sara and Amanda would have been surprised with her for taking such painstaking means, but today she felt the urgency to look her best. There wasn't time to analyze her reasons—perhaps she didn't even know herself. All she felt was the feminine urge to look pretty.

When she walked into the front room, Karl was reading his scriptures and Millie was in the kitchen adding sliced carrots to the crock pot. Karl gave Shelby an appreciative glance, but Millie showered her with compliments.

"I think our son caught the prettiest fish in the sea!" she exclaimed, causing a faint color to spread across Shelby's cheeks.

"Thank you, Millie." Shelby sat in the rocking chair to adjust her sandal straps.

Karl closed his scriptures and zipped them up in their case. He checked his watch and furrowed his brow. Then he wandered into the kitchen. "I don't think Cam's coming to church today, do you?" he questioned Millie. "It's about time to go."

Millie answered vaguely, "Um . . . let's just give him a minute. He might."

When Cameron appeared ten minutes later, his father had his answer.

Cameron looked like he had stepped out of the latest men's fashion magazine, but he definitely wasn't modeling church clothes—more like men's sleepwear. As Cameron yawned, Shelby noted his sleep-rumpled hair and had to tear her eyes from the thick blue robe that barely concealed the muscles of his chest. Making a concentrated effort of delving into the scriptures on her lap, she wished she had Amanda's often-quoted Youth Standards pamphlet to occupy her attention.

Millie looked up from the glass she was drying with a worn dish-towel and instantly reacted.

"Cameron Edgar Thompson, don't you *dare* traipse out here half naked or I'll swat your behind!" Millie began to twist her damp dish-towel into a dangerous flicking implement.

"Mom, I'm almost thirty years old! If I want to take a shower then—"

Cameron let out a whoop as he raced ahead of her into the front room, not seeing Shelby sitting in the rocking chair. As he rounded the rocking chair, he swept a quick look behind him to check his mother's progress and found his eyes locked with Shelby's instead. He stared down at her in discomfiture, raking a hand across the back of his neck.

"Oh. Uh . . . hi," he said, smothering a guilty laugh. His hands roved through his hair, making it even more disheveled than before.

"Hi." There was teasing laughter in her eyes. "Edgar, huh?"

Cameron cringed in mock aversion at the sound of his middle name. Just as he opened his mouth to reply, the dishtowel suddenly snapped against his covered thigh with a resounding crack, turning the start of his retort into a yelp.

"Mom, you're lethal with that thing!" Then, turning back to Shelby, he winked conspiratorially. "She's lethal with names too."

Millie grabbed her son's arm and wagged a finger in his face good-humoredly. "Edgar is a very respectable name, and don't you forget it! Your great-grandfather was a noble man."

"Anything you say, Mom," he laughed.

"Hey, at least you got a middle name," Shelby remarked playfully. "I used to pretend I had a middle name as a kid because everyone who was anyone had one, except for me."

Cameron looked down at her, the expression on his face changing. Shelby's cheeks reddened. She had only meant to play along, not try to get sympathy. When Shelby felt his blue eyes lingering on her, she cautiously looked at him and felt her heart stop.

"You look . . . nice," he said.

She could barely find her voice. "Thank you."

Seeing the look on his face, the blush spread. It seemed completely unfair that people had no control over such things. *If I don't stop blushing soon, I'll look like a field of wild Indian paintbrush.* Desperately hoping he hadn't noticed, she dropped her face and searched studiously through her scriptures.

Apparently unaware of Shelby's discomfort, Karl wandered in to say fondly, "We're going to have to go now, son. Will we see you there later?"

Cameron made a face. "Uh . . . maybe."

Shelby saw the pained look on Karl's face that he tried so hard to conceal. It must be difficult to be a parent, she thought. But her thoughts instantly turned to her own parents, and she had to quickly block them out. She didn't want to think about their parenting skills right now. It definitely wasn't a good time.

The drive to their ward building in Bozeman was long enough for Shelby to take in the beauties of the area. She commented on the dramatic mountain ranges and masses of wildflowers. They pointed out bare fields which, by the end of summer, would be filled with golden wheat and other crops swaying their bounty in the gentle breeze.

When they pulled into the church parking lot, Shelby's interest turned to the tan brick building with several tall gothic windows—slender at the bottom and arched to a peak at the top. It was an older style, and Shelby wondered when it had been built.

From the moment they walked inside, members surrounded her in happy welcome. Millie didn't miss the chance to bustle over and introduce Shelby to several people. They congratulated her on her engagement, wondered how she was surviving without Brad, and questioned her about things down at "the Y." She felt hopeful that she could make some friends with the members during her stay. Wouldn't Brad be pleasantly surprised to come up and find her fitting right in?

Although she received several curious looks when they sat down in the chapel and she had the uncomfortable impression that a few people were whispering about her during Sunday School, she was able to bask in the kindhearted welcome everyone extended to her. Shelby saw the way Millie and Karl interacted with others, giving and receiving love and affection. It helped put at ease even more throughout the meetings, and she felt blessed that someday she would be a part of such a good family.

It was a feeling that lasted until she was in the restroom adjusting her slip in one of the stalls. The three girls who came in must not have realized that Shelby was still in there. *There's no way they'd be blabbing like this if they knew I was here.*

"My sister told me that she's pregnant!" one with black shoes said with a wad of gum in her mouth.

"You're kidding!" gasped a hand washer.

"And I heard that people were accusing *him* of being the father," came a loud whisper. Shelby rolled her eyes in disgust at the gossiping females. She decided to stay concealed in the stall rather than barge out there to show that she'd overheard their private conversation. She hoped they would leave soon.

The black shoes tapped. "My aunt heard someone in his ward say that he totally refused to marry her. She totally *begged* him not to leave her, but he did anyway. Can you believe it?"

"What a loser!" bleated the whisperer.

Shelby looked at the ceiling, rolling her eyes.

"And here he is back at home like nothing ever happened. Poor Brother and Sister Thompson. They're so nice, they'd probably believe anything he said."

Shelby's eyes turned round as saucers the second the Thompsons' name was mentioned. *No way. They couldn't be talking about . . . No, they must have been talking about some different Thompsons. Why would anyone say something so vicious about Brad's family?* It couldn't be true, but a nagging thought murmured that if it were true, then the "loser" they had spoken of would have to be Cameron.

There was an obnoxious bang of the paper towel dispenser, and then the girls scuffled over to the door. One of them yapped something indistinct, and they all filed out of the bathroom, leaving a trail of laughter behind them. The door closed, snuffing out the noise, and Shelby walked out of the stall in bewildered silence.

When the meetings were over, Bishop Parker vigorously shook her hand, and Shelby stretched her mouth into a smile to greet him. But confusing thoughts were attacking like a swarm of bees. Was all that gossip really about Cameron? Brad's voice echoed in her mind, "He's not dependable . . . He avoids being around people . . ."

Would he have done anything so terrible?

"I understand that you'll be staying here for a few weeks, Sister Hamlin," the bishop was saying. "We'll have to put you to work!" His suit jiggled when he laughed, reminding her of a very realistic Santa Claus she had seen with her dad when she was young.

"I'd be happy to help out, Bishop."

And she meant it, even though her voice sounded hollow. Participation in Church activities held a lot of meaning to Shelby: acceptance and being a vital part of something good. The bishop invited her to participate in the summer activities with the ward and then moved on to shake hands with an elderly man. But all she could think about was the overheard conversation in the bathroom and what it meant.

* * *

Millie had suggested a picnic dinner for Monday's family night, but Shelby had a suspicion that they often had to include outdoor activities in the plans in order to get Cameron to come along. She could only imagine what he'd do if they offered to give a lesson on the three degrees of glory or the blessings of genealogy and temple work. Feeling completely ill at ease around him, Shelby almost wished he wouldn't come. She knew it was none of her business but couldn't help wondering about what he had done.

What was going on in the head of this man who was to become her brother-in-law?

While Cameron was working in the Hyalite Canyon that day, Millie and Shelby went into town together. First they stopped at the fabric store in the Gallatin Valley Mall. They had both agreed that they should buy some tulle to decorate with. The filmy white material would be pretty just about anywhere. They also found a green metal arbor Shelby thought could be decorated nicely with ivy and silk flowers and arranged somewhere at the reception. She thought Brad had favorably mentioned that idea once. The last purchase was a large spool of pale yellow organza ribbon.

As Shelby saw Millie's enthusiasm over the reception increasing, it seemed more and more unlikely that she would be able to get out of having one. And Millie really did have some fun ideas for decorations and centerpieces. They spent a few minutes looking through the pattern books for wedding gowns, but Shelby didn't see a style that seemed right for her. After paying for the items they had chosen, Millie drove east into the older part of town.

Historic Bozeman was a delightful place, with quaint old shops, art galleries, and restaurants. Baskets of red, white, and purple petunias hung from charming lampposts along the sidewalks. People were friendly and helpful, giving Shelby even more of a warm feeling for this place. They opted for getting some lunch at a small restaurant on Main Street where they could eat outside near the sidewalk and watch the people who passed by.

A toothy waitress with bleached hair and heavily mascaraed jet black eyelashes came to take their orders. Her smile instantly froze on her face when she looked down at Millie. The girl wiped her right hand distastefully on the apron wrapped around her tiny waist. Then she backed up and dropped her pen.

"Oh—I uh . . . wait a minute."

The distressed waitress fled, nearly taking down a customer who had just stood up. Shelby gave Millie a questioning look.

"What was that all about?"

"Probably her first day on the job."

After several minutes the waitress hadn't come back so Shelby excused herself to find the restroom.

"If anyone comes to take our order, I'll have the turkey sandwich and a glass of water," she told Millie and then made her way back inside the building.

As she walked past the steamy kitchen, distant voices inside slashed through the air with angry accusations. The words weren't clear but Shelby caught a few slanderous phrases.

". . . not going back out there . . ."

". . . refuse to serve anyone related to Cameron Thompson . . ."

". . . mother of the swine who destroyed my little sister . . ."

Motionless in front of the restroom door, appalled by what she had just overheard, Shelby's blood began to boil. How could anyone speak behind Millie's back like that, regardless of what her son had done?

Shelby forced her feet forward and walked inside the restroom. *Is the whole town gossiping about Cameron? How could he have done such a despicable thing? Is he capable of destroying a young girl's life by getting her pregnant and then abandoning her?* The thought made her feel sick. If this was true, then Cameron's "problems" Brad had mentioned were much worse than she had imagined.

But poor Millie! Even if Cameron was a depraved jerk, that waitress had no business shouting about it in a public place.

Shelby abruptly stormed out of the restroom, fuming in silent rage. When she reached the table where Millie sat—still waiting for service—Shelby threw her napkin on the table and reached for Millie's hand.

"Come on, Millie. Let's leave. I can't believe any place could be so . . ."

Shelby clenched her fists and let out a strangled sigh of frustration. *What am I thinking? I can't let Millie know anything about what I just heard! She'd be shattered to know people were talking about her family in such a way.*

". . . so slow. They're so slow here that we could go somewhere else and be finished before our waitress found her way back to our table!"

Millie smiled sadly. "You overheard something, didn't you, Shelby?"

Shelby looked painfully into Millie's eyes.

"Don't worry about protecting me." Her words were bitter. "I know how gossip spreads around here."

Shelby suddenly had no idea what to say. As if by mutual consent, they quietly left the table and walked back to the car. Millie drove down Main Street in silence, looking like she had something to say but didn't know how to say it.

"I'm sorry, Millie."

"Heavens, there's nothing for you to be sorry about. You did nothing wrong."

Shelby waited for her to continue.

"I . . ." Millie faltered. "Cam is too proud. He made me promise not to discuss anything about the whole darned mess with anyone—"

"It's all right, Millie," Shelby said quickly. "It's none of my business." She took a deep breath and exhaled slowly. "I just get steamed up so easily sometimes."

"No, it shows your protective nature. I think that's an admirable quality."

"Sometimes I wish I knew karate."

Millie laughed, and her face relaxed. Shelby was relieved to see it.

"Let me just say this: you can't always believe everything you hear."

Shelby had said it was none of her business, and it wasn't. Gossip was such an ugly thing. And while her mind was brimming with questions about the things that had been said behind Cameron's back, she held on to Millie's words. *You can't always believe everything you hear.*

They stopped off at a fast food restaurant, and the subject wasn't brought up again. After eating, they found a florist shop that had a few pictures of bridal bouquets to choose from. Some were painfully plain and others were so ornate they were gaudy, but eventually, Shelby found one she loved.

"What about this one, Millie?" Pictured was a bundle of pale roses and lavender statice surrounded by baby's breath, tied together by a simple organza ribbon. "Do you think it's too expensive?"

"No, it's perfect. What shade of roses would you pick?"

"Maybe the peachy pink, yellow, and cream roses. They look so pretty together accented with the statice."

"I think we should order it, don't you?" Millie asked.

Shelby gently bit her lip, considering the beautiful flowers, and then nodded with a grin.

Millie left a deposit, refusing to let Shelby help out. "The groom's family takes care of the flowers, you know."

Shelby stuttered slightly before forming the words, "Are you sure?"

"Very sure."
"Oh, thank you!"
She wrapped Millie in a heartfelt hug that warmed them both.

Chapter 6

The mere fact that it didn't require coins to operate made Millie's washing machine seem like a novel commodity to Shelby. She was actually enjoying the chore of washing and folding her clothes in the small, narrow laundry room. Warm sunshine cast a peaceful glow through the window and over the rising piles of clothes. The heady scent of lemons and bleach drifted through the room. The whole scene reminded her of Grandma Hamlin's house in Northern California where Shelby had been able to make a few precious childhood memories before the sweet lady had died.

Grandma Hamlin had red and white gingham curtains in her kitchen window that used to wave a welcome in the slightest breeze. When she was a child coming to visit in the summer, Shelby used to watch hopefully for the first glimpse of those curtains. Dad and Mom would be arguing as usual in the front seat of a rickety used car—one in a line of many—with Shelby alone in the back seat, anxiously waiting for Grandma's house to appear, almost fearing that it wouldn't. As soon as she was wrapped in Grandma's soft arms, she knew all would be well.

At least for a little while.

Tender thoughts of that sweet old lady brought a pang to Shelby's heart. If it weren't for her faith in the gospel, it would be so easy to be consumed with bitterness at life and all its unfairness. Grandma had adored her and had even asked Shelby's parents a few times to let Shelby live with her. But Shelby had never been allowed to spend more than a couple weeks at a time with Grandma during the summers.

Unbidden memories of Shelby's volatile childhood surfaced. Her father had dragged Shelby and her mother from state to state, always searching for the perfect job, the perfect situation—a sort of nonexistent utopia that had to be out there on the next horizon. "This job is really going to be great!" he would tell them enthusiastically. Realtor, sales consultant, or restaurant manager—it never mattered what the job was.

Those were the times that she remembered her dad being happy.

But gradually the smiles would fade, and he would end up as miserable as a caged bird desperate for flight. Unfortunately, that usually happened about the time that Shelby and her mother were just beginning to feel a semblance of being settled and comfortable. He was just never willing to stay in one place long enough to make it work. Shelby remembered her mother crying a lot over the years, drowning her sorrows in alcohol. She could also remember walking into the house to hear full-blown arguments raging and running away for an hour to cry because she knew the inevitable move was coming soon.

After losing so many friends with each painful uprooting, Shelby gradually felt no desire to make friends or develop any close attachments, knowing that she would just be torn away in the end.

And then one day she had learned about Grandma. Losing her to cancer was the most horrible, infuriating . . . Shelby fought the bubbling torrent of feelings and pushed the pain inside. Gripping the sides of the washing machine, she breathed deeply and sought to bring her thoughts back to the present by focusing on Brad. Becoming his wife would heal the emotional wounds she had suffered. Everything would be made right when they got married. *I know it will!* Then she would have all that she so desperately needed: love, security, and a wonderful family.

Millie poked her head in the doorway. "Are you finding everything okay in here?" she asked.

"Oh," Shelby came back to reality. "Yes, fine."

"We're going to our home teaching appointments now to visit a couple of widows. On the way back, we'll stop by the florist's shop to pick up their quote for the reception. Be sure to make yourself at home, and we'll be back around five."

"Thanks, Millie," she smiled.

The rumbling of tires over gravel sounded Karl and Millie's departure, and after Wags and Bomber barked a few times, a soothing stillness settled over the house. A bird chirped outside the window, and the dryer hummed. Shelby inhaled deeply. She really didn't mind being alone here. She tried to picture Grandma smiling down upon her from heaven, whispering words of encouragement only Shelby could hear. The comfort and peace of the Thompson home became like the healing balm of Grandma's arms. In her mind, Shelby could hear Grandma's voice singing melodies from an era long past. She began to hum in tune with the memory as she ironed her clothes.

* * *

She would never have continued had she realized that Cameron was leaning against the doorframe watching her gentle movements and the sunlight playing with the gold-red highlights in her hair. He was mesmerized by the sound of her voice. It was an image he would hide away like an unspoken secret.

To prevent embarrassment to either Shelby or himself, he silently slipped away and walked outside to sit on the front porch swing. Leaning forward, arms resting on knees, he stared down at a crack that ran the length of the porch. *What is happening to me?* She was becoming much more than a distraction. Maybe he should just get back in his truck and leave. She couldn't affect him if he wasn't around. But there were things he needed from his room.

He sat on the porch for a few more minutes until he was too restless with his thoughts to sit any longer. He stood up and went back into the house, being sure to shut the front door hard enough to be heard. Shelby's singing instantly stopped. Cameron's determination to head straight to his bedroom vanished when Shelby poked her head out of the laundry room doorway.

"Cameron!" was her surprised reaction. "I thought you wouldn't be home until later."

"Sorry to disappoint you," he teased, but there was also a question in his look as he came closer.

* * *

Once inside the laundry room, Cameron casually leaned against the wall next to her and folded his arms. He looked like he was posing for a photo shoot with his muscular arms stretching the seams of his short-sleeved polo shirt, one boot crossed over the other.

Trying not to stare, Shelby pulled an exasperated face at him. "I'm not disappointed. In fact, I'm glad we have a chance to be alone. I mean . . ." she faltered, her face turning scarlet when one of his eyebrows went up a notch. "That's *not* what I mean!" She spun around quickly, almost burning herself on the iron, and muttered, "Oh, why do I always say the wrong things!"

"What you really mean, Shelby," he said quietly to her back, "is that you wouldn't be caught dead 'alone' with anyone so depraved as me, right?"

The bitterness in his voice hung in the air. Shelby spun back to face him, eyes wide and mouth gaping, unable to find one logical thing to say.

"Which version of the story did they give you at church the other day? The one where I abandoned my unborn child or the more dazzling version where I got excommunicated? They tend to like that one."

Shelby's mouth closed, and she waited for him to go on, anxious for him to refute the terrible things that had been said. But something in his expression was understood in her heart, and she found herself saying slowly, "I . . . admit that I did overhear something at Church . . . but I really hate gossip. If there is anything that needs to be said, I'd rather hear it from you, no one else. Besides, I'm told you can't believe everything you hear."

The look he gave her was intense. She thought she could almost see moisture filling his eyes. But when he walked up to her side, what little grasp she still had on rational thoughts vanished. He took one of her hands and held it gently in both of his own.

"You are an incredible person, Shelby Hamlin."

She must have lost her voice. The only thing she was aware of was the beating of her heart as he studied her. He stood there for a moment longer, appearing to have something to say but struggling to find the words.

Then without warning, he dropped her hand as if he had been burned and turned to walk away without a backward glance. Shelby stood motionless as she watched Cameron go, wondering what he kept locked away in his burdened heart.

* * *

Shelby sneezed for the third time as Sister Lockland pulled another sewing pattern out of an old dust-covered box. She handed the pattern cheerfully to Shelby.

"What about this one? I made this for my daughter's wedding. It's got a pretty train."

Shelby took the pattern, and her heart sank. Brad would have loved it. Three rows of ruffles decorated the skirt, and the sleeves were gargantuan poufs. *Holy cow*, she thought miserably. Perhaps the train had some possibilities.

Millie had graciously driven her all the way over to the Lockland's home in town, and Shelby was becoming more worried by the minute that this trip would be a waste. Sister Lockland had shown her several patterns for wedding gowns, but they were either a decade (or more) outdated or too frilly for her taste. How could she graciously get out of there without offending someone? The last thing in the world Shelby wanted was to hurt this kind lady's feelings, especially when she had so generously offered to help.

"Um . . . you're right, it is a pretty train," Shelby offered before passing the pattern on to Millie to see what she thought.

"I could combine patterns too," Sister Lockland said. "But if there's nothing here that interests you, let's go to the fabric shop and see what they have."

Shelby smiled gratefully. "It's so thoughtful of you to help me out. I've just had such a hard time deciding on anything. But I do like this skirt over here."

They continued discussing and planning as they drove over to a wedding shop to get more ideas for Shelby's wedding gown and bridesmaid dresses, Sister Lockland giving Shelby some helpful hints that she might not have thought of on her own.

So far, Brad's plan was to get married in the Idaho Falls Temple and then have the reception that night at their ward building in Bozeman. If she had to endure a reception, Shelby wanted her roommates to be her bridesmaids. They would be the only part of the ordeal that she would be able to cling to as her own. But Sara and Amanda still hadn't let her know yet if they would be coming.

Shelby noticed a narrow beam of sunlight highlighting a swirl of dust in one corner of the shop. Everything in her life was beginning to feel like that dust in the air, stirring around in confusion and never settling. There just wasn't enough time.

Searching through a rainbow of brocades, silks, and chiffon, Shelby quickly became overwhelmed. She should be doing this with her mother, not with strangers. And having no help from home, how would she ever come up with the money for the prices she was seeing? Frustrated with herself, as well as with the entire situation, Shelby felt the sting of hot tears forming in her eyes.

When Millie and Sister Lockland disappeared down one aisle of wedding supplies, Shelby took several deep breaths and tried to compose herself. She could handle this. If she could handle being disowned for joining the Church and getting herself through her undergraduate work, then she could handle making a few decisions for a simple, yet lovely, wedding. It would be easier if Brad were here to help out. But that darn internship—well, there was no use brooding over that.

Shelby thought about the fifty-dollar bill in her wallet. She could get the case of wedding bubbles. She stopped. No, not the bubbles. Brad might think they were tacky. As she stood there debating over various items, Millie returned with laughter in her eyes.

"Look what I found."

It was a lavender guest book dotted with sage-colored leaves. Shelby looked at the book and then up at Millie. Suddenly they were both laughing as they recalled Sister Brown's warning words. Standing there in the middle of the aisle, Shelby's heart was lifted at the humor they shared. It really felt good to laugh.

At that moment, she decided to try being more easygoing and to enjoy preparing for her wedding as much as she could. Shelby left the store feeling much better because of Millie's support and Sister Lockland's enthusiastic ideas.

Even the nagging thought that something was not right was firmly shoved away by her hopeful new attitude.

Chapter 7

"Laura and Bruce are coming next week!" Millie was exuberant as she hung up the phone.

Karl looked up from reading his newspaper in an overstuffed recliner. "What day?"

"They said they're coming on Wednesday and want to stay for a few days with us. Now you'll be able to meet them, Shelby."

"I can't wait to meet them, after all the stories you've told me," she grinned, setting the dinner table.

"You'll see how fun they are—and that Tara . . ." Millie rolled her eyes. "She's such a little character. She follows Jared and Brandon around like a mischievous elf looking for trouble."

Shelby laughed and decided she especially wanted to meet the children.

"Karl, they're bringing their WaveRunners and want to go to Hebgen Lake."

Karl didn't look up this time but simply answered, "That should work just fine," and continued reading.

Just then, Cameron came through the back door. "Did I hear someone say Laura is coming up?"

Millie answered with an enthusiastic "Yes, on Wednesday!" and went to give him a kiss. "Did you have a nice day?" she asked, barely allowing him to nod before launching into the details of Laura's visit. "They want to go to Hebgen Lake, Cam. Are you heading down there anytime soon?"

"I've got the day off tomorrow. Did you want me to talk to John about reserving us a spot?"

"Yes. That would be terrific. And Shelby, I bet you'd love the drive. Would you like to go with Cam?"

Shelby looked over at Cameron, but he was intently fiddling with his watch, purposely not looking at her. Would he want her tagging along or did he want to be alone? She thought of his cutting words the other day about her not wanting to be "caught dead alone with anyone so depraved" as he was and found herself saying daringly, "I'd love to go."

Cameron looked up at her in astonishment. Millie began chattering about the scenic drive and sights that Cameron should take her to see. Even Karl offered a few ideas. Before either she or Cameron knew what was happening, Millie had planned an entire outing for them both, complete with a picnic and fishing and historical sites.

Shelby wasn't so sure about the fishing part. "I really don't know how to fish, so I'll just watch Cameron."

"You've never been fishing before?" Cameron asked, his tone implying that any existence without fishing was no existence at all.

Shelby shrugged. "Just once. When I was about ten." She had gone with her dad after he and her mom had fought about one of their moves. Her face clouded over as she stuffed the memories inside.

"It must not have been a very good fishing trip."

"Why do you say that?"

Cameron was searching her face. He just shrugged, but his penetrating eyes never left hers.

"We have plenty of rods. I can teach you." He seemed perfectly comfortable with the arrangements. In fact, he actually appeared somewhat pleased.

Later that evening, when dinner was nearly over, Brad called. Millie's eyes were shining when she told Shelby who it was. With a little embarrassment, Shelby asked if she could take the call in the other room.

"Go right ahead, dear."

It felt like several pairs of eyes were boring into her back as she walked away from the table. Shelby wondered why she felt so self-conscious.

"Hello?"

"Hey, good looking," Brad's voice called out enthusiastically. "What's my bride-to-be up to these days?"

"Um . . . well, I'm supposed to go to Hebgen Lake tomorrow with Cameron and—"

"He's still around?" Brad interrupted with a tone of sudden annoyance.

"Yeah. Laura's family is coming on Wednesday, and your mom asked him to go talk to someone about all of us coming to the lake."

"Humph."

"I wish you could come up too," Shelby continued. "I'm loving it up here. We've driven into downtown Bozeman a couple times, and I'm amazed at how beautiful everything is. I love how green the mountains are—and the trees! You know Brad, I think I could live in Montana forever!"

"Well, don't get too used to it."

His words were like a splash of cold water in her face.

"What do you mean?" Shelby said, apprehension seeping through her body.

Brad's voice was drenched with confidence and excitement. "I've been offered a job with Baxter and Wells in their San Francisco office. This is huge!"

Shelby was stunned. It felt like her brain had just been given a huge overload and couldn't process what he was saying.

"As soon as we're married, they're going to fly us out there to see how we like it. They have a bunch of recommended neighborhoods for us to see. It's like a dream come true!"

Her apprehension grew into panic, choking the words in her throat. "Wait a minute. What are you talking about? We're finishing up our degrees at BYU this fall, right?"

"I found out about a program that would allow me to finish my degree out there."

"But wh—"

"Shelby, they offered me a $60,000 salary!" he enunciated each syllable of the figure to get the full magnitude across.

Shelby paused before quietly responding. "That's a lot of money."

"Absolutely. Look, I know we sort of planned things differently, but there's no way I could turn this down. This is a once-in-a-lifetime chance."

Her next words were almost a whisper. "But what about me, Brad?"

The other end of the line was quiet.

"What about my degree? I'd always hoped to finish at BYU."

When he finally spoke, Brad was more amenable. "I've been selfish, haven't I, Shelby? I'm sorry. It's just—I can't believe how fast this has all happened, and I'm really excited. But I should have discussed all of this with you. What if I give you a little time to think about it, okay? We can talk everything over later."

Shelby took a big breath. "Okay."

"So," Brad changed the subject. "Have you and my mom had any luck picking things out for the wedding?"

"I think so. I found a dress pattern that Sister Lockland might sew for me."

"What does it look like?"

Shelby couldn't explain why she felt like telling him it was none of his business. Why was she being so defensive? She could have used his opinion at the fabric store.

"Isn't it traditionally bad luck if I tell you?" she teased, but there was audible strain in her voice.

"I just . . . wondered. I mean, shouldn't I be involved in the wedding?"

"Do you think I'm incapable of making good decisions on my own?"

"Shelby, don't be ridiculous. Why are you acting like this?"

She was beginning to drown in confusion. "I don't know." Was it normal to feel like this before your own wedding? The girls in her BYU ward who got married always seemed so blissful. They acted like they could walk into a wall and not notice!

In the past it had seemed so easy just to follow Brad's good advice. But there were so many things that were beginning to gnaw at her. Maybe she would feel different if she could convince Brad to have a small, quiet gathering in lieu of the big reception he wanted. There wouldn't be many other chances to convince him. It was now or never.

"Brad, there's something I want to ask."

"Yeah . . . ?" There was definite irritation in his voice.

"What if we invited all your family and closest friends over here after the wedding. It's so nice here at your home and—"

Brad's voice raised in pitch. "You already agreed that we should have a reception. We can't change everything now, especially when we're sending out announcements soon."

"I agreed because you always seem to be right. But it isn't what *I* want. How would you like to stand there with hundreds of strangers, knowing that *not one* of them had come to see *you*? Only if I'm lucky will Sara and Amanda be there. Besides them, I'll have no one!"

"That's completely absurd, Shelby! Those people will be there to see you just as much as me!" He was yelling now, and Shelby was on the verge of tears.

"You don't understand at all. You don't care what I'm really feeling."

"Look, if you want family at the wedding, why don't you forget your pride and invite your mother? You should have done that a long time ago!"

Tears were streaming down her cheeks as she gulped out a garbled noise. This wasn't going well at all. She held the phone in trembling hands, hearing Brad's voice in the distance but not registering the words.

She needed to get away. Far away. She had to dam the torrent of emotion that threatened to flood her soul. It couldn't be allowed out or she might not recover from such exposed pain.

She heard his voice making an apology and telling her he loved her, and somehow she choked out an appropriate response. But once she was off the phone, Shelby slipped out the back door, hoping that no one had seen her hurried escape.

She began running into the night, behind the house and up the hill. She continued through the dense trees, staggering over unseen rocks as she got farther from the thin fingers of light that came from the house. She made her way to a grassy clearing where she sank to the ground in a heap and let the moonlight float down the stream of her tears.

* * *

Cameron was the only one facing the back door when Shelby left. He could tell something wasn't right. She would have come back to the table, otherwise. But instinctively, he knew something was bothering her. It didn't appear that his mom had noticed her leave. She was refilling her glass of ice water. Cameron looked at the enigmatic expression on his dad's face. Sometimes Karl observed a lot more than he let on, even if he didn't say anything.

Cameron set his fork down. *She shouldn't be out there alone.* Should he do something? *No, she obviously wanted to get away.* He of all people knew what that felt like.

But also knowing what it felt like to be in pain, he made up his mind.

His mother's voice penetrated his thoughts. ". . . was a good sport when Sister Brown came by," Millie was saying while Karl chuckled.

Cameron cleared his throat. "Um . . . thanks for a great dinner, Mom." He kissed her cheek and walked outside, his parents staring after him. Millie looked at the closed door in bewilderment.

"Now what's bothering him tonight?" Cameron heard her ask her husband as he crossed the porch. "If that little—"

"Millie," warned Karl.

"—monster of a girl is stirring up more trouble, she'll hear from me . . ." Cameron's jaw stiffened, and he quickened his pace to distance himself from his mother's fading voice and the thoughts her outburst stirred in his own mind.

He grabbed a lantern from the shed and looked around the immediate area for any sign of Shelby. If she had ventured away from the house, the property was large enough that she could get lost in the dark. Or lose her footing on the uneven hillside.

He grabbed his jacket from his truck before setting off to find her. Listening carefully, he also checked the ground for any signs that would indicate her direction. There was an urgency inside him that quickened his steps.

"Shelby?" he called out gently.

There was no response so he tried again as he walked down by the fire pit. Scanning the road out front, he decided to head around the back of the house. She had to have been pretty upset to take off like this.

What did Brad say to her? he thought heatedly. If his brother had hurt her feelings, then by dang Cameron would—What would he do? He had no place doing anything. It was none of his business. How could he forget that?

He came to a halt. *I should just turn around and go back in the house.* But if she was upset, he couldn't just leave her out here alone in the dark. Cameron decided to find her just to make sure she was safe.

As he walked through the trees with the lantern, tender images rose in his mind, combining gentleness, beauty, and vulnerability. There was something about Shelby that made him want to protect her.

Yesterday his dad had told him that she had been disowned when she joined the Church. He couldn't imagine having no family to turn to. No matter how much they drove you crazy, family was everything.

In the moments he had observed Shelby—unbeknownst to her—he had seen such sadness in her eyes. He wondered if there were other things that had contributed to that sadness. And in spite of it all, she maintained her cheerful, upbeat attitude. He admired her for that.

Cameron cocked his head to one side when he heard a muffled sound ahead. He picked up his pace and continued searching through the moonlit pines.

"Shelby, are you out here?" he called out as he came up to the clearing.

When he finally saw her huddled against a boulder, he stopped in his tracks. He had never seen anyone look so alone before. It twisted him inside to see her in such a state. He approached without a word, the swoosh of his boots in the tall grass the only disturbance to the silence.

When Shelby saw him, she curled away and hid her face against the rock. She looked like she didn't want him anywhere near there. But Cameron cautiously sat down, leaning against the trunk of an old aspen and setting the lantern down to his side.

Shelby began wiping at her eyes. "You must think I'm crazy," she said in an attempt at light-heartedness. When he said nothing, she turned to peek at him and then faced her boulder again.

"I'm sorry if I worried anyone. I'm all right." She sniffled, wiped a sleeve across her face, and took a deep breath. "I'm okay now."

"Are you trying to convince me or yourself?" he asked quietly. She shot a quick look at him but didn't respond.

Cameron's eyes didn't leave her face as he tried again. "Shelby," he began gently, "what made you so upset?"

There was a light fluttering of aspen leaves overhead and Shelby raised her head to see them dance. Cameron could see conflicted emotions rush behind her eyes as they slowly filled again with moisture. She took a deep breath and blinked the tears away before they could begin to fall.

After a brief moment, all she came up with was, "It really wasn't anything. I think I must be tired." Her voice was hollow and unconvincing. She didn't look at him as she picked up a small rock and intently fingered the grooves in its surface.

Cameron didn't give up. He moved closer and rested a hand on her arm. "Maybe you don't feel like talking about it, but it hurts a lot worse to stuff things inside than to just let them out."

She continued rubbing her fingers agitatedly over the rock—back and forth—and then stopped. She turned to look at him and whispered helplessly, "I . . . I can't."

The emotion expressed in those two words tore at Cameron's heart. He put his arm around her shoulders and felt her soft hair on his cheek as she yielded to the warmth of his hold.

"It's okay, Shelby," he soothed. "You don't have to. But I want you to know that you have a friend here if you ever do want to talk."

Cameron wrapped the jacket around Shelby and held her close. Since Grandma Hamlin died, Shelby couldn't remember a time that she had received such tenderness from anyone—not even Brad. It would be unexpected for tenderness to cause damage of any kind. But with torrential force, the dam that had held her emotions in check for so long finally crumbled.

There was nothing left to do but surrender to the pain of allowing herself to feel.

Chapter 8

Shelby had never had a hangover before, but when she woke up the next morning, she could swear that she was having one. Her eyes and nose felt swollen and her head was pounding. She pulled her pillow over her head to shield her eyes from the bright rays of light streaming into her room. How would she ever be able to get out of bed to tell Cameron she wouldn't be going with him today?

Shelby's eyes flew open when she thought of Cameron.

Last night he was a completely different person. He had held her while she cried, never once asking for an explanation or offering advice. He had simply let her cry and then walked her back to the house. Before going inside, they had stopped at the back door. A slow smile spread across her face when she remembered telling him he was the best brother-in-law anyone could ask for. Cameron had wrapped her in a big, comforting hug and had told her that, though it was hard to imagine, he actually was a good listener whenever she needed one.

He would have made the best big brother. If only she could have had one.

There was a soft knock at her door, and Millie poked her head in. "Good morning," she said brightly. "I brought you some orange juice and a muffin."

Shelby rubbed her eyes with embarrassment. "Thanks, Millie."

Millie and Karl must surely know about last night. They had already gone to bed by the time she and Cameron had come back, but there was something in Millie's face right now that spoke of compassion. Shelby sat up and massaged her temples as Millie came into the room to set a small tray on the nightstand.

"How are you feeling this morning?"

Shelby smiled ruefully. "Actually, I could use some Tylenol. I don't think I'll be going with Cameron today."

Millie placed one of her soft hands against Shelby's cheek in a motherly gesture of concern.

"I'll run and get you some." She patted Shelby's shoulder and left the room. It made Shelby long for her own mother's touch.

And suddenly she felt like one burden had been lifted. In her heart she knew that something had to be done to reach her mother. Brad was probably right, as usual. She should invite her mom to the wedding—or at least let her know that she was about to be married. She just wasn't sure if she had the courage to deal with the confrontation. It could be awful.

Shelby took a bite of the muffin and drank some orange juice. Then she closed her eyes and sank wearily back against her fluffy pillow. She had to close her eyes against the pounding in her head. She just needed a few more minutes to rest. . . .

The sound of knocking called to Shelby in her sleep. She was barely aware of Millie putting the promised Tylenol tablets next to her cup. But when Millie grabbed her big toe that was poking out of the quilt, Shelby shot up in bed with surprise.

It wasn't Millie in her room; it was Cameron!

"What . . . ?" she began in sleepy confusion. Some remote part of her brain took in his tousled hair, low-slung black sweats and bare feet. Her thoughts were fuzzy. *I've never even seen Brad's feet before. He's always in a suit or something. But hey, it's not like it's a requirement to see your boyfriend's bare feet before becoming engaged, right?*

Belatedly realizing she was giving Cameron a pretty good view of her nightshirt and legs, she flung the covers up around her chin. "What're you doing?"

Cameron was trying to suppress a grin, his gorgeous blue eyes full of mischief. "We have somewhere to go today, and I've come to drag you out of bed if I have to."

"But I don't—"

"I won't take no for an answer. We'll skip the fishing today, but everything else is still on. Either you're ready in thirty minutes," he raised one dark eyebrow, "or I'm coming after you."

Shelby's mouth dropped wide open. So much for him being a great "big brother" type. This could possibly pass as cruel and unusual punishment! Didn't he remember how awful she felt last night?

Cameron pointed to her tray. "Your Tylenol is right there." He winked and left her gaping after him.

Twenty minutes later, in her best jeans and a white shirt, Shelby stood in the front room armed with blankets and an overstuffed picnic basket that Millie had magically—if not conspiratorially—produced. When Cameron sauntered in wearing a leather cowboy hat, faded jeans and heavy boots, he gave Shelby an approving look.

"So," he looked smug, "you got ready after all."

Feeling more alive, Shelby slanted an irked look at him. But Cameron saw the definite quirk of her lips and laughed. Millie came in from the kitchen then to hand him a wrapped loaf of banana bread.

"Cam, will you give this to John for me, please?"

He eyed it hungrily. "Sure, if I don't eat it first."

Millie huffed in playful exasperation. "I already packed some for the two of you, so hands off." Cameron quickly moved out of range of her poking finger with another laugh.

"Thanks for the lunch, Mom." He kissed her cheek and then asked Shelby if she was ready to go. When she nodded, he picked up the blankets and picnic basket, and they headed outside.

"I hope you're feeling better," Millie smiled uneasily.

"I am, thank you," Shelby replied gratefully.

"Have a nice day!" Millie called before shutting the front door behind them with a hesitant expression lingering on her face.

Cameron was run down by Bomber and Wags before he had the chance to help Shelby into his truck. He put everything into the back of the truck and then bent down and rubbed both dogs' ears back and forth, calling out endearments to the canine competitors. Finding an opportunity to ace out Bomber, Wags snuck over to Shelby's side where he eagerly received several pats. He barked triumphantly, making sure Bomber noticed that he'd been bested.

Shelby laughed at the sneaky tactics. "Did you see what Wags just did? These dogs are hilarious."

"Yeah, they crack us up."

"Do they always try to outdo each other?"

"Ever since they were puppies. I came home with Wags one day after I found him injured and alone. My parents let me keep him, so Brad decided to try it the next week."

"He did?"

"Yeah. He couldn't stand the fact that I got a dog and he didn't, so he showed up with Bomber. After a big scene, Mom and Dad said Brad could keep him. Little did they know that it would be the beginning of a never-ending contest."

"Between the dogs or between you and Brad?"

It was out before she could stop the words. But Cameron's expression barely flickered as he laughed and slanted a sheepish look up at her.

"Both, I guess."

After tossing the dogs a few slobbery tennis balls, Cameron washed his hands in the faucet on the side of the house and came over to join Shelby in the truck. He shut her door, made sure the shell was locked, and then climbed in beside her.

"I guess we're ready." Cameron adjusted the brim of his hat and then looked over at her questioningly. "I hope you aren't too mad at me for making you come."

"No, I'm not mad. Besides . . . I think you did it for my own good, didn't you?"

Their eyes met for a serious moment. When Cameron looked away, he turned on the engine and said, "I just thought getting out would be better than lying in bed feeling miserable. I wanted to do something to cheer you up."

Shelby was touched by his concern. "Thank you, Cameron. You're a good friend."

He paused before quietly voicing, "You're welcome."

"Look, Cameron . . . about last night," she began to say nervously, "I just wanted to say . . . I'm so sorry . . ."

"Please, don't apologize."

Shelby exhaled. "It really meant a lot to me what you did. I won't forget it."

He smiled. "Hey, what are friends for?" He took her hand in his and gave it a gentle squeeze. "Friends?"

She smiled back and nodded her head. "Friends."

Withdrawing her hand, Shelby looked out her window as he turned the truck around. She became aware of the gray-blue sky with round, puffy clouds, the angled peaks of pine trees and the cool morning air. She took a deep breath. "You know what? This *is* better than staying in bed." When she looked over at Cameron and saw the warm expression on his face, she added, "A lot better."

As Cameron drove down the gravel driveway onto the road, Shelby suddenly felt a flutter of excitement. They had an entire day planned with all kinds of fun things to do. If she had looked deep into her heart, Shelby would have been a little disconcerted to realize that there was nothing she wanted more than to spend her Friday with Cameron.

She took a quick look at him as he drove south. He possessed a certain strength that was unmistakable in everything he did. Maybe it was the same strength that she had recognized in Brad.

Shelby still couldn't figure out how Cameron could have done anything wrong in the past. It just didn't seem to be in his character. She wondered if he would ever tell her what had happened. But people had a way of keeping their secrets hidden. She should know—she was an expert.

Cameron glanced over. "Does it matter to you where we go first?"

"No," Shelby answered easily. "By the way, who is the man we are supposed to see at Hebgen Lake?"

"He's an old friend of the family. You'll like him. He runs a small campground down on the lake that we really like. Since it's tourist season, we just have to make sure he's got a spot for us. But he usually saves us one, anyway. It's kind of a tradition."

"How long of a drive is it?"

"About an hour."

The way he said it, it sounded like just a short little hop down the road. Things were certainly spread far apart out here. Shelby surmised that people here must be used to traveling longer distances to get where they want to go.

They continued talking easily, while in the back of her mind Shelby thought about last night and the way Cameron had comforted her so tenderly. Perhaps he *would* make the best big brother in the world. But there was just one problem with that idea. Sitting next to him while he drove, Shelby's thoughts were decidedly anything but sisterly. The first few buttons of his tan shirt were unbuttoned, giving her the slightest glimpse of his broad, muscular chest. She noticed the grip of his large hands on the steering wheel. Those hands looked worn and rough, but a contrasting memory pushed its way into her thoughts, one of soft, warm fingers touching her face the night they had eaten s'mores by the fire.

Shelby quickly turned her thoughts to the scenery outside her window but found it difficult keeping her interest glued to grasses and shrubs. Her eyes gradually made their way to the lock of hair above Cameron's ear. Shelby liked how it curled up under his cowboy hat. The little waves in his hair gave him a boyish appeal, but at the same time, Cameron exuded an air of complete masculinity. The fact that it was unintentional did nothing to lessen the impact he had on her rising pulse. *Stop staring.*

She had never felt such a reaction to a man before. With Brad, she had secretly longed for a little more passion in their relationship, but feeling so comfortable with him had always seemed to compensate for her frivolous desire.

When Cameron suggested they roll down their windows to make use of the cool breeze, Shelby sat back and closed her eyes to enjoy the feel of the wind whipping through her hair and fanning her flushed cheeks.

"Shelby . . ." his voice drifted over.

"Hmm . . . ?"

"I was going to tell you . . ."

"Tell me what?"

"I'm sure Brad tells you this all the time, but . . . your hair is incredibly pretty." He swallowed and kept his eyes on the road.

She turned to look at him with surprise and was touched by his admission. "Thanks, Cameron." *Admit it, you're more than touched,* said a tiny voice inside her head. She felt like she was glowing enough to light up the Lavell Edwards Stadium.

"It's . . ." He didn't finish.

Shelby waited for him to say something more, but he just continued to watch the road. They drove on in silence, each wrapped in their own disquieting thoughts.

Shelby took in the steep mountains rising above them. They were densely covered in dark green pines except for occasional strips where it looked like the mountain had been shaved. Flanked by yellow-green grassy meadows, the winding road followed the curve of the Gallatin River that glittered in the morning sun as it flowed vigorously over submerged rocks. Tall old trees, their gnarled roots heavily exposed, decorated the water's edge.

When a group of river rafters came into view, Shelby perked up.

"Wow, that looks like so much fun! I've never done that before."

"It is fun," Cameron agreed, enjoying her enthusiasm.

"Do you go river rafting a lot around here?"

"Not really. It's mostly tourists—I pretty much stick to fly-fishing. But if you've never been river rafting before, then you should go. The youth are going next week, and they could always use extra supervision."

Her eyes lit up. "Do you think they could use my help? I'd love to do that."

"I'll let them know. Based on the way they're always roping me into helping out, they'd probably welcome another recruit," he said acerbically.

Shelby laughed. "Thanks, Cameron."

She continued watching the rafters floating down the river until they were no longer in sight. Then there was only a landscape as stunning as a postcard. For a moment, she fixed her gaze on the puffy white clouds drifting lazily overhead in the vast blue sky. Why was Brad so eager to move away from this heavenly place? She had grown very fond of Provo but was sure that if she were to move to Montana she could be happy here forever . . .

Shelby was startled from her reverie when Cameron suddenly pulled off the road into a secluded shady turnout that paralleled the Gallatin River. He stopped at the side of the road, leaned over so that his shoulder was barely touching hers, and pointed out two elk that were eating near the grassy shore. The touch was like a bolt of electricity that rendered her incapable of concentrating on anything outside the window. All thought was focused on his nearness and how it was affecting her. She felt his breath close to her cheek and wondered if he could hear the pounding of her heart.

Shelby tried to think of something rational to say. "That would make a nice picture."

"It's a photographer's paradise around here."

Shelby glanced back at him. He wasn't looking at the elk. He was looking at her.

Cameron cleared his throat and scooted away. "When we go to Yellowstone, you'll be amazed at the beauty. I've taken a bunch of high school students into some primitive areas there for an extracurricular program. We taught them about the various species of wildlife and vegetation. It was great."

"You must like teaching to be able to survive all those teenagers!" she laughed breathlessly.

Cameron shifted the truck into first gear and pulled back onto the road. "Actually, I do. I've been working in partnership with the university on a few programs for the students. It's a lot of hard work and little compensation, but I really like working with those kids."

Shelby sat back to look through the window as they continued on their journey, wondering if Brad would like teenagers. She had a sudden picture flash through her mind of Brad in his gray pinstripe suit trying to organize a chaotic group of wild teens in the wilderness, and a laugh escaped her.

Cameron gave her a close look. "What's so funny?"

She thought for a second and finally said, "Nothing."

She looked down at her lap, but when she peeked up at him, unable to keep the smirk from her face, Cameron persisted.

"What are you thinking about?"

That just made the smirk become more mischievous.

"Oh, it's just that I was picturing Brad managing a bunch of wild kids and . . ." she shrugged and couldn't control her giggles. It must have been contagious because Cameron laughed too.

Then they both stopped and looked at each other guiltily.

"I'm sorry. I don't know why I'm laughing," Shelby said penitently.

He paused for a moment and then said thoughtfully, "I guess you just know him well enough to know it would make a funny picture."

He kept his eyes on the road ahead again and a sad, far-away look came over his features. He remained silent as he drove for a few miles.

Shelby wondered what he was thinking. When he finally spoke, she was surprised by what he said.

"I'm sorry I laughed too, Shelby. Brad is a much better person than I am, and you're lucky to be marrying him. He's so close to being perfect that you'd wonder how someone like me got to be his brother."

Whoa, what do you say to that? What was he inferring? Was he trying to imply that he really *had* done something terrible? Maybe he would tell her about it some day, but she was beginning to dread hearing any part of the story and couldn't even explain why.

After a fairly large body of water came into view, Cameron turned right onto Highway 287, which wound its way along the north side of scenic Hebgen Lake. Across the lake were mountains covered in pine trees, creating a wall of green almost from shore to sky.

"Hey, look," Shelby said, pointing over the dashboard. "There are some abandoned cabins over there."

"That's the remains of the old grayling station. From the 1800s."

"Like a ghost town?"

"Sort of. Do you know about the Hebgen Lake earthquake?"

"No. When was that?"

"In 1959. It was so massive that everything around here shifted and changed. We'll go to the Quake Lake lookout later where they explain what happened. It's pretty cool."

After a few miles, Cameron pulled into a cozy campground area with rustic log cabins and a small marina across the lawn. He parked the truck in front of a small wood building that had the words *General Store* painted on a rough piece of wood that hung over the door. Shelby thought the sign was a bit overstated when she walked inside with Cameron and saw four plywood shelves of sparsely stocked items and a rickety, spinning postcard rack. No one was behind the desk.

"John is probably in back." Cameron walked over to a doorway and shouted, "Hey, John! Are you here?"

The sound of labored shuffling came from a back room. A carved wooden cane appeared first, followed by a slightly bent silver-haired man with the kindest face Shelby had ever seen. Cameron was instantly by his side and wrapped in a bear hug.

"Hey there, you rascal, what are you up to?" The man turned to Shelby and, pointing at her with his cane and a knowing grin, he demanded, "Introduce me to this beauty of yours!"

Shelby's eyes flew to Cameron's at the old man's assumption, and Cameron began stammering, "Oh—this isn't—I mean . . ." He looked flustered but recovered enough to make the introduction. "Shelby Hamlin, I'd like you to meet John Conrad. Shelby is . . . Brad's fiancée."

A fleeting look of disappointment crossed Mr. Conrad's face, but it disappeared as he shuffled over to Shelby and extended his thin, gnarled hand to her. His grip was surprisingly firm.

Shelby smiled as she shook his hand. "It's nice to meet you, Mr. Conrad."

"The name's John around here. And I'm very glad to meet you." He patted her hand and smiled back. "Now what is everyone up to at your place? Are you going to make it down this summer?"

"Actually, that's what we came to see you about. Laura and her family are coming up from Idaho Falls on Wednesday. We were thinking about coming to the lake the next day. Will that work for you?"

"I'm sure that'll be just fine." Mr. Conrad shuffled over to the small desk in the corner and pulled out a binder. "Let's see now . . ." He thumbed through several sheets of paper. When he came to the page he was looking for, he reached for a pen and slowly scribbled something down with a shaky hand. "You're all set. You can take your usual spot."

"Thanks, John." Cameron turned to Shelby but stopped short. "Oh! I almost forgot the banana bread. My mom will have my hide if I don't give it to you!" He dashed out to the truck, the screen door banging behind him.

Shelby looked at Mr. Conrad and smiled self-consciously. He walked closer to her and gently pounded his cane up and down on the wood floor.

"He's a good boy, that Cameron."

Shelby's eyes drifted out the window to rest on Cameron, her thoughts far away.

Mr. Conrad's watchful eyes didn't miss the expression on her face. "Yes sir, a *good* boy," he repeated.

With another bang of the screen door, Cameron came back in and set the bread down on John's desk. "Here you go."

"Please thank your mother for me. She knows how I love her treats. Now then, the two of you can stick around if you'd like and take the canoe out."

Shelby glanced at Cameron in question, and he answered, "Would it be okay with you, John, if we just walked around a bit?"

"Sure, sure. You know you can come and go as you please." He waved them out the door calling, "Be good now, you two."

Shelby wasn't sure why she was blushing, but they both thanked Mr. Conrad and waved as they headed down the path that led to the lake. Cameron shoved his hands in the pockets of his jeans, and they walked side-by-side in an awkward silence. Shelby wondered if he too could feel the old man's eyes boring into their backs as they walked away.

Chapter 9

Watching Cameron stop to skip a rock across the lake, Shelby asked, "How long have you known Mr. Conrad?"

"It seems like forever," he said reflectively. "I like coming to see him. He's been kind of lonely since his wife died, and he likes having us visit."

Shelby admired Cameron's friendship with the elderly man. "I like him."

Those simple words seemed to mean a lot to Cameron, and he brightened. "I'm glad you like him. He's a great man."

They continued walking until they reached a dock where they found a weatherworn bench. Cameron suggested they sit down. He seemed nervous.

"So . . ." Cameron started as he tapped his fingertips on the bench, "do you like Montana so far?"

"I love it," Shelby said brightly and then frowned as she remembered her conversation with Brad. She saw Cameron studying her expression and looked down at her feet. "Brad was offered a job in San Francisco," she said flatly.

Cameron inhaled as if in understanding. "And you don't want to go."

Shelby struggled with her thoughts. "That's not . . . really what upset me last night. Not just that." She looked up at Cameron and seeing the look of interest and compassion, found the courage to go on. "I guess there were just a lot of things building up inside me. You might think I'm crazy, but I've never wanted a wedding reception. To me it would just emphasize how alone I am in the world. Brad's guest list would be enormous, and I'd have ten people at the most—all friends, no family."

"Shelby, it's your wedding day. I think you should have it the way you'd like it." She knew it didn't seem like Cameron to be disloyal to Brad, but she appreciated his thoughtfulness.

"There was also the whole wedding gown thing—" She broke off, but when she saw the look of confusion cross his face, she tried to explain. "We couldn't agree on what it should look like."

Cameron was even more confused. "I thought that was totally up to the bride."

Somehow that struck a cord, and she bristled in frustration. "How am I supposed to know about tradition and etiquette when I don't have a mother, a sister, or anyone to consult with?" Shelby stood and walked to the railing by the water's edge, covering her face with her hands. The wound had been reopened. She felt like she was falling down a suffocating, dark pit.

A strong arm rescued her as it was wrapped around her shoulders. Shelby took a deep breath. "I'm sorry. I didn't mean to explode like that."

"No, it's all right," he said gently.

There was a heavy pause. Then Cameron added bleakly, "I know how stressful a wedding can be."

From the far-off look on his face, Shelby knew he must have been thinking about his own wedding that never happened. Eager to turn the conversation away from her problems, but not sure Cameron's troubles were a safe topic either, all she could do was sigh as she looked out across the ripples on the lake. Shelby noticed two men fishing from a small boat in the distance.

She cleared her throat. "Where had you planned on fishing today?"

"Back on the Gallatin River. There are some spots up there that I really like."

"I'm sorry you couldn't go today."

"Don't be," he squeezed her shoulder. "There are plenty of other days I can go."

"Do you go fishing a lot?"

"Yeah—when I get the chance." He turned reluctantly to look out across the dark blue lake with melancholy etched in his features.

"Actually . . . that's how I met . . ." he swallowed painfully, ". . . my fiancée, Camille."

Camille? Shelby suddenly felt knots in her stomach. *Here it comes. Why am I so upset that she has a name?* They sat back down on the bench behind them, and her hands gripped the seat in preparation for the words that would come. When he spoke, his words were deliberate and marked with emptiness.

"I don't know how much you already know, but I met her last year when I went fishing with some friends. Someone had invited her brother Craig, so Camille just tagged along. She liked to party, but she was spoiled—used to having her own way, I guess. For some reason she latched on to me, and I was flattered by the attention. In less than two weeks she was convinced we should get married. It all happened so fast that I felt like I was spinning in a whirlwind."

He looked down at his shoes and shook his head. From under the brim of his cowboy hat, he briefly looked at Shelby sitting quietly next to him and then turned away in silence.

"Did you love her?" Shelby's words were so softly spoken that Cameron had to turn to be sure she had spoken. It took a minute for him to form the answer.

"I thought I did. I don't know. That's the worst thing of it all. I just wanted to get married, to get on with my life. Laura is married, has three kids and a home; Brad was getting a doctorate after graduating with honors, and I guess I figured I should hurry up and get married before . . ." he trailed off.

"Before Brad could beat you to it?" she finished. His eyes bored into hers, but she just returned his stare with one of sincere concern. He acknowledged her with the barest nod.

"So what happened?"

He stood abruptly, walked over to the water's edge and leaned against the wood railing. Shelby watched him, longing to say or do something but feeling only helplessness wash over her. Finally, Shelby came close to his side and rested her hand on his upper arm.

"You can tell me, Cam. We're friends, remember?"

His eyes found hers, and he smiled sadly. Still leaning forward, looking out over the lake, Cameron muttered bitterly, "She told me the week before the wedding that she was pregnant." He heard

Shelby's quick intake of breath and closed his eyes to shut out her shocked expression.

Cameron's next words came tumbling out in a surge of emotion. "Shelby, I've never talked about this to anyone other than my family, but for some reason I want you to know the truth. I never slept with Camille. She might have been pregnant before I even met her. I don't know. But she came to me in such a pitiful state that night that I felt like the best thing I could do was stand by her, give her and her child a name, and that everything would work out in the end."

His eyes were filled with torment. "I promised I would help her . . ." He picked at the splintering wood of the railing until a large enough piece was torn away to be thrown in the lake.

"When I admitted that marrying Camille was the wrong thing for us both, she turned into this raving maniac. She screamed and yelled, threatening that if I didn't do exactly as she said, she would tell everyone I had done this to her and was abandoning *my* child, along with a host of other accusations. I honestly couldn't believe what was happening and how I could have ever gotten myself into such a mess. But the bottom line is, I broke my promise."

"Oh, Cameron . . ." Shelby rested her forehead on his upper arm and let out a deep breath. "Why didn't you defend yourself?" Shelby's voice increased in tempo as she looked back up at him. "She's the one who deserves to be disgraced! How can you let her get away with this?"

Cameron turned to face her. He briefly raised his fingers to the soft skin of her cheek as she earnestly searched his face.

"I didn't think that I should have to go around defending myself. I just thought it would all blow over and that we'd go our separate ways. I never knew it would turn into such a nightmare. When someone slashed the tires on my truck one night, I decided I'd had enough." He chuckled mirthlessly.

Shelby was appalled. "So you came home to find a little peace and quiet."

She thought about the girls at church and realized Cameron hadn't found much solace here either. This Camille person had woven a pretty strong web of deceit, like a spider relentlessly hunting its prey. Shelby felt an urge to turn the tables, hunt her down, and punch her in the nose.

Cameron covered her white-knuckled fists with gentle hands, and Shelby tried to calm her thoughts as he said, "Thanks, Shelby."

Suddenly, her arms reached around his neck in a sympathetic hug. He was so surprised by her impulsive gesture that at first he just stood with arms at his sides. But when he caught a hint of fragrance at the curve of Shelby's neck and her golden hair brushed against his face, he couldn't help himself. His arms went around her back, and he drew her closer. For one heavenly moment she was his. He savored her nearness, the warmth of her body pressed close to him, and felt certain she could feel the pounding of his heart.

Wishing the moment could go on forever, Cameron suddenly was gripped by reality. This was his brother's fiancée. She was in love with Brad—and it was crucial that he remember that!

With great effort, Cameron pulled away from Shelby, and they stood gazing at each other, blue eyes fastened to hazel.

When Cameron wrenched his eyes from hers, he cleared his throat and attempted a casual offer to take a ride in one of John's canoes. A safer distance would be good, and at least in a canoe she would be farther away from him than if she were sitting beside him in the truck. After a few minutes, they had an eager Mr. Conrad giving them oars and life jackets as he rehearsed the same instructions he gave to all his renters.

"Be careful now and don't go farther than the bend down there."

"Thanks, John," Cameron called out.

Mr. Conrad waved to them as they walked back down to the dock. "See you later." He stood there, staring at them for several minutes. Then he scratched a tuft of gray hair at the back of his head. "Hmph . . ." he grunted before shuffling back inside for a nap.

* * *

Sparkling rays of sunlight ricocheted madly across the small waves that rippled around the canoe as Cameron paddled at a steady pace. With eyes closed, Shelby let the sunlight play on her uptilted face while one hand drifted idly through the cold water. She listened to the swooshing of the breeze in the pines and heard the distant call of a noisy bird. The even rhythm of the paddle pushing through the water was soothing her into a peaceful lull. There could be few things on earth as wonderful as this.

"Hey, lazybones," Cameron teased. "I'm withering away over here while you get to rest."

Shelby peeped at the brawny muscles of his arms flexing with each stroke and laughed at the inaccuracy of his words.

"What?" he demanded innocently.

"Oh nothing," she said vaguely and closed her eyes again, basking in the sun. "Let me know when you faint, and I'll take over."

Cameron saw the teasing smirk and thumped the water with one of his hands, sending a shower of water across her upper torso. Shelby bolted upright with a scream but realized in a hurry that she had made a mistake. He dropped the paddle and jumped to steady her as she tottered precariously back and forth over the edge of the canoe.

"It's okay; I've got you," he laughed as she clung to him.

"Cameron Thompson, I should push you in! That was cold!" Shelby retorted in mock indignation, her eyes dancing with their characteristic mischief.

"Then you would end up falling in with me," he pointed out, still grinning as he gripped her arms.

Looking down at the swaying canoe, she answered dizzily, "Good point. Maybe I'll just sit down."

After they were both settled, Shelby helped Cameron fish the floating oar out of the water, and he took up the job of rowing again. She noticed his firm grip on the paddle.

"Do you really want me to help?" She finally asked. "I'd be happy to, you know."

"No, I'm just giving you a hard time. Besides, I'm glad to see you enjoying the lake so much."

"You know, once I lived near Lake Lyndon B. Johnson in Texas," Shelby remembered, "and it was pretty—but nothing like this. This is so green, and being surrounded by forests and mountains makes it perfect."

Cameron jumped at the opportunity that had just opened up to learn more about her. "How old were you when you lived in Texas?"

"Almost thirteen."

"What was it like there?" he asked hesitantly, hoping that she wouldn't end the conversation or steer it away from herself like she had before. He watched her carefully as she picked at an invisible spot of dirt on her jeans.

Perhaps it was due to his earlier moment of shared confidences, but when she began to open up and share some parts of her life with him, Cameron felt like he'd been given a precious gift of trust. Shelby told him about some of her moves, funny childhood happenings, and times spent with her Grandma Hamlin. She reminisced about stumbling across the Hill Cumorah Pageant in Palmyra the summer they had moved to New York and how that had eventually led to her joining the Church.

But by the look in her eyes, he could tell some memories were still painful. Maybe someday she would tell him more. He hoped so. He wanted to know everything about her—just as a friend, of course. But for now, Cameron was content with watching her gentle movements, reveling in the glory of her golden hair, and listening to the sweet melody of her voice.

Twenty minutes later, the sky had darkened with heavy, gray clouds that threatened to ruin their picnic. They returned the canoe, and then Cameron suggested they drive on to the Earthquake Lake Visitor's Center where they could stop and eat in the back of the truck if it did rain.

As they rounded a bend in the road, they passed Hebgen Dam. Shelby looked over in surprise when Cameron turned left off the road to what looked like an old boat ramp overgrown with tall grass and wildflowers.

"There's something here I want you to see first," Cameron explained.

He drove down the narrow slope and stopped almost at the joining of pavement and water. Shelby looked out the front window as Cameron walked around the truck to her side. From the small cove looking out across the still water, ash-colored, skeleton-like trees stuck out of the water in eerie stillness. The jagged rock in the mountain protruding through the trees loomed over the water, blanketing the area in a darker gray than the misty clouds overhead.

Cameron opened the door for her. "I just felt rain drops, so we'll have to hurry." He grabbed her hand to help her out, and they ran down to the water's edge. "This is the old highway everyone used before the earthquake."

Shock registered on her face. "This road going into the water?"

"Yep. Those trees," Cameron pointed out, "used to be at the side of the road."

"So where did all this water come from—Hebgen Lake?"

Cameron nodded. "When the north end of the lake sank, it caused twenty-foot tidal waves that swelled over the dam and flooded this canyon. Up ahead is the gigantic landslide that tumbled into the Madison River. The landslide blocked all the water from the river and the tidal waves, creating Quake Lake."

Shelby listened incredulously as Cameron described the massive earthquake and resulting destruction of land and lives, campgrounds and homes. He seemed in his own element, and it was easy for Shelby to picture him working for the Forest Service during the summer months. In fact, now she could picture him standing in front of a big group of students as well. Contrary to her first impressions, Shelby could imagine all the teenage girls who would think they were in love with their gorgeous teacher.

Quickly changing that train of thought, she focused on a gust of wind that came through the canyon, whipping their hair and bringing with it a steady sprinkle of rain. The surface of the lake rippled with the splatter of raindrops. They dashed back up to the truck, but before Cameron got inside, he pulled a jacket out of the back.

When he hopped in beside Shelby, she noticed the trickle of water dripping from the brim of his hat. There was a gentle smile on his face as he offered her the jacket. It was the same one he had given her last night, and rekindled memories of his tenderness filled her mind. The desire to experience the feel of his arms around her again caught Shelby off guard.

"Thank you, Cameron," she said slightly out of breath.

Locked in his gaze, Shelby felt warm awareness building between them. Cameron slowly leaned closer and brushed a few raindrops from her cheeks with the back of his hand. It was a small gesture, but it felt like a caress.

"My pleasure," he said quietly.

Somehow his long fingers had found their way to the damp strands of hair near her ear. Shelby felt like she was falling into the deep blue of his eyes. His fingers released her hair but accidentally brushed against her collarbone. Her heart hammered in her chest and waves of warmth spread through her body in a way she had never felt before.

Unable to make sense of her reaction to him, Shelby turned away and dedicated all her attention to the task of putting on the jacket. Cameron headed back up to the highway without saying a word.

Shelby watched the wipers swipe back and forth at the rain hitting the windshield.

Within a few minutes the curve in the road brought the most astounding sight directly into view. It pulled her from a state of confusion to one of wonder. Off to the left up ahead there was a massive, gaping emptiness where the mountainside had tumbled down into the narrow canyon of the Madison River.

"Look at that!" Shelby gasped incredulously. "I can't believe that an earthquake did that."

"Yeah, it's amazing." Cameron pointed out the visitor's center high on a hill, directly across from the landslide.

"I wish I'd brought a camera today. I never have one when I should."

Without hesitation, Cameron offered, "I can bring you back here whenever you'd like."

When they reached the summit, Cameron parked in the visitor's center parking lot and spread out blankets in the shell of the truck. With the picnic basket between them, they listened to the metallic tapping of rain over their heads while feasting on roast beef sandwiches and potato salad.

"Mmm . . . your mom is the best cook," Shelby mumbled between bites.

"I bet you can cook just fine," Cameron smiled. "You've had to survive at BYU, right?"

Shelby grimaced. "I was always the roommate who made the fire alarms go off or forgot the most important ingredient in a recipe."

Cameron laughed enough that he almost choked on his food.

"Hey, it was humiliating!" Shelby smiled back indignantly but couldn't resist laughing with him. It had been funny. Then, a little more serious, Shelby surprised herself by asking, "Could Camille cook?"

Cameron lay on his side facing Shelby. "Yes. She was a good cook."

Of course! She probably knitted and sewed too.

Cameron was perceptive enough to see the look on Shelby's down-turned face, and he reached out to cover her hand with his own. "There are a lot of things that are more important to a man than whether or not his wife can cook."

The warm pressure of his hand was distracting. When his fingers began moving rhythmically over her knuckles, Shelby pulled away and glanced over at the visitor's center.

"Have you ever worked here before?" she asked casually.

"Yeah, I did actually. A couple years ago."

"It looks like the rain has let up a little. Should we go inside?"

Cameron nodded perceptively. "Okay."

As soon as they had dashed inside, Cameron was practically attacked by a questionably blond female whose ample chest stretched the limits of her green Forest Service shirt.

"Cameron Thompson, it's been too long!" she gushed.

"Hi, Chandra."

She was like a starving piranha. It took all the efforts in the world for Shelby not to glare at her.

Glued to Cameron's arm, Chandra flashed a toothy grin. "It's so good to see you!"

"Uh . . . thanks." Cameron managed to pry his arm away. "This is Shelby Hamlin, my . . ."

He was about to say more but stopped. Chandra gave Shelby a bored glance through long, fake lashes to size her up. Shelby could tell she'd been given the "sadly wanting" stamp from Chandra, but it didn't faze her. She knew she looked good in her jeans and white shirt. And by the way Cameron had looked at her this morning, he thought so too. With a little boost of confidence, Shelby smiled her best smile. "Nice to meet you, Chandra."

"Thanks," she said insincerely before turning away. "So Cameron, what's new?" And with that, Shelby was dropped.

The mostly one-sided conversation that ensued was laced with inside jokes and Forest Service lingo that intentionally left Shelby out. But when she attempted to casually drift over to a Richter scale exhibit describing the fateful night of the big earthquake, Cameron desperately reached out for her, drawing her close to his side. It was such a sudden motion that Shelby had to brace herself from tripping by wrapping one arm around his hips.

Chandra immediately stopped mid-sentence, and Cameron jumped in. "I think Shelby and I are going to look around for a minute. Does the movie start soon?"

"Uh, yeah. In five minutes. Here come some more guests, so I'd better go." With one last attempt, she batted her eyelashes at him suggestively. "See you around."

Cameron pulled Shelby with him over to the rows of large windows that provided a panoramic view of the fallen mountain and Quake Lake. He let out a deep breath. Shelby gave him a knowing look with one raised eyebrow.

"Don't say it!" he whispered in her ear with a grin.

Shelby made an attempt at feigning innocence to the obvious effect he'd had on Chandra, but couldn't quite pull it off while she was smothering a laugh.

She only hoped the effect he had on her wasn't as obvious.

Chapter 10

"Thanks for calling, Sister Lockland. I'll be sure to tell Shelby you called."

Millie hung up the kitchen phone with troubled eyes. That was the second call for Shelby. Millie wiped her hands on her apron and stirred the chili again. She glanced at the tole-painted clock on the wall. Almost seven o'clock.

Karl sauntered into the kitchen and reached over Millie's arm to get to the cookie jar.

"No snitching—we'll be eating dinner in a minute," she slapped at his hands playfully. Karl retreated and grabbed a handful of potato chips from a bag sitting out on the counter.

"Cam's not back yet?" he asked.

"He and Shelby should have been here over an hour ago. I don't know where they could be. I'm starting to get worried."

"Now don't go fretting over nothing." Karl patted her shoulder. "I'm sure they're just fine. Maybe they drove into West Yellowstone. If that's the case, they won't be back 'til much later."

Millie wrinkled her eyebrows. "She missed Brad's call."

They chatted about Brad's internship and about how much he seemed to be enjoying it. But all the while certain thoughts formed by motherly intuition kept churning in the back of her mind. And when Millie got worked up about something, she cleaned.

As she worked on scrubbing the sink and Karl on finishing up his handful of chips, they stopped midmotion as they heard the dogs bark and a vehicle rumble up the driveway.

Karl looked out the front window. "You don't have to get worked up anymore, Millie. They're back." Then he sneaked into the family room with a concealed bag of potato chips.

Millie sighed with relief. She was bustling about in the kitchen when Cameron and Shelby walked in the house with smiles and laughter abounding. They were so absorbed in the story Cameron was telling that Millie's relieved hello went completely unnoticed. With hands on her hips, Millie poked her head into the living room to repeat her greeting.

"Oh hi, Mom. What's for dinner? We're starved!"

"I made chili. So . . . where have you both been?" She looked pointedly at each smiling face. "We expected you back a long time ago."

"We ended up taking a walk around Quake Lake and lost track of the time, Mom. I'm sorry."

"I hope you weren't worried, Millie," Shelby said.

"Not really, dear. I'm just glad you had a good time."

"Millie, it was incredible! We walked up to the memorial boulder and saw the view of the canyon. It was so pretty after the rain cleared."

"Brad called to see how you were."

Shelby's face fell. "Oh . . ." she faltered but recovered with a smile and asked how Brad was enjoying his internship, purposely avoiding Cameron's face.

Millie filled her in on all the news, and Cameron slipped away. Shelby's eyes trailed after him. Why did she feel like a traitor? And who was she really betraying?

". . . don't you think so?" Millie asked about something while she filled the glasses with ice water. Shelby blinked at Millie but couldn't come up with any logical answer. She wasn't even sure what the question was. Relief washed over her when Millie continued chatting.

"Sister Lockland called about wedding gowns. She said to give her a call tomorrow morning." Shelby agreed to call her and helped Millie dish the chili into large stoneware bowls.

After eating a somewhat subdued dinner and washing the dishes, Shelby went to her room to call Brad. There was no use avoiding this phone call. She had to let him know how she felt about moving to San Francisco.

Brad picked up on his end sounding short of breath. "This is Brad."

"Hi, it's me," Shelby said. "You sound like you've been working out."

"No, just really busy . . ." his voice trailed off as though he had moved away from his phone. Shelby heard a thin rustling sound before his voice came back. "Sorry, I've been preparing something for tomorrow."

"Maybe it isn't the best time to talk," she replied.

"No, no, it's fine. I'm done. What's up?"

"Um . . . I've been thinking about what you said last night."

"Oh, last night. Yeah. I'm sorry, Shelby, I was way too uptight."

"So was I. But I'm really concerned about going to San Francisco, Brad."

There was a heavy sigh on his end. "I know. All I ask is that you think about it a little longer. Think about what it could mean for us, how it could bless us as we begin our family."

Shelby knew she didn't want to give it a lot of thought. She'd been so against the idea from the moment he'd mentioned it. But to be fair, she decided that she should give it a little more consideration. That's what marriage was all about, wasn't it? A lot of give and take, working together for the good of the whole?

"All right, Brad. I'll think about it some more."

After talking a few more minutes, Brad needed to finish up his paperwork. Shelby hung up feeling a bit disappointed with their conversation. She tried to call Sara and Amanda, knowing they could cheer her up, but they weren't home. Shelby pulled out her bride magazine. Maybe looking at gowns and bridesmaid dresses would be a good idea.

Thumbing through page after page, her mind wandered over the events of the day—driving to Hebgen Lake, meeting John, talking with Cameron. He had been so amazing today. Shelby thought about Cameron's pain-filled face when he told her about Camille and the way he listened to her open up about her life. She remembered the distracting sight of his sculpted, muscular body and the playful gleam in his eye after he had soaked her in the canoe . . . When she realized she was smiling ridiculously at her magazine, she tossed it on the floor, flopped facedown on the bed, and groaned in frustration. *What is wrong with me? What am I feeling?*

Swirling in confusion, thoughts of the afternoon harried her mind. It didn't sound like Cameron had his feet planted deeply in the gospel, judging by the way he'd been involved with someone like Camille. Did he ever attend church on Sundays, at least for some portion of the meetings? Had he been strong and active on his mission? Maybe he became lazy with his testimony when he got back. A couple guys she knew at BYU were like that.

Shelby sighed. She didn't like feeling so confused. When she had called Brad, she'd hoped for the reassurance she always felt with him. He was certainly not lazy in his testimony. He probably never had been and never would be. There was an ever-present feeling of constancy when she was with him. She'd needed the reassurance he always provided that everything was right. But the phone call hadn't really done that.

"It doesn't matter," she said aloud. "I love him, and I know he loves me. We can make everything work." She knew what she wanted, and she wouldn't do anything that would cause her to give up that dream.

There was a light tapping at her door. Shelby hurriedly composed herself and then called hesitantly, "Come in."

It was Millie. "You are getting popular around here!" she declared.

Her thoughts still with Cameron, Shelby stared blankly, wondering if this was an accusation. Did Millie think she had spent too much time with Cameron today? *She's probably right. I'm engaged to Brad.*

"It's Julie White on the phone," Millie explained. "She's the Young Women's president."

"Oh!" Shelby jumped up. "Thank you, Millie."

As Shelby headed to the kitchen phone, Millie put one arm around her in a brief embrace. That single touch meant so much to her.

As it turned out, Sister White enthusiastically asked if Shelby would be interested in helping out the Young Women with some of the activities that would be coming up. Shelby felt her spirits leap and tremble at the same time.

"We have a river rafting trip next week and the annual stake barn dance is coming up. We'd love to have your help."

"I'd like to help, Sister White. But I should warn you, I don't know anything about the Young Women. I joined the Church after high school. I'm not sure I'm the best example."

"Good heavens, the girls will love you! They'd really look up to someone from BYU."

After hanging up, Shelby told Millie about the phone call, and somehow her concerns about not having grown up in the Church surfaced.

"The only ward I've ever been in is the student ward at BYU. I have never seen what a family ward is like with kids growing up in the gospel."

"Shelby, you were a teenager once. You've experienced all the emotional ups and downs that they're feeling. And you have a testimony of the gospel. That's what's important." She sent an encouraging smile to Shelby. "I think the girls in our ward will be very lucky to have you at the activities."

Shelby's heart swelled with gratitude. "Thank you, Millie."

"And another thing. You don't have to be raised in the gospel to be a good mother or wife. I don't know if you worry about that, but I want you to know that I think you'll be wonderful at both."

Shelby was more moved than she could say. She always wondered if she was worthy of marrying Brad, how he could have chosen her above other girls with prestigious LDS families. But Millie didn't find her wanting! That was so comforting.

"Thank you for saying that, Millie. It means a lot to me."

Millie patted Shelby's left hand but in doing so was poked by the solitaire. "My goodness, I haven't seen your ring up close yet. It's lovely."

"Thanks. Brad picked it out." She said, catching sparks of light as she moved her fingers.

"Did you let him know what you liked or was it a complete surprise?"

Shelby laughed a little and said, "He surprised me."

Millie struggled, as if she wanted to say something, but turned instead to look out the window. She was quiet for a moment and then looked back at Shelby.

"Would you like to toast some marshmallows? It looks like Cam has a fire going again."

Shelby suddenly felt the uncomfortable lurch of her heart. Maybe she ought to go straight back to her room. "I don't know . . . Are you and Karl coming too?"

"You go ahead," she said as she pulled the marshmallows out of the cupboard. "I'll go see if Karl minds being pulled away from his game on TV long enough to come outside with me. Maybe we'll come down in a little while."

Shelby took the bag of marshmallows and went out the back door into the black night. Overhead, an infinite scattering of stars gleamed through sporadic, moon-laced clouds. She drew a deep breath, filling her lungs with the sweet smell of pine and wildflowers mixed with burning wood. Down the hill, the campfire was going strong, sending curls of smoke heavenward. Wags padded over, his collar jingling at his neck.

"Come on, Wags." She slapped her leg and the loveable dog waggled quietly beside her as she made her way down to the fire.

When Shelby noticed that Cameron was staring pensively into the flames, she stopped. His profile was magnificent in the firelight. His elbows rested on his knees, while his fingers were laced together supporting his chin. He must have been deep in thought.

Not wanting to intrude on his silent reverie, she began to move back. It was better not to be alone with him anyway. Something kept happening to her whenever he was near. That wasn't a good thing for someone who was engaged.

When Cameron suddenly looked up from the flames, she was drawn in by the expression of pleasure that appeared so naturally on his face.

"Hi."

"Hi," she answered shyly.

"Are you here to burn some marshmallows for me?"

Shelby laughed and said, "If I do, they're still mine!" She took in the smug look on his face. "But I might let you have the ones that fall into the fire."

The dimple in his cheek appeared with that comment. He grabbed two long sticks off the ground while Shelby sat down on the log next to his. Wags lay on the ground with his chin on her foot. When Cameron had the sticks ready, Shelby handed him some marshmallows, and he poked them onto the sticks.

"Here you go," he said, handing her one of the sticks. Then, noticing his sleeping dog beside her, he commented, "It looks like you've got an admirer."

Shelby smiled as she patted Wags's brown head affectionately and then positioned her stick near the edge of the fire. Cameron positioned his by the center flames. Shelby watched the crackling fire and listened to the chirping insects. She felt his eyes on her and tried to think of something to say.

Glancing over, she said, "Thanks for an awesome day. I had a lot of fun."

His eyes held hers. "I'm glad you came, Shelby. I had fun too."

Her name on his lips felt like a caress, and she was grateful for the orange glow of the fire that disguised her blushes.

After a pause she decided to tell him. "I guess I'll be going on that river rafting trip."

A look of pleasant surprise came over him. "Did they call you? That's awesome."

Shelby looked down at her feet. "The Young Women's president called a few minutes ago to ask if I could help them out with a couple activities."

"That's great, Shelby." He actually sounded excited. "You're perfect for that."

Shelby turned her marshmallow over and said, "I don't know about that. I'm scared to death to be around those girls!"

"Why?"

She shrugged. "I don't know how to explain it."

"I think you'll do a great job. They probably need someone like you."

"Someone who would tip them all over or fall off the raft? In case you haven't noticed, I'm a klutz! Not to mention the fact that I'm always putting my foot in my mouth." She didn't add anything about her inexperience in the gospel or youth Church activities.

Cameron moved closer to put an arm around her and squeezed her shoulder. "You are a good person, Shelby. Don't doubt yourself. You'll be great."

Just as she leaned toward him, he let go of her and the slight chill of the night replaced the comforting warmth where his arm had been. Shelby was left feeling strangely empty and cold.

"And, hey, I'll keep a close eye on you. Make sure you don't stand up in the raft like you did today."

What a smug look. Shelby held back a grin as she thumped him on the arm.

"Hey!" he cried, in a pathetic attempt to appear hurt. Shelby laughed.

A sudden breeze filtered through her hair and wound its way across her bare arms.

"You didn't wear a jacket again," Cameron said when she shivered.

"I'm okay."

Cameron set his stick down and took off his denim jacket. "Here," he said as he wrapped it around her. "It can get chilly around here at night."

Shelby was enveloped in the protective warmth that the jacket provided and breathed in the same masculine scent she had noticed whenever she was near him.

"Thanks, Cam. That's nice of you."

His eyes held hers for a moment in a silent expression of tenderness and yearning. Her beauty mesmerized Cameron. But he was equally amazed by her inner beauty. There were moments when she was a little insecure, but she was also fun to be around, gentle, and caring.

Now longing to run his fingers over the smooth skin of her cheek, Cameron agonizingly restrained himself. Turning away, he cleared his throat and stared at the fire a few seconds. The flames were escalating. Definitely escalating. In fact—Suddenly a slow grin spread unexpectedly across his face. "I think you're making that marshmallow for me after all," he said, pointing to Shelby's flaming stick.

"Aww!" she cried out in frustration and blew repeatedly until the fire was out.

Cameron ate his oozy dark marshmallow while Shelby pulled hers off the stick. Then he eyed her with a gleam.

"Don't you dare!" she laughed and pulled the burnt offering out of his reach. "I'm still going to eat this."

He watched her pick at the flaky, black shell. Then, with a look of determination, Shelby popped it into her mouth and gave Cameron a triumphant look. He laughed at her adorable face, and they continued roasting more marshmallows, enjoying the playful banter of conversation. But as the hour progressed, an undercurrent of deep emotion drew them nearer.

Later, as the fire was dying down, Cameron and Shelby were still talking, both completely oblivious of the time, neither wanting the night to end. Cameron was pointing out various constellations, touching briefly on some of the legends behind them. As she listened to his deep voice, Shelby looked at the twinkling stars above her and was amazed at the endless expanse of heavens. How was it possible that the splendor of a midnight sky had never been as palpable as it was tonight? It was as if her senses had been awakened to a greater acuteness since she had come to Montana, and she wasn't sure why.

Cameron was pointing northward. "Do you see that cluster of stars that looks sort of like a 'W'? No, farther this way." He leaned closer to Shelby, their heads nearly touching, and she followed the line of his arm out to the tip of his finger.

"Right over there?" She looked in the direction he was pointing and then stole a quick peek at his face. It was so close to her own that she could see the faint stubble on his cheeks and a small scar below his chin.

"Yeah, right there. That constellation is Cassiopeia. It's also known as 'The Queen.'"

"From Greek mythology?"

"Yeah. She was the mythological queen of Ethiopia who was . . ." There was a slight pause as Cameron glanced at her. ". . . completely gorgeous. She offended the sea nymphs by boasting of her beauty, so she got punished by having to sacrifice her daughter Andromeda to a sea monster."

Shelby chuckled. "Greek mythology is so dramatic." She turned slightly to the left, eager to learn more. "What's that star over your shoulder—the one that's really bright?"

Cameron followed her heavenward gaze and answered, "That's Vega. It's the brightest star you can see during the summer."

"Is it part of a constellation?"

"It's part of Lyra—the harp. It's one of the three stars in the summer triangle."

As he pointed out the stars that made up the triangle, he stole a glance at her upturned face. The sparkle of moonbeams danced in her eyes. It took his breath away.

With a great deal of self-control, he stood up and turned his back to her. He closed his eyes for a moment and drew in a long, painful breath. When he opened his eyes, he focused on the western sky.

"What are you looking for now?" she asked.

Cameron rubbed his hand along the back of his neck. "I wanted to show you Leo . . . but the trees are in the way. Maybe if we head up the hill we could see some other constellations—if you want."

Shelby took his proffered hand and stood up. "I'd like that."

They faced each other with fingers intertwined. For a moment neither of them was conscious of the fact that he was still holding her hand. Cameron captured her eyes with his and an undeniable intensity flared through his gaze. The sensation stirred emotions in her chest like the rushing current of a waterfall as it plummets to the ground. Then he turned and led her up the hill, still pulling her by the hand.

When he stopped in a clearing away from the trees, Cameron gently pulled Shelby in front of him and motioned to the western sky. With him standing behind her so close, she could feel the warmth radiating from his body. He pointed out Leo above the horizon.

Shelby wasn't certain if it was her eyes or the night, but she couldn't seem to find the constellation at all. She couldn't concentrate on anything but the pressure of Cameron's hand on her shoulder and the feel of his breath at the back of her hair as he spoke. A strange fluttering erupted in her chest. Feeling her legs weakening, Shelby closed her eyes for a moment and drifted backward against him. When she suddenly trembled, Cameron's hands were promptly turning her around to face him.

"You're still cold. Maybe we should go back inside."

"No, I'm fine."

His hands were still on her arms, their bodies almost touching. Cameron looked into her upturned face and felt a compelling force drawing him closer. "Are you sure?" Cameron asked quietly.

As the gentle night breeze teased her hair, he lifted one hand to her face to brush a few wayward strands out of her eyes. The contact of his hands on her face sent a fiery current between them.

"Shelby . . ." he whispered unsteadily.

His gaze lingered agonizingly on her mouth, his eyes a reflection of the burning flames down the hill.

"Yes . . . ?" she softly murmured as he gently traced his fingers down her cheek.

Her heart was hammering now. Had she ever felt this way before? It couldn't be right to feel such an intense physical response to a man as she did right now. And yet she didn't want this feeling to ever stop.

With great shock, they were suddenly assaulted by two glaring headlights. The clamor of a car engine whined with its approach, and the dogs were instantly flung into a state of uproar.

"Oh no . . ." Cameron moaned.

Sister Brown was on the loose.

Chapter 11

"Mmm hmm," Elvira Brown huffed accusingly. Her wrinkled lips pressed tightly together, forming a row of lines like a picket fence across her mouth.

Expanding the gap between Cameron and Shelby with a dangerous swish of her cane, she militantly grabbed Shelby's arm and propelled her toward the house. Extremely embarrassed and decidedly perturbed, Shelby glanced back in Cameron's direction, but he was no longer there.

Surprising Millie with her earsplitting calls through the front room, Sister Brown hunted down the Thompsons.

Shelby saw the look of shock on Millie's face. "Elvira! What brings you here this time of night?"

"I came to make sure everything was all right over here. I saw fire again."

"It was just Cameron's campfire. There's nothing—"

"Do you think he should be making fires like that?" the elderly woman asked, still keeping a tight hold of Shelby's arm. "I've seen TV programs about people that can't stop making fires and end up—"

"There's nothing to worry about, Elvira! Cameron knows what he's doing." Millie said defensively.

Karl walked in on the conversation, the smirk on his face held barely in check. "Which pyromaniac are you talking about, Sister Brown?"

"Well, it's not, I mean . . ." she stammered, obviously flustered by Karl's directness. "Oh, I'm not talking about a pyromaniac, for heaven sakes! I'm just doing my Christian duty as a good citizen and making sure my neighbors are safe. What with fires and all . . ."

She released Shelby, flung back the curtains, and peered through the front window, glaring into the darkness outside. Millie looked at Karl, who was rolling his eyes. Shelby wondered how long the Thompsons had dealt with Sister Brown's idiosyncrasies and rudeness.

Elvira turned around to face them. "Well, there's nothing more I can do I suppose," she mumbled, deflated. Then she eyeballed Shelby a moment before saying, "When is your outstanding fiancé coming up to be with his bride?"

Shelby was taken aback. "I'm . . . not sure when. Just as soon as he can."

A bony finger was pointed at her in warning. "You just be careful until then." With that, the ever-vigilant neighbor stalked back to her car and rumbled back home.

Shelby wished she could crawl into a deep hole and disappear.

* * *

On Sunday after sacrament meeting, Shelby was stopped in the hall by the Young Women's President, Julie White. She introduced herself warmly and made Shelby feel completely at ease with her.

"Would you be willing to come to Young Women's today so we can introduce you to the girls?"

"Okay," Shelby said hesitantly. "Where do you meet?"

Julie explained how to find them and waved a cheerful good-bye. Then Shelby walked down to the Sunday School room. It was difficult to pay attention to the lesson while feeling nervous about meeting the young women.

When Sunday School was over, Shelby walked down the hallway. After the first intimidating minutes of being introduced to the Young Women, Shelby's heart settled, and she came to the conclusion that she could actually enjoy being with them. There were only eight girls, and they all seemed nice. She couldn't help wondering if any of these girls were the ones she had overheard in the rest sroom but tried not to notice any black shoes or gum-chewing. It would be better not to know.

There was one girl who stood out because she sat by herself. She had long black hair and expressive dark eyes. She seemed somewhat unresponsive and downhearted. Shelby felt compelled to find out more about her.

After Church, she was making her way to the Thompsons' car when Sister Lockland flagged her down excitedly. Almost out of breath, Sister Lockland said, "I'm sorry I wasn't home when you returned my call yesterday. I've been dying to tell you that I found a dress you might like! It was at the mall *and* on sale." She hurriedly handed Shelby a folded piece of paper.

"I was trying on formal dresses when I happened to see a wedding dress hanging there like it was meant to be! Here's the name of the gal who put it on hold for me, and this is the model number. You've just got to look at it! I think it is much closer to what you had in mind. But if you don't like it, let's get together again and see what we can come up with."

"Thank you, Sister Lockland."

Shelby waved as the other woman ran off to a minivan being driven by an impatient teenage son. Then she walked over to the Thompsons' car, where Karl and Millie were just getting in.

"Hello, dear," Millie greeted. "How did it go with the Young Women?"

"Fine," Shelby answered with a smile. "I thought the girls were nice."

"Everyone ready to go home?" asked Karl, hunger written on his face.

Before they made it home, Cameron sped past them in the opposite direction with a hasty wave at his parents and a cloud of dust trailing behind him. He had completely avoided everyone this morning and was apparently going to keep it that way. After last night's embarrassment, Shelby was only too willing to keep a distance from him as well.

Sister Brown had certainly made her disapproval of Cameron quite clear. By the way the old neighbor had stormed up, you would have thought she was breaking up some sort of scandalous interlude! Nothing had happened, for crying out loud! It was almost like Sister Brown had been deliberately sniffing out trouble. Did the poor woman have so much time on her hands that she had to spy on the neighbors for entertainment?

A silent inner voice pricked at her conscience. *That was not fair, Shelby, and it definitely wasn't kind.* But she had been embarrassed by

Sister Brown's unwarranted implication that something had happened between Shelby and Cameron. *But something* had *almost happened . . .*

Shelby quickly looked out the window, unwilling to think any more about it. But as she watched the rolling green hills pass by, the image of Cameron's face last night entered her mind. Again she saw the way he had stood so close, the expression in his eyes. If their neighbor hadn't come, how would that night have ended? Her mind replayed the memories of every touch, causing a tight quiver in her chest.

Shelby closed her eyes and with a shake of her head resumed her study of the rolling hills and tall trees. Brad might not want to live here, but with such exquisite beauty, how was she to prevent herself from falling in love with Montana?

* * *

Shelby quickly discovered how busy the Young Women's program was. Julie White and her counselors were very friendly and made Shelby feel instantly needed and useful. They explained Shelby's assignment with the youth on the river rafting trip and with organizing the barn dance at Brother and Sister Lewis's farm. The Young Women were in charge of this particular activity, but all youth and adults would be invited. It sounded like a fun thing to work on.

When Shelby had asked about the dark-haired girl who had sat alone in class, Sister White had told her some interesting things.

"Her name is Rose Blackburn. Her parents live up north on the Flathead Indian Reservation, but she lives with her aunt and uncle and their three children on the outskirts of town."

Sister White had also mentioned that Rose often looked angry or sad and that she didn't seem to get along with any of the other girls in the ward. Shelby's heart was touched. She had distinct feelings about helping Rose yet didn't have the slightest idea what she could do in the short amount of time she'd be in Montana. It was apparent that Shelby would have the opportunity to practice faith and to rely on Heavenly Father's guidance.

* * *

Monday morning, Cameron woke up still determined to stay away from Shelby. There was no way on earth he wanted to put himself in a vulnerable situation again. He stood too great a chance of getting his heart involved in a completely impossible, hopeless situation. And he just couldn't risk that. He'd been forgetting his resolve lately to stay far away from women, and with Shelby it was becoming harder to do. *She's just so . . . never mind.* Today he would get himself back on track.

After getting dressed, he found his mother alone in the kitchen, busily preparing breakfast.

"What are you cooking up?" he asked her hungrily.

"Plans," she stated meaningfully.

Sneaking a piece of hot bacon, he asked mischievously, "What kind of plans?"

"Wedding plans," she laughed, but not before noticing the passing look of disappointment on her son's face. Millie ached for him, wishing she could do something to help him out of the misery he'd been going through. "Shelby and I are going into town today for some things. But Dad and I want to take her to the canyon for a picnic. I think she'd love to see Hyalite Reservoir and some of the waterfalls."

"Mmm, that's nice." Cameron hoped his voice sounded noncommittal.

"Do you want to come too? We'd love to have you join us." Millie asked hopefully.

Cameron rubbed the back of his neck. "I don't think so. I have some things to do before the river rafting trip tomorrow." He'd invent some things to do if necessary.

"Come on! Please come with us. We need your expertise on the trail to the falls," Millie coaxed.

"I really am busy today, Mom."

When Millie's face fell, Cameron felt guilty. His mother was the last person in the world he ever wanted to disappoint. She had stood by him through thick and thin throughout his entire life. Then came the nagging thought: *So why can't I just tell her the truth?* Instead of answering that question, Cameron took off in a hurry, leaving Millie to stare after him in confused speculation.

* * *

After breakfast, Millie drove Shelby into town to see the dress Sister Lockland had put on hold for her and to visit the florist shop. But when they got to the mall, not one sales associate could find the dress. It wasn't hanging in the closet reserved for items on hold, and it wasn't on the racks.

"Perhaps it has already been sold," a woman with heavy red lip liner said condescendingly. "It was a clearance item, after all."

Those jeweled fingers have probably never ever touched anything as low as a "clearance item," Shelby thought. "All right. Thanks for your help," she said, trying not to sound sarcastic.

Millie suggested that Shelby try on a few wedding gowns anyway, just to get a feel for styles. Shelby didn't feel like trying anything on with the rude woman around. But thankfully, she left, and a younger girl helped her bring dresses into the fitting room.

Millie loved nearly everything Shelby tried on, exclaiming how beautiful a bride she would be. Shelby decided there was only one of the dresses she could afford, but it would have to be altered quite a bit to be modest. She really liked another dress, but it was a fortune. They decided to keep looking.

At the floral shop, it was a challenge selecting boutonnieres and corsages for the reception. There would be no purchase for her father. She pictured him wearing a boutonniere, playing the part of proud father of the bride. She tried to imagine what it would be like to have brothers and sisters surrounding her at the reception. She forced herself to dismiss the wave of loneliness pressing down on her. But when she thought about a corsage for her mother just in case she could come, her efforts to be upbeat weren't very effective.

Not wanting to worry Millie, she tried to conceal her feelings by maintaining her outward expression of cheerfulness. Fortunately, it wasn't too difficult a task because Millie was so pleasant to be with. It was heartwarming to be able to laugh and talk with her like they were old friends. There were few things she wanted more than to have such a good relationship with her mother-in-law.

On the way back home, Millie enthusiastically described the Hyalite Canyon and its many beauties that they would enjoy for their picnic.

"I can't wait for you to see it. There are so many things to do—camping, fishing, hiking to the waterfalls and lakes. It's breathtaking! Romantic too," Millie said dreamily. "I don't think I mentioned it before, but Karl proposed to me at Palisade Falls."

"Wow! That *is* romantic."

"It really was," she reminisced. "We were standing together at the base of the waterfall, and he was so shy and nervous that I thought he'd fall in the water." They both laughed. Then Millie unexpectedly said, "You know, I wish Cameron could have come with us today. With all his experience in biology and the Forest Service, he makes a great guide."

At the sudden change in subjects, Shelby became quiet. She could easily imagine Cameron pointing out interesting facts along the way with his calm expertise. It would be more enjoyable to have him along too, since he had such a playful nature. Maybe not constantly, but she had definitely seen that side of him and liked it. She wondered what his reaction would be if she were to tickle him. She savored that thought for a moment.

When they got home, Karl helped load up the car, and they set out for an adventurous picnic up the Hyalite Canyon, Shelby concentrating on keeping her mind on the lush forest setting.

* * *

In utter frustration, Cameron yanked the expensive calendar off the wall. *This is ridiculous! My apartment is a breeding ground for unwanted memories of my ex.* Perusing the Twelve Months of Luxury Destinations calendar, he couldn't help remembering the day Camille had stuck this on his wall with a hint that they should save up for some of these places. *Yeah, right.* He chucked the calendar into the garbage and then slumped onto his futon.

He shouldn't have come here, of all places. There was no reason for him to be here alone, facing gruesome ghosts of the past, when he had a completely acceptable alternative. No one should have to be alone when he had family that wanted to spend time with him.

Cameron's thoughts turned to Shelby. There was loneliness in her eyes today as he had watched them all leave for their picnic. The last image in his mind was that of Shelby sitting alone in the back seat. She had turned to wave back at him with a smile that didn't quite reach her eyes. He couldn't stand the thought of anyone feeling so alone in the world. Even though he'd had his share of times when loneliness had overcome him, he'd always had his family to rely on.

Somehow he longed to erase the loneliness from Shelby's face. If he could just help her feel welcome and be her friend, he would be doing a lot. Such strong feelings took him by surprise. He had no desire to get involved, but the inclination to extend basic human kindness persisted.

She needed a friend. That's all there was to it. And they had agreed that they were "friends" the day they went to Hebgen Lake together.

Cameron wondered how well Brad knew his future wife. It seemed strange that Shelby could be engaged to be married and yet still have that overwhelming loneliness. Then again, maybe it was better just to mind his own business. His imagination could just be running wild. But there wasn't a single thing wrong with plain old decency and kindness. It was time to face the facts. If she was to be his sister-in-law, what was wrong with being her friend? They might as well take the opportunity to get to know each other better. As friends. Close friends.

Now that he had come to a decision, a new sense of urgency swept over him. He practically leapt from the futon, grabbed his keys and wallet and ran out the front door of his apartment. He drove past the MSU campus and headed south into the canyon, hoping all the way that he wouldn't arrive too late to find them.

Twenty minutes later he was losing hope when he caught a glimpse of gold in the sunlight. Shelby! She was walking through a grove of trees in the Hood Creek Campground.

Cameron quickly pulled into the first available parking space. As he strode in her direction, she turned and caught sight of him. She made a small wave with one hand. His heart lurched inside his chest. He sternly reminded himself that the only purpose in him being here was for their friendship and to please his mom.

"Millie, Karl," Shelby called out through the trees. "Cam is here." Millie couldn't have looked more pleased.

"Did you save me any food?" he asked eagerly.

"We have more than enough," Millie said, walking over to squeeze his arm affectionately. "I'm so glad you found us, Cam. Come on over to the picnic table and grab a plate."

Karl looked surprised. "Did you finish up all the things you had to do at your place?"

Three pairs of eyes waited for his explanation. Cameron thought about all the "things" he had done: gathering every last thing in his apartment that had the slightest connection to Camille and paying a visit to the big metal dumpster out back. Oh yeah, he was finished! He never wanted to set foot in that apartment again.

"I got done a lot sooner than I'd thought, so I decided to see if I could find you guys."

Millie said, "I just wish you could have come sooner for our walk to Palisade Falls. Now all you're in time for is lunch."

Shelby looked at his plate being heaped with food. "Perfect timing," she laughed, and Cameron returned her smile with one of his own over a big bite of chicken. He was amazed at how different he felt now compared to an hour ago. *This is so much better.*

Shelby placed two cans of soda pop in front of him. "Root beer or lemonade?"

"Root beer, please."

"Oh yeah, I remember the caseload of root beer you brought home," she teased.

"You should hear some of the stories we have about Cameron and root beer," said Karl.

"Dad . . ." Cameron warned with an exaggerated groan. "No one is interested."

Shelby's interest heightened. "What stories?"

In spite of Cameron's humorous glare, Karl went on. "Once when he was about twelve and Scott was a toddler, Cam was drinking some root beer. Baby Scott was pulling on Cam's sleeves to get a sip, but Cam didn't want to share. Scott kept saying 'Boot Reer, me boot reer.' Cam thought Scott said to boot him in the rear, and he laughed so hard that he sprayed a mouthful of root beer out of his nose all over the kitchen and his brother."

Trying not to become a visual aid for the story, Cameron choked down his mouthful, smothering his laughter. The others had no need to do so, and their laughter could be heard throughout the campgrounds.

"That's so unfair!" he laughed.

Shelby was so captivated by the transformation that his smiles and laughter created that she didn't even see the ground squirrel that scampered beside her shoe. A loud chattering finally took her notice, and she gave the animal her full attention.

"Hey, little guy, what are you trying to tell me?"

Karl snickered. "This is a stick up. He wants your lunch."

"Here," she said, tossing a small breadcrumb beyond the table, into the bushes. "But don't come back for more." The ground squirrel darted for the offering.

"Uh-oh. You did it now," Cameron accused dramatically. "You'll never have a moment's peace from now on. He'll be back swearing his undying devotion to you."

Shelby smirked but raised her eyebrows when the animal returned, chattering even more loudly than before.

"Oh boy, this is bad," Cameron said mysteriously. "I think we'd better get out of here before he makes the signal."

"What signal?" asked Shelby, doubtfully.

"*The* signal," he continued importantly. "Some animals have an inborn signal that when sent out summons all others of its species to its aid."

"They do?" she asked incredulously.

"Yep. If he transmits that signal, you could get attacked by a herd of ground squirrels—BAM—just like that."

Shelby looked aghast until she heard Millie snickering. Looking at Karl and Millie's faces, she realized that she'd been had. Turning back to Cameron's innocently placid features, she cried out laughingly, "You . . ." as she elbowed him in the ribs.

Unprepared, Cameron yelped and nearly jumped out of his seat. "Hey!"

Millie shook her head in mirth. "You have to be careful around him, Shelby. He's the biggest tease I know."

"Then I'll have to plot my revenge," she said with a flair of dramatics.

"Ooohh, let me help you," Millie conspired. "I'm his mother—I know his weaknesses!"

Cameron reached for his fishing gear and declared, "Not *all* of them, Mom. And I think I'd better get out of here before you ladies gang up on me."

Karl called out, "Wait up, son. I'm with you," and hurried after him with his fishing gear in tow.

"Don't overdo it, honey," Millie called out, unconvinced her husband had listened.

The ladies watched the men walk down to the water's edge, a trail of hefty laughter following in their tracks.

Chapter 12

Shelby sat on an old wool blanket in a shady patch just a few feet from the water's edge, a towering pine tree covering her with its cool shade. Her back against the rough bark of the trunk, she watched Cameron cast out his line and whip it back and forth in perfect rhythm. Sunlight framed him in nature's spotlight, outlining his masculine physique. Rays of light sailed gently over masses of ripples in the water.

Millie sat nearby in a lawn chair, her rhythmic breathing indicating she had dozed off. She was such a sweet lady. She always had something funny to say, and yet she would be serious when her feelings were deep. It seemed remarkable to Shelby how much she grew to love Millie the more she was around her. It was beginning to feel like a healing balm, long needed.

While Millie dozed, Shelby continued to observe Karl and Cameron while they were fly-fishing. Karl was a handsome, older version of his sons. Though perhaps not as lithe as Cameron, he seemed to be just as absorbed in the rhythm of the fly-fishing.

Her eyes trailing back to Cameron, Shelby watched in fascination as he teased the fish below the surface with his line. There was a magical beauty to the pattern woven in the air with his fishing line. At the end of the line, the small fly would land gently on the water and almost dance as it imitated a hovering insect.

There was no question about it. Cameron was magnificent to watch.

When he suddenly looked her way, Shelby felt a jolt course through her—as if she had been caught in the act of stealing from the cookie jar.

"Come on over, and I'll teach you," he called out casually.

Resisting, Shelby glanced to see if Millie was awake yet. Karl had moved farther down along the bank. "I'm not so sure . . ."

"It's really fun," he coaxed. "And it's easy."

"Easy, huh?"

"Piece of cake," he grinned. "Come on . . ."

She stood up, brushed off the seat of her pants, and walked closer to the water's edge. Small ripples flowed in against the bed of large rocks. "Will I be getting my feet wet?"

"No, I'll come out."

He walked up to her, making a sucking sound in the mud as his waders emerged from the water. Shelby looked warily at him and all his equipment. She eyed the sharp hook stuck to a fuzzy, homemade "mayfly" at the end of the fly line. This probably wasn't a good idea. It was all too easy to visualize the wrong places she could sink that hook into.

Seeing the look on her face, Cameron asked, "What's wrong?"

"I'm having nightmares already just thinking of what could happen with that hook!"

Cameron threw back his head and laughed. Shelby loved how his face lit up like that. She grinned back at him and waited for his response.

"It's easier than you think, I promise."

"What if I snag the trees or hook myself?"

"You won't. Here, I'll stand right behind you—like this—and guide your arm."

When he moved up close behind her she could feel the tools and rough flies on his vest jacket through the shirt on her back. His arms were warm against her, and he smelled of clean soap.

"This is the fly rod, and this is the line. Take the line with your left hand like this. Yeah, that's it . . . Now grip the rod on the cork here with your right hand. Good."

With confidence he guided her hands with his own, giving her the feel for the basic movements. She felt cradled with him behind her, encircling her with his arms. Warm sunshine bathed them with light. It was all too easy to remember the contrastingly chilly night on the hill when he had stood behind her pointing out constellations.

She was keenly aware of his taut, muscular arms and broad chest as he spoke.

"Okay, let's try it together," he was saying. "Forward, snap. Back, snap."

She let him guide her movements as the line was thrown straight out and then abruptly snapped back behind them. There was a loud swoosh sound with each stroke in the air. He repeated this procedure several times until she started to get the hang of it.

"That's the basic technique. From here there're a lot of methods of presenting and playing the line that take some practice."

"You know, this is kind of fun."

"Wait 'til you catch your first fish." There was a smile in his voice. "Then it will be *you* that's hooked!"

"As long as I'm not literally hooked!"

A slight bobble at the end of the line interrupted their laughter. "Hey, we got one!" Cameron cheered and hurried back behind her.

Shelby screamed. "You do it! Here!"

"Hang on, you're doing fine," he laughed as they reeled in a shiny, fat arctic grayling that flipped about wildly in the water. He walked into the water to scoop the feisty fish up in his net. Then he raised it triumphantly in the air.

"Who caught that one?" Millie's voice called out from behind them, having woken with all the shouting.

Shelby turned and chuckled. "Mostly Cam."

"Looks like we're having a fish fry tonight!" They all turned to see Karl returning triumphantly with his catch of two cutthroat trout. Millie was first to notice his limp.

"Honey," she cried. "Did you hurt your knee?"

"It's nothing," Karl said. But he winced as he leaned against a tree.

"Here, Dad, let's get you over to a chair," Cameron coaxed.

"I'll be fine in a minute. Nothing to worry about."

Once Karl was settled in a lawn chair, he and Cameron compared the fish they had caught, both playfully claiming the winner's title. But Millie noticed her husband instinctively rub at his knee several times.

Hands on her hips, Millie stated, "I think we should head back home now."

"What's the hurry?" Karl protested. "We're having a good time."

"It's been quite a day," Millie said. "Aren't you tired?"

"Of course not," he huffed, unmindful that he was rubbing his knee again.

Wagging a finger at him, she answered, "Your knee is giving you more trouble than you're willing to admit."

Knowing how stubborn his dad could be, Cameron came to her aid. "I'm getting a bit tired too. I'll help you pack everything up, Mom." Shelby agreed and began to place food containers in the picnic basket.

Karl frowned at them all and then turned away and muttered, "Tired, my foot," and something about party poopers. The others exchanged conspiratorial grins. Cameron walked Karl over to the car, leaving Millie and Shelby to finish gathering food.

"I feel bad that we have to cut our day short. I really wanted to show you more of the canyon," Millie said regretfully. "But Karl has a bad knee, and I think he really should get off his feet for a while—"

"Don't worry, Millie. Of course we should take care of Karl. Maybe another day."

"We'll have to come back," said Millie. "There's so much more to see!"

Cameron strode up just then. "More of what to see, Mom?"

Millie turned to him to explain. "I just wanted to show Shelby some of the other waterfalls and views of the canyon. I feel bad cutting the day short, but with your dad's knee . . ."

"It's no problem, Millie," Shelby reassured her, touched by Millie's sincere regret for not being able to finish their outing. "There are plenty of things to work on for the wedding."

"I . . . could show you around," Cameron said with only a trace of uncertainty.

Millie brightened considerably. "Oh, Cam! Would you? There's still enough daylight to enjoy more of the area."

Karl muttered from inside the car, "Thought you were tired." caused a warm flush to spread up Cameron's neck, but he ignored his father and turned back to his mom. "No problem."

Shelby gave him a friendly smile. "Thank you, Cameron. But I don't want to inconvenience you."

It was decided that Millie would drive Karl home and Cameron would bring Shelby back a little later. They gathered the few things that remained and took them to the car. Sitting stiffly in his seat, Karl apologized for his "bad timing," and Millie started the engine.

"You just get some rest, Dad. And don't worry, Mom. I'll be showing Shelby so much of this canyon that by the time we get back she'll be sick of Montana!"

Shelby laughed. "As if that were possible! I could never get tired of this place."

Millie waved from the car. "Thanks again, Cam. We'll see you later."

Cameron and Shelby waved back, watching the car disappear from view in companionable silence. Then Cameron turned to face her dutifully.

"So . . . what would you like to see first? Your wish is my command."

"Oh really?" Shelby's eyes sparkled mischievously.

"You know I'll get tortured if I don't do what Mom says."

"My, aren't you obedient," she teased.

"No, just terrified of her! She knows all but one of my weak points."

"Only one, huh? What would that be?"

Cameron looked down into Shelby's shining face. Bracing himself he just smiled mysteriously. "I'll never tell."

Shelby thought the look was unbearably handsome. "Let me guess," she joined in the game. "You're secretly working for the CIA?"

He laughed. "That's a good one."

"How about . . . I don't know . . . your entire back is covered with tattoos?"

He gave her a look of pseudo indignation and then claimed, "Of course it is."

Shelby laughed. They had almost reached his truck, parked under an enormous pine tree, when she said, "You know what? I can't imagine anything topping Palisade Falls. It was completely amazing."

Cameron chuckled. "That's where my dad proposed to Mom, so they don't think anything can top it either."

"A waterfall plummeting from eighty feet off a cliff is nothing to scoff at. You know, I was serious when I said I could never get tired of this place. I love it here. I just want to see as much as I can before I go back to Provo."

Cameron didn't say anything about her having to leave. He merely nodded. Hearing those words helped remind him of his resolve just to be her friend. They had reached his truck so he helped her in and walked to the driver's side.

"Do you feel up to a small hike?" he asked as he fastened his seat belt.

"Sure."

"There's a great trail with a lookout point over the Hyalite Canyon that we could see. It's one of my favorite places. On the way up there you pass several different waterfalls. When you see the massive cliff walls and mountain peaks it will knock your socks off."

"Sounds perfect."

As the engine rumbled to life, a lively beat of harmonizing voices burst through the cab. Judging from the elevated volume level, it was obvious Cameron had been enjoying the music before he had left his truck earlier.

"Woah . . . sorry about that," he said as his hand shot out to turn the CD off.

"No, don't turn it off. What group is it?"

He scratched his forehead. "Alabama."

"I liked it."

"You did?" He glanced at her, and she nodded happily. "Are you sure?"

"Yeah. I'd love to hear it."

Cameron grinned broadly and turned the music back on before pulling out of the parking lot. They rolled down their windows to let the cool mountain air in, and Cameron assumed the position of tour guide. Accompanied by energetic and heartfelt melodies, he pointed out logging roads and names of mountain peaks. Shelby listened and commented in fascination, absorbing every bit of information that he had to offer along the way.

When they stopped, Shelby asked, "Is this the spot you mentioned before?"

"Yep. It's the Hyalite Creek trail head. It'll take us there."

He grabbed a bottle of water and a small daypack from the truck and then led the way up the trail. They climbed steadily through the towering forest amid lodgepole pine, Engelmann spruce, Douglas fir, and aspen trees.

Shelby pointed out tiny yellow flowers that drooped like umbrellas along the edges of the trail.

"They're glacier lilies," he explained. "They only bloom early in the season, so you're lucky to see them."

They followed the trail to Grotto Falls, a wide magnificent waterfall. They continued to climb through the dense undergrowth, and Shelby noticed how much wetter this forest was than the ones she had seen in Utah. There was moss growing on tree trunks and rocks, and green ferns grew at the base of trees and clumps of shrubs.

Cameron pointed out a strangely shaped mountain on the west canyon wall. "That's Elephant Mountain." Close beside her, he pointed out the swoop of stratigraphy creating the image of an elephant's head and trunk.

"Hey, I see it!" Shelby said excitedly as she stared in delight.

Just beyond that point in the distance were partially frozen twin waterfalls dripping down the sheer cliffs. A couple stood in the way taking pictures, so they continued on to Arch Falls, named for its natural rock arch.

"Look how the falls take a sharp turn just to go under the arch," Shelby exclaimed in awe. "That's amazing!"

Cameron just grinned, engrossed more by her than the falls.

Back on the trail, they reached a fork, and Cameron guided Shelby to the left where a wooden sign pointed the way to Silken Skein Falls.

"This takes us up to the point I wanted to show you. It's steep but worth it."

They crossed a creek and climbed an immensely steep, narrow path. Cameron held Shelby's hand in a tight grip until they reached a slim, graceful waterfall cascading down the mountain in several levels. Each paused to catch their breath after the strenuous climb.

When he came up close behind her, Cameron held her upper arms and turned her around. "Look back this way," he said quietly. When Shelby turned to see the view, she gasped. It truly was breathtaking. "Do you mind if we stay here for a while?"

"Actually . . . I was hoping you'd say that. If you like to sit and appreciate the world around you, there's no better place than up here in Hyalite Canyon."

They sat on a boulder for a while, sharing from his water bottle. Cameron couldn't help certain feelings rising within as he drank from the same spot where Shelby's lips had been. Though feeling like a foolish, teenage boy, it still made him long to know the feel of her mouth against his own. *I've got to get this under control.*

When they had backtracked down to the main trail, it wasn't long before Cameron found a fairly level clearing without too many rocks. He pulled a small blanket out of his daypack and spread it on the ground for them. Shelby sat down and feasted on the scenery.

To Cameron, she almost looked like a little elf, with childlike joy in something so simple as the earth and sky. Camille had never enjoyed hiking or being outdoors. She wanted more material things—even expected them, like the luxury destinations he'd tossed out. So had most of the other girls he had dated. They wanted nicer things in life than he could ever afford. It was refreshing to see a woman enjoying the outdoors as much as he did.

They talked for a while about so many things that neither could have remembered. They mused over school and work, hobbies and books. Words came freely, friend to friend.

"So where did you go on your mission? I don't remember if you told me," Shelby asked.

"Costa Rica."

"So you speak Spanish?"

He grunted. "Un poquito," he said, making a tiny measurement with thumb and pointer finger. "I've forgotten a lot of it."

"What's it like in Costa Rica?"

He picked at a weed beside him and thought a minute. "Tropical. But there are mountains, volcanoes, and beaches. It rains a lot so it's really lush and green. The people are wonderful too."

"It *sounds* wonderful."

"Yeah, I'd really like to go back someday. I always thought I could go there on my honeymoon—" He stopped and laughed harshly. "I guess that won't be happening."

"Why not? You could still go."

He made a funny face. "By myself?"

"You'll get married someday. Then you can go."

He looked at her pointedly. "I doubt it."

"I wanted to go on a mission. I thought it could sort of make up for all the years I wasn't in Primary and seminary."

Cameron looked at her warmly. "You would've been a great missionary."

Shelby looked down at her shoes, a thoughtful expression playing on her features. "Can I ask you something?"

"Sure."

"Why did you stop going to church?"

He looked away, and she worried that she had offended him. Then he said, "At first I just missed every once in a while. Being lazy, I guess. Then there was Camille. I was angry—livid, actually—that a few of the people I *thought* were my friends, who I'd known my whole life, would turn on me. They automatically believed her, never once trying to find the truth. They were such hypocrites, coming to church and preaching to everyone else when they were in the wrong. I didn't want to have anything more to do with them."

"It must have been terrible, Cam," she said. And yet she wanted to help him see how much better his life could be with the gospel. She wanted him to be happy again. But he had to want those things for himself. "Hasn't anyone in the ward supported you?"

He rubbed his chin pensively. "Yeah. The bishopric and their families have been good to me. So have the Lewises . . . Actually, there've been a lot of people who have been kind and supportive." The tone of his voice made it sound like he'd never realized it before.

Cameron's forehead wrinkled. "What about you, Shelby? When you joined the Church, did other people treat you badly?"

"Not the Church members, of course. I didn't know anyone well enough in our apartment complex for them to care. But my friends from school sort of cut me off. They must have thought I was a freak or something," she laughed humorlessly. "My mom was the worst, though. The things she said . . ." He shook his head sympathetically. "We haven't spoken since the day I left for BYU."

Cameron watched her pick at a blade of wild grass, twisting it until it was in shreds. He said quietly, "You must miss her."

"I do. I mean, she was hardly ever there for me, drinking away her own problems, but I still love her. I just think she didn't know how to be a mother to me. She was so unhappy . . ."

"Have you ever written to her or tried calling?"

"My letters were all marked RETURN TO SENDER. I tried calling only once. She hung up on me as soon as I said hello." She shuddered at the memory.

"Aughh . . . that must have hurt."

Shelby nodded bleakly. "It was bad enough that I joined the Church. But when I told her I'd be leaving . . ." She shuddered. "I've never seen anyone so angry! She was already a widow. I basically made her childless as well by coming out to BYU."

"You didn't purposefully hurt her. You only did what you thought was right."

"I know. It's just that . . . I wish she could have understood that I never wanted to cause her any pain. I wasn't trying to destroy our relationship."

"How long has it been since you last tried to communicate with her?"

She hung her head sadly. "Four years."

He shook his head in disbelief.

"I should try to write again. But I wouldn't know what to say—'Hi, Mom. Are you still mad at me?' or 'Hey, I'm getting married; hope you can come!'"

Though hearing her sarcasm, he saw the fear in her eyes. He wasn't sure what to say. "If you could only tell her *one* thing, what would it be?"

She turned away to focus on another tall blade of wild grass. *One thing?* So many thoughts passed through her mind. But she knew the answer.

"I need to tell her that . . . that I love her. It's just hard to find the courage. I don't remember anyone in my family ever saying 'I love you' out loud."

Though somewhat astounded, he tried not to appear so. "Someday the time will be right, Shelby. Some kind of opportunity will open up for you to talk to her. And when that time comes, I think you'll do fine."

She sighed. "Thanks, Cam."

Cameron unexpectedly stretched out on his back to look at the sky. Bending his arms back to prop up his head, he watched a lengthy cloud float slowly along. He drew in a deep breath.

"Sometimes when I watch the clouds drift through the sky, it feels like all my troubles drift away with them. Just for a while."

"Really? I wish it worked."

Cameron nodded. "You should try it." He patted the blanket beside him.

Shelby lay back on the blanket beside him and watched a fluffy mass of clouds until she could detect their slow movement across the sky. An unseen bird sang an enchanting duet with the trickling water of a nearby stream. She breathed in the clean air, which carried a lingering scent of pine and wildflowers. They didn't speak. Thoughts of their conversation faded as the surrounding calm enveloped them.

Then she turned her head to Cameron. "This is amazing. I could stay here forever . . ."

"Me too," Cameron said lazily and then yawned.

Drowsy warmth of afternoon sunlight draped over them. Shelby closed her eyes, listening to nature's melodies around her.

She awoke with a start.

Where am I? Seeing Cameron sprawled out on the blanket beside her, sound asleep, she sprang up to a sitting position. *I fell asleep . . . We both fell asleep.*

Not wanting to wake him, she quietly stared out at the rugged mountains covered with dark green pines, the verdant canyon below, and the clear blue sky above. Wildflowers sprang up all over the hillside, and the creek bubbled merrily down its way. The sun was lower in the sky, casting a mellow glow over the landscape.

A low rumble of snoring drifted up behind her, interrupting her silent reverie. Shelby turned around with a grin to watch Cameron as he slept. *He must have been tired.*

Turning back to the scenery, she wrapped her arms around her drawn-up legs. A hawk soared high overhead. An insect landed on the blanket next to her feet. All was still except for Cameron's gentle snoring, and even that had a soothing, rhythmic sound that didn't bother her at all. She was amazed at the grandeur of the mountain peaks and steep canyons below and felt privileged to be able to sit quietly and enjoy it.

Shelby closed her eyes and imagined that with each breath she took, all her surroundings became a part of her, never to be forgotten. This moment would be engraved on her senses, cherished in her memories.

She looked down at Cameron. A lock of hair had fallen out of place on his forehead. She hesitated for a moment and then timidly brushed it back. Her awareness became centered on the rise and fall of Cameron's chest.

When a particularly loud rumble escaped Cameron's lips, Shelby had to stifle a laugh. With a spark of mischief, she considered the way his arms were propped behind his head. Then she nudged him in the ribs. He moved slightly, but the motor began to hum again. Nearly laughing out loud, she leaned over him and tickled him under his arms.

Had she known what his reaction would be, she might have thought twice about her action in the first place—especially to someone as ticklish as Cameron was. His arms instinctively bolted out to grasp the offender, trapping Shelby against his chest with a swiftness she wouldn't have thought possible. His eyes opened. The sight of Shelby on top of him thrust away all effects of sleep. She hid her embarrassment by laughing.

"Were you tickling me?" His mouth parted in amusement.

"No," she laughed even harder, trying to wriggle her trapped hands from under his arms. But the movement tickled him even more, and he cried out, "Hey, stop!" He rolled over and pinned her beneath him on the blanket, both of them laughing too much for either to realize what had happened. Cameron began to tickle her, and she let out a squeal.

"Don't you know you shouldn't wake a sleeping bear?"

"You were interrupting the quiet with all that snoring!"

"What do you mean? I don't snore!" His fingers were at her waist.

"Oh yes, you do," Shelby retorted playfully, gazing up at him.

Suddenly, Cameron became more serious. Stillness enveloped them in a soft hush. His face was mere inches from hers, unspoken messages written in his eyes. His attention centered on the sweet curve of her mouth.

Beneath him, Shelby saw the look on his face and instantly held her breath. The fire in his eyes made rippling sensations course through her midsection. He searched her face for a moment and then suddenly pulled away.

They both stood up, each painfully aware of the other. What had happened? What had been meant to be a mere kidding around with a buddy had almost resulted in something entirely different. That's not what she had intended. She was just having fun, playing around. He was fun to tease. *He's also not someone you should be pinned under,* she told herself sternly. *You shouldn't have been so impulsive!*

Cameron brushed off his pants, his eyes slanted briefly in her direction. "I guess we should head back."

She knew a sinking disappointment in the pit of her stomach. "Probably."

She wanted to stay here with him or go for another drive. She was even willing to ignore the little voice inside her head that was asking for an explanation for these irrational desires.

"But . . ." began Cameron. Shelby looked up hopefully. ". . . we can't go until—" he started walking to her purposefully, and her heart began to thump wildly.

"Until what?" she asked breathlessly.

"Until I get even."

Comprehension hit her with full force. She laughed and screamed at the same time, running out of his reach. He chased her up the hill and around a tree until his arms drew her in easily. She found herself hoisted ever his shoulder, her arms and legs dangling to the ground.

"Cameron Edgar Thompson, you put me down this second!" she shouted over her frantic laughter. He didn't listen, just strode over to the stream.

"I'll tell your mother!"

He moved closer to the water.

"You wouldn't dare!"

He stepped in up to his ankles with a chuckle and started lowering her. "Say 'uncle.'"

"What?" she screamed.

"Say 'uncle.'"

"Why?" Shelby couldn't believe this. Her head was almost touching the water, and he wanted her to call him 'uncle'? He was nuts! "You aren't my uncle!"

Cameron started laughing. He put her down carefully, hilarity dancing in his eyes. "Haven't you ever heard that phrase before?"

"No." Smiles belied her indignant tone of voice as she clung to him so she wouldn't fall into the water.

"You say 'uncle' so I'll stop," he explained.

Somehow the word came out barely more than a whisper. "Uncle."

Again, the anticipation of being kissed swept over her body in one ecstatic moment. Trembling with anticipation, she felt her knees weaken. Cameron's lips parted as he gazed intently at her mouth. He stepped forward and drew her more fully into his arms. Cupping one side of her face with a warm hand, he tilted his head slightly and very slowly lowered his face until his mouth was inches from hers. Shelby's eyes drooped closed as she waited for his kiss.

But it never came. Instead, she felt the brush of his lips on her cheek. Shelby's eyes flew open. Cameron pulled her into a hug with a sisterly pat-pat-pat on her back. Then he said, "I'm glad we're friends, Shelby."

She didn't detect that *his* words were completely ragged and forced. She only knew that she had made a fool of herself. As affectionate as it felt, he was merely offering friendship, and she had mistaken it for more.

The worst realization was that she had *wanted* more. So much more.

Chapter 13

He shouldn't have done it. It was a bad idea, and he knew it. But later that night, after Shelby had spoken with Brad on the phone, Cameron found himself asking Shelby if she would like to see a Forest Service cabin the next morning.

"I have to check up on one of the cabins up the road tomorrow before we go river rafting with the youth. Would you be interested in coming along?"

"Sure. That sounds great."

And that was that. He should have never mentioned it. But this "bad idea" was creating delicious anticipation inside him.

"You might want to bring a camera. There's a path of wildflowers with some great views."

"I will. What time should we leave?"

"Let's try to leave here before ten. Then we can grab some lunch before river rafting."

Filled with an equal measure of enthusiasm and trepidation, Shelby wondered what tomorrow would bring.

She awoke early the next morning, unable to sleep any longer. Lying in bed, she tried to push away the memory of the day before, but it was useless. Everything had been emblazoned upon her senses so that she could still feel the warmth of Cameron's hand on her face, his lips on her cheek.

It should have helped talking to Brad last night. Shelby reached for her favorite photo of Brad, the one kept tucked inside her scriptures by her bedside. How strange that she couldn't picture his face before pulling out the photo and studying it closely. Running a finger over the edge of the picture, she admired the look of confidence, strength, and goodness that silently spoke to her. There were a lot of differences between Cameron and Brad, but there were definitely some similarities as well.

When Shelby finally showered and dressed, the sun was peeking over the mountains and shone down in pleasant beams of light. Searching the room, she found her camera at the bottom of her suitcase.

There was a tap at her bedroom door.

"Come in," she called out while thumbing through her purse, looking for a tube of lip balm.

Cameron walked just inside the door holding a fanny pack in one hand. "I thought you might like to use this today. There's a water bottle in the back here, and you can put anything else you want inside the other pockets. It's kind of nice to have your hands free when you're walking."

"Thanks, Cam. That was thoughtful. I don't have anything like this."

"Sorry, it's kind of worn out. It's one of my older ones. You don't have to use it if—"

"No, it's perfect!" she said, a defiant gleam in her eye as she flung it behind her back. "I want to use it."

Cameron scratched one eyebrow and grinned. He loved the many ways she could express herself with a look in her eyes or a twitch of her mouth. He loved looking at her no matter what she was doing. But watching her now in the intimacy of the bedroom was too much. Yesterday was too much. Everything involving Shelby was getting out of hand, and yet he couldn't stop himself. It was becoming impossible not to be with her, as impossible as it would be to stop breathing.

"I'll be waiting for you outside," he said. "Take your time; there's no rush."

Shelby placed a hand on his upper arm. "Thank you."

He left her to finish getting ready and went outside to the shed to haul down a new sack of dog food for Wags and Bomber. The second the dogs heard the rustling paper of the sack they came running. Cameron chuckled to himself. The rival dogs lunged into the shed, meeting him with gleeful enthusiasm. Both were equally determined to get the first bite that would fall into their dog dishes.

"Hold on, you two. If you push me down you'll be sorry. No! Down, Bomber!"

His efforts were not entirely successful due to the humorous tone of his voice.

"Hey, what's going on out here?"

Slobber and panting were halted at the sound of Shelby's melodic voice. Looking inside the shed door, Shelby saw Cameron nearly being toppled by the dogs and laughed. Her eyes caught his in a playful twinkle.

"Either they love you terribly or they desperately want what you've got!"

"These miserable, good-for-nothing mongrels . . ."

Seeing the amusement in Cameron's expression, she laughed again. "Don't tell me a couple of cute dogs can get the best of you."

"They *think* they can get away with this."

"I'd say they're getting away with it just fine."

Cameron looked up at her in mock indignation. She was teasing him, and he really liked it. A lot.

He stood up, brushed off his pants, then walked menacingly toward her. Shelby giggled at the look. Then he took her by the arm and leaned close to her face, saying gruffly, "Come on, you."

He couldn't remember the last time anyone had teased him—or more, who could make him feel like smiling again. By walking behind her with both his hands on her upper arms, he steered her over to his truck. Right before they reached her side, Cameron pulled her back against him and whispered like a western villain, "Don't tease yer tour guide, little lady. I reckon he might be forced to show you nothin' but weeds."

Shelby couldn't help herself. She burst out laughing.

They drove north alongside the Bridger Mountains on the left, and Shelby was amazed at their beauty. Fireweed grew in lavender-pink patches along the roadsides, decorating every bend.

In a few minutes Cameron turned off the road and pulled up right in front of a large metal gate with a sign: Do Not Block Gate.

She looked at him questioningly. He drawled arrogantly, "Don't worry about the sign. Since I work for the Forest Service, I can do whatever I want."

"Oh really?"

"Yep. Just watch me."

He got out of the truck, reached down for a tall blade of grass, and stuck it between his teeth. With a cowboy swagger he strolled to the gate, pulled out a set of keys from his pocket, and unlocked the gate. He turned around to look back at Shelby with a mocking grin.

She clapped and called out an exaggerated, "Bravo." He took a bow and pushed the gate open. When he came back to the truck he drawled, "Ain't nothin' that can stand up t' me, y'hear?"

She surprised him when she joined in the charade. "I hear, you villain, you. But if you don't release me at once, I won't be sharing any of them . . . uh . . . vittles I brought to snack on."

Cameron threw his head back and laughed heartily as he slowly pulled through the gate. "All right, you done it now, little lady. You ain't gettin' nothin' but weeds."

He wasn't kidding when he told her about the view before. The overgrown path they drove through crossed a green meadow bursting with millions of yellow dandelions. All play was abandoned as Shelby exclaimed, "Wow! Look at them all! I never thought dandelions could be pretty . . . but this is spectacular!"

She leaned against Cameron to see the view through his window of blue sky and the white peaks of the Bridgers towering above dense green forests and colorful flower-laden meadows below. It almost made her feel like she was somewhere like Switzerland.

"It looks like the mountains have a long ribbon of white frosting along the top ridge," Shelby pointed. "You don't see that on the jagged mountains in Provo."

Cameron could hardly contain his pleasure with each expression of Shelby's own delight. She seemed to like this spot as much as he did, and it gave him wonderful sensations to be sharing it with her. The satisfaction he felt boosted his self-assurance. And the admiration he felt for Shelby was skyrocketing.

The overgrown path curved around and up to the rustic Forest Service cabin about half a mile from the gate. Off to the right amid the pines, there were two other weather-beaten and aged log buildings that looked like a barn and shed. Shelby thought the cabin would have been a bit more modern, but the only thing around that looked like it belonged to this century was the outhouse facility. Close by was a fire pit that appeared to be well used. Black ash and burned remains of a log had been left behind by recent visitors. A fence built with log Xs joined by long log poles bordered the cabin and its adjacent woodpile.

As they got out of the truck, Shelby exclaimed in fascination, "Cam, what kind of a place is this?"

"The Forest Service has cabins in many locations throughout each district that the rangers have been using for years and years. They're rented out to the public during the summer and some even in winter to people who want to rough it."

"You mean we could stay here?"

We. What those words did to him! Was that "we" as in the two of them or "we" as in her and Brad? It was obvious, and feeling like a fool, he cleared his throat and avoided Shelby's eyes as he nodded.

Shelby hurriedly inserted, "I don't mean you and me stay here, I just mean . . . anyone can rent cabins like this?"

"Yeah, they can."

She turned around in a full circle taking in all that she could see. "Cool."

"Do you want to see inside? You might change your mind after you see how primitive it is."

"You have a key?" Excitement filled her voice.

He dangled the keys above his head with an air of importance. "Come on."

They walked around to the other side where there was a log porch overlooking the valley. There were two rooms inside. In the first room were two old metal bunk beds with bare mattresses and a potbellied stove. The other room had a wood-burning stove and a kitchen table and chairs made of rough pine. There was a counter ledge but no sink. A few windows looked out to the mountains and forest.

"I love it," Shelby pronounced.

Cameron smiled. "Looks like the last people that were here left things in pretty good shape. I'm just going to bring in a few more logs for the kitchen."

"Can I help?"

"Sure." He led the way out the door with one arm gently at her back.

Shelby tried not to remember the earlier impressions of him carrying a stack of wood, but he was impossible to ignore. When the wood was piled in a container on the kitchen floor, he locked up the cabin.

Something moved in the brush near Shelby. "Cam, there aren't any snakes around here, are there?"

"I don't think we'll run into any. Why?"

"I don't get along so great with snakes," she said, looking closely at the ground. "They make my skin crawl."

The western villain was back. "Don't worry, little lady. Ain't a snake around these parts that would dare mess with me."

Shelby shook her head in amusement. "You're crazy."

They walked along a wildflower-strewn path that was nearly imperceptible except for the slight impressions where tire tracks might have once etched their way up the hill. Shelby was ecstatic about all the masses of yellow dandelions. But as Cameron pointed out delicate stems of blue lupine, tall purple larkspur and pink-veined sticky geranium, she became enraptured with all the wildflowers as well. They had such interesting names: arrowleaf balsamroot, penstemon, and heartleaf arnica.

Then she noticed a petite blue flower with such tiny yellow-circled centers that they would go unnoticed if you didn't look at them closely. Shelby knelt almost reverently as she fingered their fragile petals.

"What are these called, Cam?"

He came up beside her to examine the cluster of flowers she held. "Forget-me-nots. They're small, aren't they?"

"Small, but so dainty. I think these are my favorite wildflowers we've seen so far. They're sweet and unassuming."

Instantly, Cameron wished he could pick a huge bouquet just for her. He had the strongest desire to pluck some right there as he knelt beside her and tuck them into her hair. Looking at Shelby, he couldn't help but associate the forget-me-not's endearing beauty to her own.

They walked on, coming to an enormous fallen tree trunk that made a picturesque arch for them to walk under. The right side of the path became steeper, while the left side dropped off. There was a merging of bright sun and gentle shade on the slope. Clouds that looked like scoops of vanilla ice cream were piled together in an endless azure sky. The air was cool and refreshing.

All too soon it was time to walk back to the truck.

"Are you hungry?" Cameron asked.

"Starved."

"Then I know just the place."

Cameron drove into town, where he bought them lunch at a pizza place laden with authentic Western décor. A friendly waiter brought them old-fashioned glass mugs filled with ice water. Shelby wondered if anyone here knew Cameron. She thought about the scene in the other restaurant with Millie. Noting all the boisterous young adults in the restaurant, Shelby said, "This looks like a college hang-out."

Cameron nodded. "MSU is just up the hill."

After enjoying the best pizza Shelby had ever eaten, they realized it was time to head over to the river rafting office. Cameron turned off Main Street and drove south through an older neighborhood with charming Victorian and cottage-styled homes, each with a nicely kept yard. Mature trees lined the cracked sidewalk, creating a heavy cover of shade.

Shelby said, "I love older homes like these."

Cameron smiled and nodded. "So do I. They have so much character."

"I've always wanted to own a h—" She broke off abruptly, her smile vanishing.

He turned to look at her. Her gaze was focused just past him, out the left side of the car. The expression on her face made him pull over.

"What is it, Shelby?" he asked, looking in the same direction and then back at her.

She sat beside him, yet she was far away, somewhere she couldn't take him.

Shelby swallowed hard. "That house," she murmured. "It's just like . . ."

Cameron looked over his shoulder at the small, white cottage. Three steps led to a spacious front porch spanning the front of the home. Overgrown lilac bushes hugged the sides, covering some of the windows.

Cameron turned back to Shelby and touched her arm. "Tell me."

Her right hand instinctively went to her heart. "That house looks almost exactly like my grandma's."

"Where did she live?"

"In California. I loved going to her house in the summer. We would sit together on her porch swing sipping lemonade, and she would tell me the funniest stories. I was always happy there."

"Is she still alive?"

Shelby felt the familiar lump in her throat. "No." But somehow she felt like talking about her grandma for once. "She died of cancer. When I was young, she wanted me to come live with her—that was when my dad was moving us from city to city with every new job." She sighed. "I wanted to stay with her, but my parents wouldn't let me. It made me so mad." She looked at Cameron and smiled sadly. "I've always had this dream . . . that I could buy a home like hers and fix it up. I'd put red and white gingham curtains in the kitchen window and plant lilac bushes and roses all over the yard. Just like she did."

"It sounds like a dream that should become a reality."

"Who knows? Maybe someday." She didn't know what Brad would think about it. But she suspected that he would prefer a brand new home with the latest modern conveniences. "I'm sorry. We should go."

"We have a few minutes."

"I don't want them to think we aren't coming."

"All right. Will you tell me more about your grandma on the way there?"

Shelby's smile was like the sunshine. "I'd love to."

* * *

Although the morning had been warm and clear, by the time Cameron and Shelby got to the river rafting office it had become quite overcast and drizzly.

"Don't worry about the rain," Cameron explained. "You'll get soaked by the rapids, anyway."

In the parking lot, they met up with some of the teenagers from the ward who had arrived in separate vehicles. One boy stood out as the main attraction to a cluster of pretty girls, the volume of his voice amplifying several notches with the arrival of a new carload of rowdy boys. Inside the office they saw more youth and leaders getting ready for the rafting trip, including Rose. Shelby stopped in her tracks when she saw her. *She actually came!* But the shy, young girl stood apart from the rest of the group.

Shelby hurried over to say hi. "How are you doing, Rose?"

With somewhat vacant eyes, Rose turned, and a spark of life lit her eyes when she saw Shelby. "I'm fine."

"Is this your first time river rafting?"

Rose shook her head. "No, I go a lot."

"Really? You must like it, then."

"Yeah, I do."

"I've never done this before, and I'm a little bit nervous!" she chuckled. But her mirth was somewhat lost on Rose.

Following an awkward silence, Shelby said, "Maybe I should stick with you, since you know what you're doing."

Rose's lips curved into the semblance of a smile. "Okay."

Cameron walked up just then. Shelby introduced him to Rose.

"Nice to meet you," he said, shaking Rose's hand.

Rose opened her mouth to speak, shook his hand, a trance-like, dreamy expression on her face. But her response was inaudible. Shelby stifled her amusement. *He has no idea what effect he has on people—female people, anyway.* She saw two other girls staring at Cameron from across the room with similar expressions on their faces as well.

"Did you see these?" he was asking, pointing to a wall with several wild photos of rafters from past runs. They were hanging on for dear life, their mouths gaping wider than mouths should open.

Shelby chewed on her lower lip, her trepidation increasing by the minute. "I think I've changed my mind. It looks too scary."

"C'mon. You're going to love it," he told her, pulling her along. "Let's go sign in."

"See you in a minute, Rose," Shelby said, pleased that Rose smiled and gave her a small wave.

They registered their names with the secretary at the main desk. She explained some brief procedures and then told them where to get their gear and where to change.

"Please be sure to remove all your jewelry," she reminded them as they walked back outside.

Cameron turned to Shelby. She was sliding the diamond ring off her finger.

"I forgot to take this off before we left," she apologized.

"That's okay. Where would you like to put it?"

"I really don't know where it would be safest."

He looked down at the long, bare finger of her left hand.

"Do you have any suggestions?" she asked him.

Cameron swallowed. He could think of a lot of ideas, but he couldn't share any of them. "I'd be happy to put it inside my wallet. It'll be locked up in the truck."

She placed the ring in the palm of his hand. "Thanks," she said, looking up at him uncomfortably. "I'm still not used to having it."

He turned the small ring over in his hands. It felt cold against his skin.

"It's nice," he said quietly.

Shelby couldn't understand the strange feeling that came over her as she looked at Cameron with her ring in his hand. She watched him turn away to walk to the truck. He was so thoughtful and considerate. And she felt so much closer to him after talking about Grandma Hamlin. She had even been able to share a few things about her childhood that she usually kept locked away in a chest of sad memories.

Cameron returned, that relaxed grin lighting up his gaze, and Shelby felt a wild fluttering in her chest. She looked away, hoping her feelings would settle and that he wouldn't see what she had plainly seen on the other girls' faces. *What is happening to me?* Fingering the bare spot where her engagement ring had been certainly didn't help. She felt exposed and vulnerable, as though she no longer had her armor to protect her.

They followed the rest of the group of youth and leaders over to an area outside where wetsuits were being selected. Shelby was handed a black wetsuit that still felt damp, some booties, a fleece jacket, and a bright blue waterproof jacket. Then she and the other women were led to a dressing room. There wasn't much privacy to speak of, so she tried to undress quickly. The form-fitting wetsuit felt cold and rubbery as she pulled it over her hips. Once it was on it felt a little heavy, and she was sure she looked ridiculous in it. But there were several other women in the same predicament, giggling over their appearances. It seemed a kind of camaraderie was forming that would probably increase by the time the trip was over.

Shelby met Cameron outside again where they were given yellow helmets that adjusted in the back like a child's construction play hat, a bright orange life jacket, and a big blue paddle.

"What else are they going to make us carry?" Shelby whispered to Cameron facetiously. "A couple of lead weights?"

He just laughed. "Here, let me carry your stuff to the van."

Shelby handed him her things, grateful for the gallant gesture. He looked absolutely incredible in that wetsuit. She wanted to ask him if he lifted weights or worked out a lot to keep in such great shape. But her thoughts remained locked up, too personal to voice aloud.

Soon everyone was loaded up into a long van. Two rafts and a kayak were ready to be hauled on the flatbed hitched behind the van. They all had to squeeze together to fit everyone in, and Shelby wondered if anyone beside herself had even bothered with a seat belt. One tour guide began to welcome them all and give some information about their trip.

"The Gallatin River is very high right now from the runoff, so you will need to pay very close attention to your guides. If your guide determines conditions are too dangerous to proceed through the Mad Mile, then you will be unloaded before we reach that section."

Shelby's eyes grew round. Leaning against Cameron, she whispered, "We're going to die!"

He chuckled but whispered back, "You're going to love it."

She couldn't decide if the goose bumps she felt were from nerves or from the words he had spoken so close to her ear.

When they unloaded beside the river, more instructions and warnings were issued. The guides went over various catastrophic scenarios that could happen and how to help the guides save a person in such situations. Shelby could envision a capsized raft and being trapped beneath, getting whacked on the head with a paddle, and a host of other horrible possibilities.

What on earth am I doing here? Shelby thought as she looked up at the darkening sky. *And all those parents let their kids go on this trip?*

Someone was saying, "Most likely nothing will happen at all, but it's important to know what to do just in case."

Without any further ado, fleece jackets were put on, life jackets cinched tightly, and helmets adjusted. The group looked like a herd of blue clones with yellow heads. If anyone had thought they might look ridiculous before, there was no question now.

Shelby and Cameron were assigned to go with Jason, a tour guide who looked very young but claimed to have been running the Gallatin for ten years. Rose made her way over to Shelby so she could be in her raft. There were six in their group including Jason, who would sit in the center back and call the commands. They helped carry the raft to the edge of the river holding on to ropes wrapped around the top edge of the raft. One by one, the people in their group got in.

Shelby and Rose sat together on the middle seat, Shelby on the left and Rose on the right. A boy named Tyler and his father, one of the Young Men leaders, sat in front of them. Cameron sat behind them. Shelby didn't have a chance to wonder if he was thinking about his promise to keep an eye on her. She felt him nudge her back below the life jacket to remind her not to stand up and tip them all over. She turned around long enough to make a face at him but smiled to herself when she heard his low chuckle behind her.

Jason taught everyone some basic commands such as "all forward," "all back," "high sides," and "hang on!" At first the water was very calm and practicing the commands went fine. But once they entered white water, Shelby found it difficult to synchronize her paddle with those in front and in back of her. Sometimes her paddle clanked into Tyler's paddle in front, other times with Cameron's in back. They began to go much faster, hitting rapids that sprayed them with ice cold water. Shelby screamed, and Rose actually laughed.

"Just wait 'til you see the Mad Mile!" the guide yelled over the roar of the whitewater.

"Yeah!" yelled Tyler. "The Mad Mile rocks!"

Cameron leaned forward and tapped Shelby on the shoulder. "How're you doing?" he asked with a grin.

She thought about the freezing water covering her feet in the bottom of the raft. Her toes were cold inside the booties, but it didn't seem to matter. She was having a fantastic time.

"I'm great," she answered him with a big smile.

They hit more rapids that completely soaked everyone. Shelby discovered that it was very difficult to paddle with the command "all forward" when they were right in the middle of a huge onslaught of water being tossed in their faces. Her initial reaction was to freeze as the raft was tossed wildly up and down and sometimes hitting air and crashing back down against the frothy waves.

Jason told them some stories along the way when the water was slightly calmer. During those moments Shelby observed the little creeks emptying into the Gallatin from the forested mountains. It was a narrow canyon with spectacular rock outcroppings towering above them. The majestic river was extremely swift and high from the spring runoff. Other than being a little cold, she found it all exhilarating.

Then it began to rain. Cameron was right—it didn't make any difference since they were already soaked. Shelby was grateful for the wetsuit and fleece she wore beneath the jacket. She was gaining an appreciation for those who took every precaution for people to enjoy their river rafting experience.

"How does everyone feel?" Jason called out. There was a cheer of enthusiasm. "I think you are all doing well enough as a team that we can proceed through the Mad Mile if everyone agrees. If you don't think you feel up to it, now would be the time to let me know so we can let you out."

Everyone shouted, "Let's go!" with great enthusiasm. Cameron hooted along with the rowdy boys, and Shelby laughed. They were headed for a wild ride! Jason became less cheerful and more demanding as the bubbling, churning whitewater became worse. He yelled out commands to push them harder and harder and keep them from disaster.

Suddenly, they were in a terrifying section of rapids with so many massive boulders jutting out of the bubbling turmoil that it looked like a death trap. With no warning whatsoever, the raft heaved and jolted everyone to the left. Tyler slid precariously close to the edge. Amid the screams, Tyler's dad grabbed for him, but the raft rocked so far over that it would surely capsize.

Shelby felt a split second of dread. Time stood still as she thought with horror, *I'm going to go over!* Then Tyler was suddenly gone, his father shouting out to him in panic.

Before Shelby could even think of what to do, she was bucked off the raft and flung into the rapids. Her body whacked into rocks and whirled horribly in every direction. The moment she rose to the surface, she gulped a breath of air before going under the ice water again, hitting boulders like she was a rag doll. Her body temperature dropped. She was moving extremely fast.

I'm going to die . . .

Chapter 14

Cameron thought his heart would stop when he saw Shelby disappear into the churning water.

"High side! High side!" Jason shouted frantically to those remaining in the raft.

With two empty seats on the left, the raft was completely off balance and tipping over. Unless they immediately corrected the high side, they would capsize.

Forced to forget Shelby for the moment, Cameron hurled himself over to the side that was suspended in the air. The raft plunged back down into the torrent of rapids and rock. Releasing a few expletives, Jason steered the raft clear of an enormous boulder. He continued shouting directions to everyone. When the raft rammed into the slope at the river's edge, he leapt out. Cameron raced behind him, followed by Tyler's dad.

Cameron searched across the water. The noise of the river was thunderous. He saw the kayak rescuer towing Tyler over to the other raft, which had stopped up ahead.

Good. Tyler's safe. But there was no sign of Shelby. *Where is she?* His heart plummeted in cold fear. *She has to be all right!*

Then he saw her yellow helmet bobble above the violent flow.

In the torrent, Shelby spluttered and coughed. Frantically, she groped for ground beneath her. Like a miracle, she suddenly stood up. She had found one single little spot that was protected by rocks where the water wasn't as swift. Right in the middle of the river.

* * *

Shelby saw the rafts all rushing downstream, leaving her behind. *Wait! Don't leave me here!* She began to panic.

Someone on the shore frantically raised both hands in the air, signaling to her to stay put. His shouting went unheard over the wild roar of the rapids. But she remained where she was, shivering in the ice cold water.

Rescuers positioned themselves with ropes along the edge of the water.

I don't want to be rescued by the rope. I don't want to be hauled back through the rapids again just clinging to a rope!

She felt unbelievably relieved when she saw the rafts stop up ahead and a few people painstakingly making their way back upstream. One pantomimed to Shelby, communicating the crew's intent to reach her with the kayak. It was not easy for them because the banks rose steeply and were completely covered in a slope of huge rocks. Shelby watched from her isolated spot in the center of the river, her legs and feet becoming numb. It was so cold!

Someone kept making signals to her by patting a hand on the top of his head. Shelby thought they were asking if she was okay, so she patted her head back, hoping that it meant she was fine. Once she realized that they were working on rescuing her, she sat back against the rock to wait. A photographer came to take pictures of her stranded in the middle of the river. At a moment like this, photographing her seemed so ridiculous that she ignored the cameraman.

Finally, the kayak rescuer was attempting to reach her, paddling against the force of the river. Shelby tried to remember the rescue procedures they had gone over before entering the river, but she didn't think they covered this particular situation. Should she swim out to him or extend her paddle. *Wait a minute, how did I manage to hold on to the paddle?* Her fingers were locked in a death grip around it.

"Just sit tight!" the guy in the kayak yelled over the roar of the rapids. "I'm coming to you. Are you hurt?"

"No, I'm just freezing!"

"I want you to listen to me carefully, now." He shouted. Shelby tried to make herself focus only on his face and what he was saying. "You need to toss your paddle in the water and the others will catch it down there. You are going to hold on to this metal ring on the kayak and kick HARD! Don't let go until I tell you."

Shelby understood the rescue plan, but she didn't want to move. *I can't do it!* It was safe and somewhat sheltered in this one small spot. She didn't want to get back in the ferocious currents. But she had no choice.

"Are you ready?" the kayak rescuer called.

"Yes," she wailed.

Reentering the water was a horrible shock to her body. Shelby clung frantically to the metal ring on the back end of the kayak and tried to kick hard, but it was nearly impossible. The force of the rapids thrashed her legs around all over again.

But her greatest fear was that she would freeze to death. She didn't want to be hysterical but she heard her voice cry out over and over again, "It's cold . . . It's cold . . ." Her legs were flung beneath the kayak, out to the left, and then the right. She couldn't possibly be doing her part.

Finally, when she thought she couldn't hang on any more, they reached calmer waters near the bank, and Jason dragged her to safety. But she didn't even notice Jason. She only saw Cameron standing on the rocky bank, a distressed look on his face.

"Cam . . ." As she called his name she was handed over to him, and he wrapped her in his arms. He did not let go for a full minute.

"Are you hurt?" he asked worriedly, pressing the warm palms of his hands on her ice-cold cheeks.

"No. But I think I'm going to have some new bruises to add to my collection."

"Come sit down."

He led her to a rock, where Jason proceeded to ask her all kinds of questions—her name, the date, if she could wiggle her fingers. Shelby realized he was checking to see if she was coherent. Both men helped her empty the water trapped within her sleeves.

"Thank you," she said. "Can I get back in the raft now?"

"We don't have to get back in, Shelby," Cam said, squatting in front of her, his hands gripping her knees. "I'll ride back with you in the van if you—"

Shelby immediately shushed him as she covered his lips with her fingers. "Please Cam, I really want to finish." Her fingers involuntarily lingered on his soft, warm lips. The pressure of his hands on her knees increased.

They both realized in the same instant that they had forgotten Jason was standing there. He had just asked something.

Cameron stood. "What did you say?"

Jason gave him a strange look. "Are you ready to head back to the rafts?"

"I'm ready," Shelby stood to answer.

They made their way cautiously back to the rafts, where everyone met them with cheers and applause. Tyler sat in the raft, as wet and cold as Shelby was, waving to her.

Seeming very concerned, Rose asked, "Are you all right, Sister Hamlin?"

"Yes. Thanks for asking," Shelby said. "Has that ever happened to you?"

"No." Rose smiled shyly at Shelby and a connection was made, a bond that could only be felt rather than described.

Once they were on their way again, someone yelled, "Three cheers for the two newest members of the Gallatin River swim team!"

* * *

"Where's Shelby Hamlin?" one of the girls at the front desk of the river rafting shop called out. "She's got to see the photos that they took of her out there! That was really something!"

Shelby felt like some kind of celebrity with all the attention she was receiving, both on the drive back in the van as well as inside the office. Now that she was warm and dry for the most part, everyone seemed to have some kind of comment for her.

"You had one heck of a trip!"

"Someone just booked a river rafting trip when they drove by and saw you getting rescued out there!"

"Did you see all your photos on the computer?"

Cameron bought her a photo package, the price of which astounded Shelby. She bought a T-shirt with the Mad Mile illustrated on it. Then the youth were picked up in several vehicles.

"See you on Sunday, Rose," Shelby called out, and Rose waved back with a smile. Shelby's heart was full.

When Cameron and Shelby finally headed back into Bozeman, they were completely exhausted.

Shelby rested her head against the back of the seat and yawned. "Wow, what a day!"

"I'm sorry it didn't turn out like I had hoped."

"Cameron, I loved every minute! And don't you forget it!"

"Every minute, huh?" he smirked. "I'll have to remember to dunk you in a bucket of ice water next time you look bored."

"I have to admit that I didn't like being so cold, and I was pretty scared at first. But I can't wait to go river rafting again!"

"Are you serious?" he asked, incredulous but very pleased. "You would really go again?"

"It was completely amazing! And I love the pictures. Thank you, Cameron, for the best day of my life!"

He glanced over in awe before turning onto the main road. "It was my pleasure, Shelby."

Cameron felt warm all over. This was one incredible woman. She had to be very tired, but she was practically glowing with happiness. He loved the youthful delight she showed in everything she did. He loved her tenderness, her kindness. She was enthusiastic as well as appreciative.

Realization sank in. He was definitely sinning right now. No matter how he looked at it, he *definitely* coveted what his brother had.

Chapter 15

As Cameron drove off to work early the next morning, Shelby watched him through her bedroom window until his truck was out of sight.

Something was happening to her. While she wanted to banish the thoughts creeping out of her subconscious, there was simply no denying the attraction she felt for Cameron. She felt so alive and happy when she was with him, and when he was gone she felt an extraordinary void. She felt a closeness to him that she had never experienced with anyone before, not even Brad.

That thought terrified her.

She knew what she wanted in life. Home and family for eternity. Sitting on the bed, she thought about Brad and knew that she still loved him. He was the one who could bring those blessings of an eternal family into her life. She had to keep her head on straight and hold true to her principles.

Besides, even if Cam was a little bit attracted to her, he was mostly just being friendly. His words entered her mind with a jolt. *I'm so glad we're friends, Shelby . . .* It was foolish to read more into his actions than that, no matter how often her thoughts turned in that direction.

Drawing a cleansing breath, she decided it was time to get her mind off of Cameron. Since Laura's family would be coming today, it would be easier to do that because of all the preparations that needed to be made for the company.

Leaving her room, she focused on all the mind-boggling room juggling that Millie had planned. It was decided that Jacob and Brandon would take Shelby's room because it had two twin beds, and Shelby would move to Cameron's room. Then Laura and Bruce could use the other bedroom and put little Tara with them. Not even slightly comfortable with ousting Cameron from his own room, Shelby offered to sleep on one of the sofas, but Millie assured her that it was all taken care of.

"Now don't you worry about a thing! Yesterday he insisted that you get his room."

Always thoughtful . . . No. Stop it! Don't read more into it than you should. He's just being a good friend.

"Cam wants to stay at his apartment," Millie continued, "but I hope I can convince him just to camp out in the family room. I want him to be here with the rest of the family."

Trying not to think about Cameron, Shelby avoided making the move to his room all day.

But Millie seemed happier than ever with the prospect of rearranging and jostling. Shelby didn't have any experience with the hustle and bustle of relatives coming to visit. And never had she seen so much baking! The cookie jar was overflowing with huge chocolate chip cookies, and the fridge was loaded with potato salad and all kinds of tempting food. There were even two cherry pies baking in the oven.

As Shelby helped Millie grocery shop, clean, and put an extra leaf in the table, Karl prepared the boat for the lake. It was kind of fun being part of the hubbub. Thinking about meeting her future sister-in-law and her family, Shelby was eager and nervous all at once. She really wanted Laura to like her.

It was strange how this day brought back memories of her childhood. Perhaps it was because there were just the three of them there, but Shelby thought about unpacking boxes with her mom and dad after having just moved to a new place. She could picture her dad's expectant face as he searched the view from the windows. She pictured her mom's haggard features as she unwrapped the same crystal vase for the umpteenth time.

It was such a different scene from the one she was living today.

Feeling a jumble of emotions, she decided it was imperative to call Brad that evening. Her world was wavering beyond control. If she called after 7:00 p.m. he should be home.

Later, as she finally gathered her things together to move into Cameron's room, Shelby noticed the piece of paper Sister Lockland had given to her after church last Sunday.

The wedding gown . . . if only she'd been able to see it.

She looked at her watch. It was almost three. If she left right now she could probably shop for a gown and be back before dinner. She stared at the paper for a moment and then hurriedly shoved the rest of her things into her duffel bag. She'd better switch rooms first.

Shelby walked down the hall to Cameron's door. Hesitation overcame her for a moment; then she walked inside. Setting her duffel bag on the denim comforter, she looked around the room. It was very masculine and smelled of pine. On one wall there were two framed prints entitled "Nature's Majesty" with photographs of a timber wolf and a bull moose wading in a stream.

A display case on another wall held a fairly large assortment of bug-like things, all of which had hooks in them. Peering through the glass of the case, she read the names beneath some of the "creatures" in fascination: Wooly Bugger, Elk Hair Caddis, Parachute Adams, Griddle Bug. She realized that those must be different flies used in fly-fishing.

Straight ahead, a bookshelf was loaded down with all kinds of books. Taking a peek at some of the titles, she saw that he had a wide range of interests. There were field guides and survival handbooks, and books on fly-fishing, agriculture, and botany. There were a few religious titles and several classics.

On top of the bookshelf, there was a small piece of paper in an aged oak frame. It looked like a story of some kind. Her interest aroused, Shelby picked up the frame to read the words. They described how some forest rangers in Yellowstone National Park had been making their way up a mountain to assess the damage after a large fire. One ranger found a bird literally petrified in ashes, perched statuesquely on the ground at the base of a tree. When he moved the bird, three tiny chicks scurried from under their mother's wings. Although she had died by protecting them, those under the cover of her wings would live. At the bottom of the page was the scripture Psalms 36:7—*How excellent is thy lovingkindness, O God! therefore the children of men put their trust under the shadow of thy wings.*

"Wow," she thought aloud before replacing the frame on the bookshelf.

The powerful message of that story sank deep in her heart. It must have meant a lot to Cameron too, for him to have had it framed. Shelby wanted to ask him about it.

As she was organizing her things before leaving, Shelby noticed a snapshot on the nightstand. Out of curiosity, she walked around the bed to look at it. Cameron was posing with his arm around a striking, long-haired brunette.

Shelby felt an awful sinking sensation in the pit of her stomach. She was certain that it wasn't Laura. Could it be Camille? No. Why would he keep a picture of her around after all that she had done? Unless . . . could he still be in love with her? Somehow she doubted it.

A more likely answer was that this was his *girlfriend*. An attractive, shapely girlfriend! How foolish she had been to think that he had any interest in her! A feeling of jealousy welled up inside her that she couldn't understand. *Why would he have any interest in me? I'm marrying his brother!*

Finally, Shelby returned the picture, forcefully grabbed her keys and purse, and stomped out of the room with grim determination. She had a wedding dress to buy.

"Millie?" she called.

"I'm in here," came a voice from the other end of the house.

Shelby walked briskly down to the laundry room.

"Oh hi, Millie." When she saw her future mother-in-law cheerfully folding sheets, Shelby forced her mouth into a smile. "Would you care if I ran into town to look at wedding dresses?"

"Good heavens, no! It would be wonderful if you found something today."

"I hope I can."

"Just take as long as you need. I'm about done, anyway."

"I shouldn't be too long. I hope I'll be back before dinner."

"Don't rush back. Just have fun." Millie patted her shoulder affectionately.

"Thank you." Shelby turned to go but paused in the doorway. "Millie . . . ?"

"Yes, dear?"

"Thank you for making me feel so welcome here. It really means a lot to me."

Shelby was instantly enveloped in one of Millie's warmest embraces, causing many emotions to surge to the surface.

"We are *so* glad you came, Shelby."

Blinking away unwanted tears, Shelby smiled again and quickly left the house.

* * *

Standing on a pedestal encircled by regal mirrors, Shelby felt like a queen. It was too good to be true! This wedding gown was absolutely perfect—as if it had been made just for her. She was sure she hadn't seen this one before. How could she be so lucky?

No, this wasn't just luck. It was a blessing.

With no parents to share the costs of her wedding, she had to make her savings go as far as possible. And even though Millie had assured her they would be helping significantly, buying her wedding gown was something Shelby really wanted to do on her own.

Scrutinizing her reflection from every angle, she knew that nothing had ever made her feel as beautiful as this dress did. The princess skirt flared out from her small waist in layers of filmy, white organza. The bodice was delicately beaded and trimmed in Venice lace. A few matronly women passed by and told her she looked exquisite.

The sales lady even told her she'd be crazy not to get it. "I think that one was returned this morning," she said. "A lady bought it off the clearance rack for her daughter, hoping that with *that* price tag she'd like it." The sales lady shrugged. "Must not have worked out. But good thing for you, huh?"

Shelby grinned. "Very good!"

Twenty minutes later, Shelby was headed to the parking lot with an enormous package in her arms and triumph in her heart. She had even found a tiny crowned veil that would look beautiful when she pulled her hair up. She envisioned her wedding day, full of heavenly sunshine and glorious arrays of flowers. She would look ethereal in her wedding gown, and Brad would be dashing in his tuxedo.

An unbidden image of Cameron dressed in a tuxedo flitted into her mind.

As her heart guiltily lurched to her throat, Shelby dropped her keys on the pavement next to her car. She stumbled, nearly kicking the keys across the parking lot. *Shelby Hamlin, think about your fiancé.* Balancing her package and purse, she clumsily grabbed her keys and unlocked the car door. When the packages were carefully arranged in the back seat, Shelby got inside and let out a heavy sigh. As soon as she got home, she should call Brad.

Driving west on Main Street into the setting sun, Shelby focused her attention on things she wanted to talk to Brad about. She would beg him to come up on Friday. Though her plans weren't finalized, it might be her last weekend here. Surely he could find time, even if it was just for two days. But she knew he was extremely busy, and the internship was so important to him.

It was just that if he didn't come, Shelby was afraid that something indescribable might begin to take hold of her. She was beginning to feel trapped in the precarious grasp of the unknown, snagged by the talons of an unforeseen foe.

Chapter 16

"I'm so glad to finally meet you, Shelby!" Laura's smile and casual manner immediately put Shelby at ease.

Millie eagerly turned to the children who had whooped their way into their grandparents' waiting arms and were taking their turns petting the ecstatic dogs. "This is Jared, and this is Brandon. Over here is little Tara."

Everyone laughed at Laura's embarrassed moan when Tara stuck her finger in her nose and asked where the "chotlit tookies" were. Millie kissed her pudgy cheek and answered. "Grandma's chocolate chip cookies are in the cow cookie jar, Tara, just like always."

The boys looked at Shelby with curiosity. "Are you going to be our aunt?" Brandon asked from within Karl's grasp.

"If that's okay with you." Shelby smiled down at him.

At five, Brandon was skinny and had darker hair than his older brother. Jared was seven and tall for his age. Tara was undeniably chubby and the cutest little girl Shelby had ever seen. She was just as Millie had described her—a mischievous little elf with bundles of energy. Shelby wished she could give Tara's cheeks a soft little pinch—which felt strange because she'd never had such a crazy inclination before! She hoped the little girl would let Shelby hold her before they had to go.

"Where's Cameron?" Bruce asked, his arm around Laura. Shelby noticed he was tall with thinning brown hair.

Karl answered, "He's working near the Hyalite reservoir. But he should be home in a few hours." Then Bruce and Karl walked off together, absorbed in their conversation about water levels and pollutants, Bruce's field of work.

"Lunch is ready, everyone," Millie called out. "And we have lots of cookies and ice cream for dessert."

The boys shouted their enthusiasm and disappeared through the back door.

Laura walked between Shelby and Millie. "How long do you get to stay in Montana?"

"Until the first week of August," Shelby answered.

"What is the wedding date?"

"August 20."

Millie spontaneously added, "She bought her wedding dress this afternoon. It's just gorgeous!"

"Do we get to take a peek?" laughed Laura, her eyes sparkling.

"Sure."

Although there was no fire in the wood-burning stove, there was a rosy glow of warmth on the faces of both the children and the adults as they gathered around the table. Millie served a delicious lunch while everyone chatted about tomorrow's festivities. The boys could hardly contain their excitement about going out on the boat.

"Did you fix the inner tube, Grandpa?"

"Sure did, Jared."

"Yessss!" shouted the boys in unison as they pumped their arms back triumphantly.

"Can I go first?"

"No, Jared, you said I get to go first!"

"Boys, settle down," said Bruce between mouthfuls of his huge turkey sandwich.

"Everyone will get a turn, so don't you worry," Karl winked at the boys.

Laura called out, "Fingers out of the butter, Tara."

Shelby sat back, quietly observing this noisy, contented family. It seemed like several conversations were going on simultaneously while Tara continued to sneak her dimpled fingers into the butter with guilty blue eyes on her mother.

As an outsider looking in, she saw love, openness, and respect. It was indescribable to her. She just sat and absorbed it all with wonder.

This is what she had always imagined a family should be. It's what she would have when she married Brad. She wasn't able to sit back as an outsider for long. She was drawn into each conversation until she felt as integral a part of the group as anyone else was.

"Shelby," Laura asked, "do you know when Brad will be coming up?"

"Yeah, when is Uncle Brad coming?" Brandon joined in.

"I called him earlier, and he said that he's going to try to fly up this weekend if he can get away."

"I hope he can make it," said Laura. "It's been a while since we've seen him."

Shelby couldn't agree more. After shopping this afternoon, she'd had a good conversation with Brad, much to her relief. He had been in a good mood and was very talkative. He loved working with Baxter and Wells but never brought up the subject of San Francisco. He had asked about everything she had been doing and was very supportive. He was even glad to hear she had bought a wedding gown. When she had told him that she really wanted him to come up, that she wanted to be near him, he'd promised to try.

"If I can get all my work finished, I'll head out Friday morning."

His words weren't very convincing, but she couldn't ask for more. And if it turned out that he couldn't come, then she would just have to deal with the situation. It had made her feel so much better to have been able to talk with him.

Later that evening, Shelby gave in to Millie and Laura's persistence to model her wedding gown for them. They waited outside Cameron's bedroom door while she was changing. Through the door, Shelby could hear them talking like best friends who had been reunited after a long separation. She smiled to herself. Maybe someday she and Laura could be like that together. Looking in the mirror hanging above Cameron's chest of drawers, Shelby scrutinized her appearance. She hoped they would like the dress as much as she did.

With a few last adjustments made, Shelby opened the door.

Laura gasped with delight. "Oh my gosh! What a gorgeous dress!"

"Shelby, you look like an angel," Millie added, her eyes dancing with pleasure.

Shelby smiled shyly as she smoothed her hands over the skirt.

Laura fingered the organza delicately. “It must have cost you a fortune! It’s so elegant.”

“Actually, it was on the clearance rack. I couldn’t have afforded it otherwise.”

“And I love how it flares out. It really compliments your figure.”

Millie chuckled. “I think Brad will get a shock when he sees you in it!”

Shelby showed them the tiny, beaded spray that would crown her head. “I’ll just have to figure out how to pull my hair up.”

“I think it’s perfect. You look sensational!”

Laura couldn’t be more enthusiastic, and Shelby felt like her chest would burst with happiness. Such kind attention made her feel simply radiant. When Tara found her way over to the commotion, she made Shelby laugh.

“Ah you detting meh-weed?”

“Yes, Tara. I am getting married.”

“Mommy, tan I have a dwess like dat?”

Laura picked up her daughter with a smile. “Someday you will, sweetheart.”

“No, not Sunday, Mommy. Wight now, today.”

Shelby went over to Tara and touched her cheek. “Would you like to be my flower girl at the wedding? Then you could have a pretty new dress like mine.”

Tara nodded and lit up with smiles.

“Would that be okay with you, Laura?”

“Are you sure you want her to be a flower girl?”

Shelby took one look at Tara and said, “Yes! She’d be so cute!”

They talked about shopping together on Friday or Saturday to find a little dress, and Tara even put in her request to have a “pwincess cwown” just like Shelby’s. Then Millie took Tara into the kitchen for another cookie, leaving Laura to press Shelby with more questions.

“So what colors have you chosen?” Laura asked as she flopped down on Cameron’s bed.

“When Millie and I went to the florist shop, I fell in love with all the pastel-colored roses, but I’m not sure. I’ve had a really hard time picking things out for the reception.”

“Is there anything I can do to help?”

"If you'd be willing to shop with me while you're here, that would be great."

"No one has to ask me twice to go shopping!" Laura's statement made them both laugh.

"I guess I'd better change out of this dress. I don't want to ruin it."

Laura slid off the bed to help Shelby get undressed. She had just pulled the zipper all the way down when the bedroom door was unexpectedly flung open and Cameron walked in. He stopped dead in his tracks at the sight of Shelby's satin bra against her bare back. Spinning around, she saw him there and a soft gasp escaped her. She pressed the slipping dress against her chest, wordlessly staring at him, her heart pounding.

"Uh . . . I'm . . ." His voice was painfully hoarse, "so sorry."

He stood immobilized, eyes magnetically locked with Shelby's.

"Hey, Cam! You're home!" Laura hurried over to give her brother a hug. She got nothing more than a vague greeting and a slight pat. It was obvious what had taken his attention. But as Laura took in Shelby's stunned face and then Cameron's mesmerized one, she raised her eyebrows. There was an unspoken something arcing between them, of which she had no part.

Finally he spoke, his voice raspy. "I wasn't thinking . . . I'm sorry for bursting in on you."

"It's not your fault," Shelby said quietly. "It is your room."

"Uh . . . I'll just . . ." he pointed to the door and backed up into his nightstand. It made a loud, reverberating thud against the wall. "I'll talk to you later, Laura." Tossing a last look of agony over his shoulder, he closed the door behind him and fled.

* * *

"Jared, please don't lean over the edge of the boat!" Laura called out from her seat.

"Dude. Dad. Why not? I've got a life jacket on."

"Because it's not a safe thing to do, son," Bruce answered. "And don't call me *dude*." Then Tara squirmed out of his arms to copy her brother. "Tara, get back here, little monkey."

"But I wanna go swimming wiff Uncle Tam and Bwandon."

Laura handed Tara a piece of licorice. "Uncle Cam is taking Brandon for a ride on the inner tube. You'll get a turn in a minute, honey."

Tara heaved a big sigh. "Ohhhh tay."

She scrunched up her little nose in the best grimace she could make. Shelby had to look away. She was having a hard time not laughing when the kids were so funny!

Hebgen Lake glistened. Sunlight entwined itself in the shooting spray of water formed by skiers and other watercraft. Although she hadn't tried the inner tube yet, it did look like fun to Shelby. Her eyes followed the slack rope out across the water. Cameron disappeared under the water once before climbing onto the inner tube. Shelby could see his boyish grin as he pulled Brandon onto his lap. She wished one of those grins would be given to her, but today he had been studiously avoiding her.

She sighed. It was better this way, but it left her feeling cold and empty.

"Hit it!" he yelled back to the boat. He was having as much fun as his nephews and obviously loved being with them. It was very endearing.

Karl waved to them and slowly moved the boat forward, gradually picking up speed until Brandon's squeals could be heard over the roar of the motor. Shelby watched them with fascination as they were tossed over waves, left then right, with the pull of the boat. When Karl finally slowed down to a stop, Brandon yelled for more.

"Let's give Tara a turn now," yelled Laura.

"Yay!" Tara jumped off of Bruce's lap and headed to the stern while Brandon was hauled up. But she surprised everyone by running back to Shelby.

"Wanna go wiff me, Shebby?"

"That's so nice of you, Tara. But I think Cam—" Shelby broke off as Cameron pulled himself onto the platform and sat down, trails of water running off his muscular body, "—wants to take you."

"I want *you* to, Shebby."

Cameron spoke up. "You can take Tara if you want to."

His blue eyes met hers briefly, and her heart lurched in her chest. How could eye contact feel so physical? Why was she still having these feelings? Shelby lowered her eyes and saw Tara grabbing her hand.

"T'mon. Less go."

Shelby let Tara pull her back to the stern. Grabbing a towel, Cameron walked to the helm and sat by Millie. Bruce held the inner tube still while Shelby got on. She felt clumsy with her life jacket on. When Bruce lowered Tara onto her lap, Shelby wrapped her arms around her. She could hardly believe they trusted her with their daughter. But holding little Tara felt wonderful.

"Go weally fast!" Tara cried.

Shelby noticed that Karl was no longer driving the boat, that Cameron had traded places with him. Bruce rehearsed some instructions and signals, and then they were off. Tara screamed with delight as they went faster, hitting more and more waves. Shelby couldn't help from shouting and laughing either. She couldn't remember having this much fun for a very long time. It was like being a child again!

After everyone was exhausted, they all headed back to shore, where they feasted on Millie's sandwiches, potato salad, and watermelon. Sitting on lawn chairs under a canopy of trees, the adults watched the children digging out a city for their Hot Wheels close to the water's edge. Karl's head began to nod, and Bruce was suspiciously quiet too. Millie and Laura were talking cheerfully.

Cameron abruptly stood up and walked over to help the kids dig their city. Realizing he was avoiding her, Shelby rested her head back to look at the clouds slowly drift along in the light blue sky. She felt the peace of their surroundings pouring over her. Surely there would be a place like this in heaven, she hoped.

She was shaken from her quiet reverie when Laura called out, "Hey Cam, why don't you and Shelby take out the WaveRunners for a while? Nobody else is going to use them."

Shelby sat upright. "Laura, I've never ridden one before!" Cameron looked over at Shelby with a quirk on his lips.

Laura assured her, "It's easy. If I can do it, you can." Shelby gave her a skeptical look. "Cam, come on, show her what she's missing."

His gaze shifting between Shelby and his sister, Cameron stood up and dusted the coarse sand and dirt off his bare body. Then he walked over to Shelby with two life jackets dangling in his hands. Standing directly in front of her, he gave her a daring look.

"Come on. I'll show you what to do."

It was the first sign that he might give up avoiding her. The thought made her heart beat faster.

As he towered over her, Shelby tried not to look at his hairy legs and bare chest, but it was proving quite difficult. Even if she looked solely at his feet it had an unsettling effect on her. She thought about joking with him about tattoos covering his backside. There was nothing remotely resembling a tattoo on him. Nothing but sculpted muscle covered in beautiful flesh.

Shelby stood up and quickly took one of the life jackets from Cameron but turned to face Laura. "If I die, we'll know who to blame," she hissed.

Laura just laughed. With excited trepidation, Shelby followed Cameron down to the water's edge.

"Put your life jacket on first, and then I'll show you how they work." When he saw the look on her face, he gave her a reassuring grin. "Don't worry, you'll love it."

"Do you think I can drive by myself?"

"Yep."

"I'm not so sure."

"I promise you'll be just fine. And within five minutes you'll be trying to figure out how you could buy one of your own."

When she put on the life jacket she realized it wasn't completely dry yet. She let out a squeak when the cold plastic touched her skin, and Cameron's lips twisted into a good-humored grin.

"Are you ready?"

He took her hand and helped her get onto one of the WaveRunners. As she balanced on the seat, he wrapped a yellow cord around her wrist and pulled it tight. He explained that there was a stop-switch clip attached to the end of the cord, and if she were to fall off, it would pull out the clip and stop the engine. He showed her the throttle and everything that she would need to know to start and stop. He didn't let her go until she felt comfortable.

Shelby smiled with anticipation when she felt like she was ready. "Where will you be?"

"I'll be right beside you." He caught her smile.

Again the physical response. A longing for the friendship and fun they had enjoyed before swept over her.

She started the engine as he had taught her and gently moved out in the water. It really was easy! When Cameron gave her some encouraging words, she squeezed her fingers around the throttle and quickly began to move forward. She let out a lively shriek when the momentum pushed her backwards, and she sped across the water.

Nothing could have prepared her for how thrilling it would be to race with the wind in her eyes and hair, hanging on for dear life. And to laugh like this! She slowed down to look back where Cameron was and found him coming up alongside her. When he saw her beaming face, he laughed.

"It's fun, isn't it?"

"I can't believe it! I've never done anything so fun in my life!"

"Is your cord still tight around your wrist?"

"Yeah. Let's go!" She took off without looking back and began her screaming, laughing ride again.

Cameron watched her go with ardent wonder in his eyes.

Chapter 17

When Shelby was suddenly thrown over the handlebars of the WaveRunner into the lake, Cameron raced to help. He cautiously approached the capsized machine, searching for her head. When he saw her, face down against the other side of the machine, he jumped into the water and swam over to her.

"Shelby!"

He grabbed her from behind and turned her around.

"Shelby, are you all right?"

His hands tenderly moved over her face. When she opened her eyes, she was slightly disoriented. She coughed and sputtered out his name in a shaky laugh.

"Hi, Cam . . ." Trembling arms reached out to grasp around his neck, and he held her as tightly as the lifejackets would allow.

"Are you hurt?"

"No, I'm fine." Breathing hard, she laughed at herself. "That was crazy! One second I was zooming along, and the next I was under the water! It happened so fast!"

Cameron ran his hands over her arms as if to check for injuries. "Are you sure you're not hurt?"

"Yes, I'm sure. Just embarrassed that I did that! Between river rafting and now this, I don't think I was meant for water sports!"

Her shaky voice and lopsided smile were playing havoc with his emotions. Not to mention her nearness. From the moment she had shown up in that green bathing suit today, Cameron knew he'd have a difficult time. It made the green flecks in her eyes stand out from the brown like tiny lanterns glowing in the dusk. And even with a life jacket on, her graceful curves could be made out in the water. He had to resist the urge to pull her even closer.

Heaven help him if he even thought about seeing her undressing in his bedroom yesterday.

"You got thrown pretty hard."

"I didn't break the WaveRunner, did I?" *How could it possibly not be ruined?* she thought. The top half was completely submerged under the water, the underside gaping unnaturally above. *It must weigh a ton too.*

"The machine is fine, Shelby. The only thing that matters is that you are all right."

"Thank you. I really am fine." She turned to look at the capsized machine. "But how do you turn this poor thing over?"

"I'll do it. You just flip it . . . like this."

She stared as he maneuvered the machine upright again. "You're either incredibly strong or that was a piece of cake to do."

Cameron just smiled mysteriously and pulled her to him. "Let me help you get back on your seat."

With hands on her hips, he gently helped her up. When she had balanced herself on the seat, she reached down to grasp his hand.

"Thanks, Cam."

She leaned over her leg to see the coloring promise of a small bruise. From the water, he gently touched the skin around the area.

"Can you make it back all right?"

"Positive. Nothing is going to stop me from having more fun!" She rubbed one hand across her brow. She felt like she had swallowed half of Hebgen Lake and might have a couple bruises tomorrow, but she was ready for more!

Unmindful that his hand was still on her leg, Cameron looked up at Shelby and saw her face turn into a quirkish grin.

"You know what, Cam?"

"What?"

She patted the WaveRunner. "I *do* want to buy one of these."

Without thinking, he patted her foot and grinned back. "You're so adorable."

He caught her off guard. She felt the warmth of a blush spreading across her cheeks. But she didn't have more than a moment to worry about it. As if he had touched fire, Cameron instantly released her leg and swam back to his machine.

"Ready to head back?" he called out coolly as he started his engine. Barely looking at her, he fiddled with his mirror and throttle for a few seconds.

"Yeah, I'll be fine." She felt bewildered at his immediate indifference.

"Go ahead, and I'll catch up."

So we're back to avoiding each other again.

Shelby took off without bothering to see if he was following. Gradually making her way back to shore, she didn't hear his hushed words, spoken for her alone.

* * *

When Cameron and Shelby walked back onto the shore—Cameron ensuring they were much farther than arms-length apart—everyone asked how she had liked the ride.

"Laura, you were right," Shelby smiled as she reached for a towel. "It was a blast!"

"I got thrown my first time too, but not as hard as you did."

"You saw that?" she groaned.

Laura giggled. "Hey, you should see me wipe out. Bruce thinks I'm a goner every time."

"I can't wait to try it again!"

Cameron brought Shelby a can of pop but left her right away to join the kids.

"Shebby, look what I did." Tara held up a bandaged finger, her eyes moist with tears.

"What happened?"

"I tut it on the woot beer."

Holding back her mirth, Shelby listened to Laura's translation.

"She poked her finger inside the pop can to see if there were any fishies swimming around in her root beer and cut it on the opening."

Shelby was reminded of the story of Cameron and the "boot rear." She caught the blue sparkle in his eye and knew he was thinking of the same thing. But he quickly looked away. Neither of them realized that Laura had seen the interchange and was watching the two of them.

Brandon sauntered over, his interest based only on the discussion of blood, and importantly clarified the insignificance of Tara's wound.

"That's nothing! I cut my leg all the way open on my bike when I was little. There was blood everywhere."

"Dude, you're *still* little," added Jared. "And *I've* had the worst cut in our family. Grandpa, remember the time I had your pocket knife . . ."

The focus shifting to the boys with a full-blown dispute over nasty battle wounds and their resulting scars, hardly anyone noticed Laura grab her brother's arm as she led him away for a walk.

"Come here, Cam."

"Where are we going?"

"Let's take a walk."

Although Laura was only two years older, Cameron was used to his sister acting like a mother hen around him ever since the day she'd turned twelve and babysat for the first time. She always seemed to have a way of prying things out of him without offending him. That turned out to be a blessing for him when he was dealing with the problems Camille had inflicted. Laura had acted—come to think about it, she had acted a lot like Shelby had—like a fierce little warrior wanting to protect him. But it was best not to let his mind wander in that direction . . .

"All right Cam, what's going on?" Laura interrupted his thoughts with a start.

He spun around. "What?"

"What's going on with you?"

"Laura, what are you talking about?"

"You know what I mean. What is going on . . . with *you* . . . and Shelby?"

Uh-oh. Not this, he thought. Stopping to kick a clump of weeds, Cameron rolled his eyes at his sister. "What are you implying? She's Brad's fiancée!"

"Yeah, but I've seen the way you look at her."

Cameron laughed mirthlessly out loud. "That's ridiculous!"

"Cam, I saw what happened yesterday."

"What happened yesterday?" he asked with all the casual innocence he could muster. "I was working all day."

"When you walked in on Shelby wearing her wedding gown, you didn't even know I was there!"

He took a deep breath. "I was just surprised, that's all. I'd forgotten that she was going to be using my room."

"The look on your face wasn't surprise."

A large group of noisy campers walked by ,and conversation ceased. Relieved by the interruption, Cameron looked away from his sister and saw John Conrad sitting on the back deck of his "general store."

"There's John. Let's go say hi to him," he suggested.

Without waiting for Laura's response, he headed up the bank toward John. Though having been put off, Laura quickly followed behind, just as eager to see John. She was a fond admirer of their old friend and didn't have many opportunities to see him anymore. But she was determined to resume her talk with Cam just as soon as she was able.

"How have you been lately, John?" Laura asked affectionately, sitting down beside him.

"Fine . . . just fine. Busy as always." John grinned. Then turning to Cameron, he asked, "And what about the beauty you were with the other day? Seems like you two were having a mighty fine time together!" The old man chuckled.

"Oh really?" Laura asked knowingly.

Cameron couldn't tell if his face had paled or colored up. All he knew was that what was supposed to be an escape from his sister's conversation now felt like a trap. Laura was smirking at him, and he felt a sudden flash of heat encompass him.

"John, you know that I told you she—"

"Now, now, don't get in a huff, son." John patted Cameron on the shoulder with a shaky hand. "Just giving you a hard time. Gotta have some fun around here."

"You're absolutely right, John," Laura said. Then looking innocently at her brother, she asked, "So what were you and Shelby doing here at the lake?"

"Nothing. Mom just asked me to show her around."

"I see."

"Boy, was she ever pretty!" John added.

"So, John," Cameron said abruptly, "when will the new cabins be finished?"

"What? The new cabins? I hope they'll be done by June next year."

John told them a little about the construction and changes that would be happening in the near future. Then it was time to go. "You be sure to tell your parents to drop by and see me before heading home today."

"We will." Cameron and Laura said good-bye and continued walking east along the edge of the lake, past several older cabins.

"So . . . are the kids excited about Dad's homemade ice cream tonight?" Cameron asked before whistling an off-hand tune.

Laura looked over shrewdly. "Yes . . . but you're trying to change the subject we were on."

"What subject, Laura?"

"Shelby."

"You're being a pest, Laura! There's nothing to talk about."

"Something's going on."

"No, there isn't."

"Then how do you explain the way you've acted today?"

Now he was getting exasperated. "I didn't do *anything* today! And I've hardly said two words to Shelby in the last couple of days, so will you just drop it, Laura?"

Laura turned to him and stopped. "Just the fact that you are deliberately avoiding her tells me something is up. What are you hiding?"

"There's nothing to hide. She's marrying Brad in one month. End of story!"

Laura touched his arm and then gently asked, "Cameron, are you in love with her?"

His reaction startled her. He took off in the opposite direction, raking his fingers through his hair, and sunk onto a bench that overlooked the lake. His thoughts were racing wildly, his stomach in knots.

She can't do this to me. I can't have her breaking down my defenses! He had to calm down and breathe.

When Laura caught up to him, she sat down on the bench beside him and wrapped her arm around his shoulder.

"Cam, I'm sorry. I didn't mean to upset you. I just worry about you so much, and I want you to be happy."

He stood rigidly, staring at the water, his mouth a line of steel. She tried again.

"Please talk to me, Cam. If you really do love—"

"That's enough!" he burst out violently.

"But Cam—"

"Leave it alone! There's nothing that can be done, Laura, so just . . . don't do this." His voice was raspy and full of emotion. "It doesn't make any difference what *I* feel."

"Does she know?"

"No! And she never will."

"Cameron Thompson, how can you say that? If you are in love with Shelby, then doesn't she have a right to know?"

"No!" came the savage reply. "She's in love with Brad, and they're getting married! I'm not about to confuse her or ruin her chance of a perfect temple marriage. Ruining one wedding is enough for me."

"Yeah, and it's a darn good thing you *did* call off your wedding before ruining your life because of that immoral, scheming tramp! But this is completely different, and you know it!"

Laura was seething, her cheeks a fuming crimson. Then, in an intense but much quieter voice, she repeated her fervent plea. "This is different, Cam. Shelby is different. If I were to talk to—"

"Don't you dare say anything to her!" he spat out, pointing a finger in her face. "Not one word!"

"But what if she has feelings for you too?"

There had been several heavenly moments recently when he had dreamed that could be possible. But he refused to give in.

"You're being ridiculous, Laura! She's marrying Brad, for crying out loud! The only reason she's here is for the blasted wedding!"

Cameron rubbed his hands over his eyes. This was becoming unbearable. Once his sister got an idea into her head there would be no end. How could he make her understand?

"Laura, I refuse to be the one responsible for destroying another relationship."

"Oh brother!" She rolled her eyes in disgust.

"Laura, please. You have to promise me that you won't say a word. It wouldn't help anyone at all. You'd only be creating trouble."

"Fine! I won't tell Shelby!" she shouted furiously. "But what about *you*?"

His voice was hollow when he muttered, "Don't worry about me. I'll be moving back to my apartment."

"That's not what I mean, Cam. What about your feelings?" She nearly choked on the words, her eyes filling with tears. "You have a right to be happy too, you know."

"Oh, come here."

He promptly wrapped his sister in his arms. As he patted her back and listened to the muffled sound of her sniffling, Cameron wondered how he would endure the torment of his situation.

* * *

Late that night, after everyone had gone to sleep, Cameron lay awake on the sofa unable to sleep. His thoughts turned to the first time he had ever seen Shelby. She had entered his life like a charging bull. But as he had gotten to know her, she seemed more like a wandering butterfly, giving joy wherever she went. And soon she would flutter away from his life only to become a longed-for dream.

Driving half of the group home this evening, he'd stolen a glance in her direction in the rearview mirror. For a brief moment, melancholy was written on her face as she had stared out the window watching the mountains. He wondered if she had been remembering something about her childhood. And *he* wanted to be the one to find out about it. He wanted to be there when she needed to talk.

As he remembered talking with her several times in front of the campfire, a relentless ache formed in his heart. The two times he had almost kissed her, he had really forgotten himself. He would never be able to stargaze again or sit at his favorite spot in the canyon without thinking of her. *How could this have happened to me? How can I love her so deeply when she isn't even mine to love?*

Cameron tossed and turned on the sofa. He had to leave. *Even if it means going to my own stinkin' apartment.*

There was a chance Brad might come this weekend, and Cameron had better stay far away. For Shelby and for himself. She needed to be with Brad, and Cameron couldn't bear the thought of seeing them together. And the worst thought of all was that he would make a fool of himself by unwillingly baring his feelings in a moment of weakness.

Yes, he should definitely leave. First thing in the morning. If he was away he might have a chance to think a bit more rationally about the whole situation.

He punched his pillow a few times and tried to find a comfortable position, but he couldn't escape the feeling that he needed to get away.

It was almost suffocating him.

Finally, the feeling became so intense that he bolted off the sofa. Without making a sound, he felt his way through the dark and scrawled a few words on a piece of paper. After sticking it to the fridge with one of Millie's duck magnets, he gathered his things together and walked outside to his truck.

It wasn't until he pulled his keys out of his pocket that he remembered.

The key. The key to his apartment wasn't on his key ring; it was in a wood box on his nightstand.

Cameron groaned at his truck, debating his options. He could go back inside the house, take the note off the fridge, and wait until tomorrow. Or he could try to find the blasted key without waking up Shelby. But how could he get in his room without waking her up? Going in his room where she was sleeping was the last place on earth that he needed to be right now. Staying on the sofa was the easiest solution, but the thought of being around any longer made him feel like he would jump outside of his skin. He needed that key.

He headed back inside the house with a growl. It had been stupid to put his apartment key on a different key ring just because he was sick of the place. He should never have done that. It had just reminded him too much of the times Camille had come over. She used to list off the faults of his apartment and tell him what she could do to improve the place. It made him shudder.

Now he was sneaking into his own bedroom like James Bond—and he had brought it all on himself! *What an idiot I am!* Holding his breath, he opened the door and peeked into the darkness. The only sound came from Shelby's soft, even breathing.

He tiptoed quietly over to the nightstand and lifted the lid of the wood box. It creaked open. *Don't wake her up!* He groped inside the box, feeling around for the key. When his fingers came in contact with a small, dry bundle, he lifted it gently into a patch of moonlight. He had hidden away a cluster of the tiny blue forget-me-nots Shelby had admired. Touching the surface of the dry petals, he looked mournfully at Shelby's sleeping form and then placed them back inside the wood box. He felt inside again for his key. When he had it securely in his hand, Cameron made his way around the bed.

Moonlight cascaded through the window onto the bed, but Shelby's face was in the shadows. Easing closer to the bed to be sure her eyes were still closed and that he could make a safe getaway, Cameron's breath was instantly taken away. Shelby's tousled hair framed her head like an amber halo. One hand rested with the palm up beside her pillow, and dark eyelashes lay closed over her cheeks. The sight of her body loosely draped by his own comforter stirred overpowering emotions in his heart.

Cameron moved closer, desperately wanting to touch this exquisite vision. He wanted to know what it would feel like to brush his hand against her skin, to know the feel of her yielding lips against his own.

With a tangible ache in his chest, he pressed his fingertips to his mouth and lowered them to Shelby's lips in a feathery caress. Then he forced himself to walk away, softly closing the door on a dream.

Chapter 18

The shrill ring of the telephone the next morning woke Shelby from an emotionally draining dream. A few minutes later, Shelby heard a knock at her door.

"Shelby?" Millie called softly.

Shelby sat up in bed. "Come in."

Her head poking through the door, Millie informed her that Brad was on the phone.

"I'll be right there."

She jumped out of bed and put her BYU sweats on before leaving the room. Why had he called so early?

"Hello?" she yawned, suddenly remembering traces of the compelling dream, its dim images swirling around her head.

Brad's cheerful voice woke her completely. "Hey, Shelby, guess what? I'm leaving in a few minutes to come see you!"

"You're kidding, right?"

"Nope. I finished up my work, and I'll be there this evening." He sounded so excited.

"Brad, that's great. I'm really glad you can come."

"Is anything wrong?"

Her pause was barely detectable. "No, I'm just glad you get to come." Hazy images continued to invade her mind.

"I love you, Shelby."

"I love you too, Brad."

"Can you believe we'll be married next month? I can't wait!"

"It's . . . hard to believe. I've still got more things to do with your mom."

"I'll help you this weekend. I don't have to leave until Monday, so we can take care of a lot of things together."

"That's great," she said.

When she hung up the phone, Shelby hoped the day would go by quickly. Those intense feelings she was experiencing whenever Cameron was near were getting stronger and more distracting. Just the thought of him made her chest constrict. She needed to be with Brad again to stop all the confusion that seemed to be engulfing her.

Shelby found her scriptures and sat down on the bed to read. She found her bookmark and opened to that page.

Please help me, Heavenly Father. I'm so confused. She began to read from the book of Alma, hoping that her unease would subside. *I thought I had received an answer already. Help me to feel right about marrying Brad. He is everything that I need.*

As she read each verse, carefully searching for anything that would help her, the dream came back to disturb her. She had seen a dark cloud surrounding Cameron. It appeared to be swallowing him up in its thick haze. When she tried to reach out to him, he disappeared from view, and she had woken just as she had wanted to cry out.

Shelby thrust her hands over her eyes to block out the image. She couldn't allow herself to feel like this. What was happening to her? Cameron Thompson lacked qualities that Brad could offer her. He was not the one who could provide the stable life she wanted.

Sitting on the bed, besieged with tormenting thoughts, an idea came to her. Maybe her mind had confused the brothers and it was really Brad in the dream. That would make more sense. It was simply a matter of one brother being here and the other not. That was a completely reasonable confusion. She couldn't possibly be in love with Cameron if she was marrying Brad in a month! It was Brad who possessed stalwart strength, Brad who would provide the balance and security she needed—not Cameron! No matter how hard she resisted his undeniable magnetism, Cam wavered in his activity with the Church. He had been willing to marry Camille outside of the temple. She wasn't sure how far from the gospel he had strayed—

Shelby stopped herself. It was ridiculous that her thoughts were even wandering in that direction. All she needed was the answer from above that she was still doing the right thing by marrying Brad.

Maybe she should go to the temple to receive her endowments next week instead of next month. She had heard of the peace people had found within the temple. It was what she needed now.

Looking down at the scriptures in her lap, she prayed again that she would gain the peace that she sought and a reconfirmation of her decision to marry Brad. What surprised her was the recurring feeling that she should contact her mother. The thought persisted and terrified her. It wasn't the answer she was looking for, but she had faith it was from the Lord.

When she had read to the end of the next chapter, her study was interrupted by a loud voice calling through the house.

"Has anyone seen Cam?"

* * *

Shelby sat on a vinyl-covered chair outside the dressing room as Laura tried another dress on Tara. While she waited for them to come out, she thought about that morning. Karl and Millie had taken the news about Cameron leaving just fine, but they were somewhat subdued. Laura, however, seemed especially upset. Shelby had hoped that shopping would lift her spirits, but it didn't seem to be working.

She wondered if Laura had fought with Cameron about something. When the two of them had returned from their walk by the lake yesterday, they hadn't seemed very happy. What had made him leave so suddenly? The note he had left merely said he had been called in to work. That seemed strange, but everyone had been tight lipped about the whole thing.

Shelby shifted in the lumpy chair. Then she heard Tara's loud voice echoing through the dressing room. Skipping out to Shelby in a pale lilac dress with cascades of organza, Tara giggled with glee.

"Tara, I told you to wait for me," Laura scolded when she came out.

"But I wanna show Shebby my pwincess dwess!"

Shelby stood and held Tara's hands so she could swirl her around. "You *are* a princess! This dress is gorgeous, Laura!"

"It is cute, isn't it? I have such a hard time resisting girl things after having two boys."

"Is this one on sale?" Shelby asked hopefully.

"No, but it doesn't matter. I told Bruce it might cost this much."

"I like this one the best so far. She definitely looks like a flower girl!"

Laura made a squirmy Tara try on two other dresses before giving up and buying the lilac one. Tara jumped around, squealing her joy.

"I just hope it will look good with your bridesmaid dresses," Laura said.

Shelby's smile faded with that subject. "They still haven't let me know if they can come or not, so I might not have any."

"They can't do that! You have to give the florist your order next week."

"I know."

"I say you give them an ultimatum," Laura said with a crooked smile.

Shelby sighed and decided to confide in Laura. "You know, I never wanted a reception in the first place. I have no family that will be there, and I'll be lucky if I can drag my roommates up. I don't know what to do about it."

"What about your mom? Wouldn't she come?" Laura asked, unaware of how touchy that subject was.

Shelby picked at her fingernail before answering. "I still haven't told her about it. I haven't seen or spoken to her for years."

"Oh, Shelby, I'm so sorry. I didn't realize . . ."

Shelby waved her hand in the air as if to dismiss it. "Brad told me I should invite her, which actually really upset me, but he's right. I just don't know how to go about it."

Laura put her arm around Shelby in comfort. "I can't imagine how that would be."

"That's why I love your family so much. It's the family I never had. And the family I want my children to have."

Laura's smile was faint, and Shelby wondered if perhaps she and Cameron really had argued. Then a strange expression appeared on Laura's face. "I'm . . . glad you feel that way. You know, it's too bad you didn't get to meet Scott before he went to Guatemala. But he's a carbon copy of Cameron . . . so if you like Cameron, you'd like Scott . . ."

Shelby felt the color drain from her face. Laura watched expectantly, her inferred question hovering in the air between them. *What's she trying to find out?* Shelby's mind raced. Her heart was in her throat. But she managed to answer as nonchalantly as she could.

"I'm sure I'd like Scott too."

"Mommy!" Tara patted Laura's leg.

"What honey?"

"Less go!"

Laura sighed. "All right princess, let's go show Grandma your new dress!"

* * *

It was six o'clock, and Shelby was nervously brushing her hair for the third time. Brad would get there any minute, she was sure. The anticipation was driving her crazy. She knelt down by the bedside and said another prayer asking Heavenly Father for peace. If He could say, "Ask and ye shall receive," then she would have faith that He would send her peace.

And she hoped it would come flooding in the second she saw Brad.

Shelby set the table for dinner while Laura helped Millie in the kitchen. Bruce was wrestling with the boys, and Karl was sitting in his recliner reading a story to Tara. Seeing them all together gave Shelby an immense warm feeling inside. She had truly grown to love this family in such a short amount of time. And she felt like she belonged. Was this an answer to her prayers?

Shelby's heart almost stopped when Bomber and Wags began a tirade of barking outside. Everyone dropped what he or she was doing to see if it was Brad. Jared and Brandon put their faces up against the window to look outside.

"It's Uncle Brad!" shouted Brandon.

"I'll race you outside," Jared challenged him.

"Wait fo' me!" Tara yelled as she followed them outside.

Laura started to follow them but noticed Shelby standing in the middle of the kitchen.

"Are you coming?" she asked, searching Shelby's face.

Shelby nodded her head and followed Laura outside. When Brad saw her he held out his arms, and she ran to the comfort of his embrace. He didn't kiss her in front of his family, but she reasoned to herself that he was a very private person. After hugging everyone, Brad put an arm around Shelby and walked with her inside the house.

They all sat down to a homey dinner, very much like the one Millie had prepared the first day Shelby had come. Brad loved being home. It was written all over his face. He was the star of the evening too, carefully answering each question he was asked with great detail. To Shelby, it felt just like it used to when they had been together at BYU. While he spoke, she could picture him standing in front of their student ward bearing his testimony, and that same feeling of awe came over her. He was such an outstanding, strong person.

Once during dinner when Jared mentioned something about Cameron, Brad asked where his brother was. Karl explained about Cameron getting called in to work. Brad soon dismissed the subject, but Shelby noticed Laura glance meaningfully at Bruce. Shelby wasn't sure, but she thought she caught Karl and Millie exchanging the very same look. She wasn't sure what to make of it all.

After dinner, the kids asked Brad to play catch with them outside, but he explained that he needed to take a walk with Shelby. He led her away from the house along a grassy path to the side of the road, the amber sun setting on their backs. Brad clasped her hand and asked how she had been.

"Pretty good. I'm so glad you came. And I'm also glad your internship has been such a great experience for you."

"It really has. And that brings up the subject of moving. Have you thought any more about San Francisco? They told me that I needed to give them an answer soon, and I still feel really good about it. How about you?"

This was not what she wanted to talk about right now. She wanted to hear how much he loved her. She wanted to be comforted in his arms.

"I haven't, Brad. There are so many other things to think about right now with the wedding. Are there any other places where they could offer you a job?"

"Why?"

"It's just that . . . I'm not sure I feel good about starting a family in San Francisco. If we can't finish up at BYU or stay in Montana, couldn't we go to a smaller city than San Francisco?"

"But I would only commute there. We'd actually live somewhere else. I heard that Walnut Creek is nice."

Shelby looked at her feet as she walked through the tall grasses. "I used to live near there when I was younger. I guess that wouldn't be too awful."

"I'll show you the information I brought when we get back. Oh, and I can't forget to try on tuxedos while I'm here. Do you think you can go with me tomorrow?"

"Sure. I have a meeting in the morning, but we could go after that."

Brad seemed surprised. "Is it a meeting you can get out of?"

Shelby stared at him. "It's the last meeting before the barn dance tomorrow night, so I need to be there. Will you come to the dance with me?"

He groaned, clutching his stomach. "A barn dance? Just the name of it makes me queasy!"

Shelby shook her head. "Very funny."

"Yes, I'll come . . ." he sighed, ". . . because I love you. And so we can be together."

"After my meeting in the morning we can spend the rest of the day together."

"All right. I'll just switch some things around in my planner so we can still check tuxedos."

"What things did you have planned?"

"I just outlined some of the wedding stuff we should do and in what order, to maximize our shopping time. I thought a checklist would help us."

"Uh, thanks. But your mom and I have done quite a bit already. Other than ordering the announcements, there're only a few things that need to be taken care of."

"Oh. Okay. By the way, I called Sara a few times before I left and tried to talk her into coming up with Amanda. I really think they will, after all. Do they have dresses?"

"No, I just told them to try on a few lilac-colored dresses so they'd at least have some ideas."

"I think we should pick the style so they don't show up in something atrocious—but you know, come to think of it, Sara has really good taste. Every time I've seen her she's dressed to kill."

Shelby looked down at her tennis shoes and jeans and wished she had dressed up before Brad came. "Yeah, she does dress well . . ." *But I like my jeans. Why can't I be myself?*

When the light began to fade, they headed back to the house. Brad still held Shelby's hand as they talked. In the back of her mind, she had an endless array of questions demanding to be asked, but so far Shelby had held them in check.

"You're awfully quiet tonight," Brad commented.

Shelby shrugged as she studied the path in front of her. She watched the carefree yellow arnica sway in the gentle breeze. Then she stopped in her tracks and blurted out, "Tell me why you want to marry me."

Slightly taken aback by the outburst, Brad glanced at the road in both directions. Then he took both of her hands in his own and gave her a thoughtful look.

"I want to marry you because you're the best thing that ever happened to me, because you make me happy, because I love you—"

"In that order?"

Brad was so stunned that he had to pause before he continued. "What is this, Shelby? What's wrong? You know how much I love you!"

"I want to hear it, Brad. Tell me how much."

"All right. I love you, Shelby Hamlin! And I promise that by the end of this weekend there will be no doubt in your mind."

It was a challenge she hoped he could live up to.

Chapter 19

When Brad dropped Shelby off at her meeting the next morning, he told her, "I'll be looking at tuxedos while you're here at the Whites'. We can pick something out when you're done."

She nodded. "Sure. Thanks again for the ride."

Brad drove away, and Shelby watched him until he was out of view. *He bugs me.* Surprised with herself, she fought against such thoughts. *He's a good guy. He didn't do anything wrong.* So what was wrong with her? Probably just nerves. Every bride gets them, Millie had said. Shelby shook her head and walked to the front door, hoping that she could focus on the meeting instead of her nerves.

Sister White asked everyone who had come how preparations were going for the dance that night. With their limited budget, assignments had already been delegated to people on the committee to help out with music, decorations, and refreshments. "Is there anything else that needs to be done?"

"I think we're ready," one of the other leaders said. Everyone seemed enthusiastic about the things that had been planned so far, and several people added some very helpful suggestions that would make the dance a success.

Brother Lewis had connections with a local band that would play for them. "Oh, they're fun," he piped up excitedly, one hand drumming a rhythm on his portly belly. "We're in for a treat. And we'll teach some dances and have a square dance caller with the band." Shelby didn't know what to expect, but if there was square dancing, she wouldn't too feel awkward—she had at least done that before.

When the meeting was over, Shelby talked to Sister White about the Young Women's program while she waited for Brad to pick her up. She was amazed at how inspired this woman was, and Shelby wished she could have participated in the Young Women's program during her teenage years. It would have been such a blessing in her life.

Before leaving, Shelby asked about Rose. "I don't know why, but I feel concerned about her. She doesn't seem happy."

"Listen to the Spirit, Shelby. It will always guide you in the direction you should go. If Rose is on your mind, then you need to follow the promptings you have."

Those words repeated themselves over and over in Shelby's mind. *Listen to the Spirit. It will always guide you.* She could easily apply those words to other circumstances in her life. Such as knowing how to approach her mother. She would have to listen to the Spirit so she could be guided. Then she'd need enough faith to actually follow through with whatever the Spirit told her to do.

Shelby left her meeting feeling very uplifted. Taking care of wedding details with Brad went well too. She actually enjoyed spending the rest of the morning with him. No nerves. He was a complete gentleman and friendly to everyone they spoke to. Her heart was beginning to settle into a calm acceptance that all was right. She had been praying faithfully and was sure that her prayers were finally being heard. Everything was going to be fine.

Brad dropped Shelby off at the mall to look for a pair of shoes while he went over to his best man's house for a short visit. As she got out of the car and waved good-bye, she began to feel calmness settling over her. It lasted until she got to the mall doors and walked straight into Cameron.

* * *

"Whoa!" said a surprised Cameron, stabilizing the woman who had just run into him. When he looked down to see who it was, his surprise turned into something more like panic.

"Shelby!"

Hardly believing her fate, Shelby stammered awkwardly, "I'm sorry. Hi."

"We've got to stop bumping into each other like this," he said in an attempt at lightheartedness. It didn't seem to be having the right effect on her.

"Umm . . . I was just . . ." she scratched her head nervously. "Where have you been?"

"Uh," he shrugged, shoving his hands in his pockets. "Working."

Shelby nodded but noticed that he wasn't wearing his Forest Service shirt. Cameron rocked nervously back and forth on his heels. "Yep. Just working. Did Brad come?"

"Yeah. He just dropped me off . . ."

In desperation, she turned to catch sight of Brad's car. He was nowhere in sight. Looking back at Cameron, Shelby could think of nothing to say. How could her voice abandon her in such a cowardly way? She wanted to know why he had left so suddenly but couldn't seem to bring it up. She could only manage to focus on the striking blue polo shirt that defined his chest and broad shoulders. His hands still hid in his pockets, but she could easily visualize his long fingers. She tried not to remember how those fingers had felt on her cheek. It was an impossible task.

"So . . . how are plans shaping up for tonight?" Cameron asked.

"Tonight?" she asked blankly, wondering what it would feel like to trace the slight cleft in his chin with her fingers.

"The barn dance with the youth?" he reminded.

"Oh . . . of course. I think it'll be great."

"You're coming aren't you?"

Shelby nodded. "I think Brad will be coming with me."

She wasn't certain but she thought she caught a faint look of regret cross his face, but it vanished just as quickly as it had appeared.

"Then I guess I'll see you there," he said.

"What? You're coming?"

Cameron grimaced. "Another ploy to keep me active. They want me to chaperone."

She nodded, but couldn't stop thinking, *He'll be there tonight.* "Will you be coming home before then?"

"No," he said, nudging a rock with the tip of his boot. "With as much work as I've got to put in, I'm better off at my apartment."

"Oh."

Having exhausted safe topics of conversation, their eyes met briefly and then wandered to the mall doors.

"I guess I better get going," Shelby smiled shakily, not wanting to leave. What else could she say? *We may have a small problem here. I think I'm falling in love with you.*

"Me too." Cameron cleared his throat. "Shelby . . . I . . ."

Her heart nearly stopped as she waited for him to finish.

"I'm . . ." After a long pause, he waved his hand to gesture that it was nothing of significance. "I'll see you tonight."

Letting out a breath of disappointment, she answered, "See you tonight." She moved to open one of the heavy glass doors. Cameron promptly reached for the handle and held it open for her. Shelby thanked him and walked through the doors into the mall but couldn't stop shaking. Unable to resist the urge, she turned around.

Cameron stood in the same place, watching her intently. Shelby turned back, pressing a hand to the ache in her chest and quickly making her way around the corner of a shop.

Determined to settle her racing heart, she tried to focus on the errand she had come for and headed for the nearest shoe store. She tried on several pairs of shoes, all the while thinking about how she had run into Cameron.

Finally, the incongruity of the situation hit her. *What am I doing? How can I be sitting here looking for shoes for my wedding—my wedding to Brad—when all I can think about is Cameron?*

She left the store and found a bench to sit on. Staring at the geometric pattern in the floor tiles, her thoughts raced. *How can I care for them both? I don't know what to do . . .* She should talk to Brad. But what would she say? How could she explain anything to him when she couldn't admit to herself what she was feeling? There wasn't time to talk tonight. They had to leave for the barn dance in just over an hour. But maybe tomorrow they could take a drive and she could talk to him.

Later that evening, they drove to the Lewis farm in her car. Although she wanted say that she needed to talk to him, he was in such a good mood that she didn't have the courage to bring it up. He was joking about some of the barn dances he had attended in his youth and confessed that it definitely wasn't his "thing." But he wanted to support her, so he promised to be a good sport and be right by her side for every slow dance. She would have laughed if she hadn't felt so anxious about finding time to talk to him.

Remembering that Millie had given her directions to the Lewis's house, she reached into her purse and pulled out the small sheet of paper. She looked over the map but didn't give it her full attention. There were so many things on her mind.

"What's that?" Brad asked. Before she could answer, he said, "If it's directions on how to get there, we don't need them. I've been there hundreds of times."

"Millie gave them to me in case I had to drive there myself," she said, slightly perturbed.

"Okay."

After they had descended from the mountains, Brad headed south on a long, flat road that divided several hay fields in the valley.

When he finally pulled up to the farm and parked the car under a large tree, Shelby held her breath as she nervously scanned the line of cars out front. There was no sign of Cam's red truck. Shelby felt a conflicting flood of disappointment and relief wash over her. But he would probably show up soon. How would she react when she did see him?

Walking alongside Brad, she looked down at her black jeans and periwinkle stretch shirt and hoped she fit the "casual dress" standards. At least it was her favorite outfit. The blue of her shirt reminded her of the forget-me-nots growing on the hillside by the Forest Service cabin that Cameron had shown her.

Interrupting her thoughts, Brad took her arm and said, "You look great tonight, Shelby! I'll be the envy of every man here tonight." His teasing compliment made her smile.

"Thanks, Brad."

The path to the old barn was lit with a long strand of lights. Decorations were being hung outside on the splintery, weathered boards of the barn. Walking up the path, Brad put his arm protectively around Shelby as they greeted several ward members who had shown up to help. Then they went inside the big open door propped open by a bale of hay.

"Shelby, over here!" Sister White waved from behind a long table covered with an assortment of cookies and brownies and an enormous round thermos. As they made their way over to Sister White, Shelby noticed a couple of men and a woman setting up musical instruments, amplifiers, and other equipment in the back of the barn.

"Hello, Brad," greeted an enthusiastic Sister White. "It's great that you could be here tonight!"

"It's great to be here," he replied with a meaningful squeeze around Shelby's shoulders. The band started tuning various instruments in a cacophony of sound, which drew the attention of everyone gathered.

"Is this the band Brother Lewis was going to try to get?" Shelby asked amidst the noise.

"Yes," Sister White nodded. "They call themselves the 'Bridger Band,' and from what I've heard, they're pretty good."

Shelby wondered for a moment if that was supposed to be a joke. From what she was hearing, there was no indication yet that they were good. Maybe Sister White had only meant that someone had *told* her they were good. *Let's hope so! Otherwise, we're in big trouble!*

Over the dissonant wailing of a violin being tuned, Brad excused himself to walk over to some old friends he hadn't seen in a long time. Shelby stayed to help unpack paper plates, plastic cups, and napkins while she glanced curiously at the band. They had a guitar, violin, keyboard, drums, and a few other interesting instruments lying about. Shelby kept a watchful eye on them as Sister White helped her arrange the napkins in a fan shape.

Soon the discordant notes were magically transformed into a vivacious melody that left her in no doubt that they were good. Very good!

"I wonder if I'll be able to do any of the dances they're going to teach us tonight," Shelby mused.

Sister White laughed. "I used to think the same thing before moving here, but it's really fun. The caller will walk you through each step."

Shelby kept arranging and decorating as she listened to Sister White's amusing story of her first "contra dance," where she got so winded that she collapsed on the floor. She made it sound like a free for all where no one ended up with the same partner for more than a few seconds and everyone—old and young—danced with each other.

"But don't worry, Shelby," Sister White consoled her. "There will be plenty of time to take breaks when they play the popular stuff for slow dances." She rolled her eyes. "The kids couldn't survive without that!"

Shelby chuckled as they began arranging a collection of mismatched chairs around the perimeter of the room. She turned at the sound of boisterous laughter coming from the entrance to the barn. Several boys surrounded an attractive Mia Maid as she enthralled them with a story about a teacher from Bozeman High. Shelby couldn't keep herself from eavesdropping, wondering if they were talking about Cameron. She'd stop them in a hurry if they were. That was simply intolerable.

When Sister White excused herself to get more desserts from her car, Shelby straightened some chairs close to the group of gossiping kids and listened. But their conversation was cut short when another vanload of giggling girls arrived. Within a few minutes several more vehicles pulled up to the farm, and the barn was filled with the cheerful chatter of members from all over the stake. Shelby didn't see Rose anywhere yet and wondered if she would come at all. This could be an intimidating activity for someone who was shy.

Her thoughts turning to Cameron, she wondered why he hadn't shown up yet. She thought about their conversation in front of the mall. He did say he was coming, so any minute now he would probably walk in looking utterly gorgeous. No matter what he wore tonight it would be tough for any woman to restrain herself from ogling. He'd look good in anything. And when he smiled that certain way . . .

The mere anticipation of seeing him tonight had such an unsettling effect on her that she began to feel excessively warm. Stepping outside the barn into the cool darkness, she walked through the crunchy dry grass and paused to admire the last hint of fiery orange and faint purple on the jagged, black horizon. As the hum of an engine drew near, Shelby checked nervously to see if it might be Cameron. But a green Expedition stopped to park, and a flood of rowdy youth made their way to the barn. She was beginning to wonder if something was wrong. *Why isn't he here yet?*

"Hi, Sister Hamlin," came a timid voice from behind her.

Shelby turned around and lit up with pleasure when she saw Rose. Although the girl stood looking awkward and unsure of herself, Shelby was amazed at how lovely Rose looked. Her long black hair was curled at the ends and gleamed like onyx. With long lashes framing them, her dark brown eyes were striking.

"Rose! I'm so glad to see you!" Shelby put an arm around her. "How are you doing tonight?"

"Fine."

"You look so pretty!"

Rose immediately dropped her eyes to the ground and mumbled her thanks.

"Hey," Shelby started, "Do you know how to do any of these dances they're going to teach us tonight?"

"Yeah, some." She shrugged. "I like to dance."

"That's good. I'll know who to ask for help when I'm lost!"

With a shy smile, Rose glanced at a group of noisy boys and then back again at Shelby. It seemed like she wanted to say something, but Shelby thought that perhaps it was just Rose's uneasiness that gave that impression.

"Would you like to come help me with the refreshment table?" Shelby asked hesitantly. She didn't want to scare Rose away. But to her surprise, the young girl nodded and followed Shelby back into the barn.

A man was organizing couples into sets for a reel while the band began to play a lively tune. Shelby saw Rose's unmistakable look of longing at the dance floor. Glancing around the room, it appeared that the popular kids were all lined up to dance, but there were a few still standing around talking. Shelby set a bowl of potato chips on the table and wondered if it would be too transparent to find a partner for Rose.

The problem nearly solved itself when Shelby noticed one boy who kept making an appearance at the refreshment table. Though he didn't say much, he stared at Rose while stuffing his mouth with chips and gulping down a cup full of punch. After repeating this procedure twice, the boy sat down across the room to steal frequent looks at his quarry.

"Rose, I think we're done setting up here, so if you'd like to go dance you can."

Rose looked uneasy. "I wouldn't know who to dance with."

"It looked like some of the girls were asking the boys to dance." Shelby watched for any reaction from Rose. "Is that common at this type of dance?"

Rose shrugged. "Yeah. Everyone sort of dances with everyone. Until they play normal stuff."

The boy across the room was still staring at Rose with exaggerated nonchalance. There was another boy next to him who looked like he probably came only for the food. His plate was filled to capacity, and he appeared to be quite contentedly settled back in his chair. Since Brad didn't want to dance, she might have to resort to drastic measures in order to help Rose.

"I'd like to learn some of these dances." Shelby pointed casually in the boys' direction. "What if we both walk over there and each get a partner? Then maybe we could be in a group together."

Rose blinked at Shelby in surprise. "I don't know . . ."

Shelby took the plunge. Putting her arm around Rose, she said, "Come on," and led her over to two very shocked boys.

"Hi," Shelby greeted them. "Would you like to dance with us?"

One was thrilled, the other one stunned. But within minutes the four were whirling and stomping around to a lively tune as the caller led all the dancers through their moves. Shelby discovered that it really didn't matter which partner she started out with because she was constantly moving and finding herself next to someone new. Once their group made a big mistake that had them all laughing hysterically as they tried to recover into the right formations.

It wasn't until their group was making a humorous attempt at forming a star that Shelby had a strange feeling come over her. She wasn't sure why she turned instinctively to look across the room at the doorway, but when she did, her eyes locked with Cameron's for a heart-stopping moment.

She wondered how long he had been watching her and why she hadn't noticed him standing there before now. She smiled at him and waved before having to promenade with her short, starving partner. When Cameron winked back, her heart fluttered wildly inside her chest. He disappeared from view as Shelby's group did an allemande. But when she saw him again her heart sank like a lead weight.

Draped on his arm was the brunette from the photo on Cameron's nightstand.

Chapter 20

As the band continued their next vivacious tune, Shelby's partner escaped to fill his plate with brownies, leaving her standing alone at the edge of the dancers. When she saw Cameron leading the brunette out to the dance floor, she forced herself to look away. From the way the woman smiled up at Cameron, it seemed quite obvious that they knew each other well.

Seeing him laughing and smiling down at the pretty stranger had done something terrible to Shelby's heart. Wrenching clarity pierced her with the knowledge that her heart would never be the same again.

Feeling the need to get some fresh air instead of gawking, Shelby made sure Rose was still with her admirer and then headed purposefully toward the open barn doors. She didn't make it outside before Brad snatched her up for several rounds of introductions to old friends. When she became lightheaded, she asked Brad if they could go outside for a few minutes.

"What's wrong?" he asked in concern.

"It's . . . nothing, really. I just need to get some air."

Brad put his arm around her and quickly led her outside, nearly bumping into a couple locked in a heated embrace. Only half aware of them, Shelby didn't see Brad's look of disdain slanted at the passionate twosome. They continued walking around the side of the barn and into the grassy field. Stopping next to a barbed-wire fence, Shelby tried to think more rationally by taking a deep breath.

"Are you okay, Shelby?"

"Much better. Sorry about that. I'm not sure what made me feel so claustrophobic."

"Maybe I should take you home."

"No, I'm fine now. I still have things to do."

"Are you sure you want to stay?"

Shelby nodded her head. They stayed outside for a few minutes longer until she was able to put on a good "having-a-great-time" face, despite the strange ache that remained inside. Just as they entered the barn again the band began to play a slow song, and Brad turned to Shelby.

"Do you feel like dancing?"

She gave a quick perusal of the room but didn't see the brunette or Cam. "Uh . . . sure."

Brad led her out to the center of the room and swept her into an appropriate Church dance hold. They danced smoothly together and looked like the ideal couple. With the novelty of their forthcoming marriage, it was natural for them to receive many admiring glances.

Shelby couldn't have felt worse.

When the dance ended she walked to the refreshment table to see what help Sister White needed, so Brad excused himself to say hello to Brother and Sister Lewis.

"Can I help with anything else?" Shelby asked.

"Later on we can refill the thermos. But for now, just have some fun!" Sister White looked closely at Shelby. "Are you feeling all right?"

Shelby brushed off her hidden feelings and changed the subject so easily that it would have taken a very astute person to suspect anything was bothering her. Or someone who seemed to know her very soul . . .

When Cameron suddenly glanced her way, Shelby quickly looked down at the refreshment table and picked up a cup of ice water. After taking a few sips, she nearly choked when she looked up to see Cameron walking toward her with the brunette at his side. *Oh help! What am I supposed to do now?* There was no way to escape.

"Hi, Shelby," he smiled warily. "How are you doing?"

Exchanging pleasant greetings with each other seemed mundane and ridiculous when her heart was about to burst. Who was this woman?

As if in tune with her thoughts, Cameron answered. "This is my friend Kerri Mullins. Kerri, this is Shelby Hamlin, Brad's fiancée." He wrapped an arm around Kerri.

"Nice to meet you," Shelby forced a smile.

"It's nice to meet *you*," Kerri said. "I've heard a *lot* about you."

Shelby could have sworn that she saw Cameron thump Kerri in the back, but they were standing too close to each other for her to be sure. Besides, Kerri was still smiling.

"Well," he began uncomfortably. "We're on chaperone duty. I guess we'll . . . see you around the dance."

Shelby nodded stiffly. "It's nice to meet you, Kerri."

"See you later," Kerri said with a friendly smile. Then they left.

Shelby closed her eyes in relief.

* * *

As the evening wore on, things improved. Shelby got to visit with Rose and found out that she worked during the summer at a pizza restaurant, played basketball during the school year, and enjoyed many crafts in her free time. But her best friend lived two hours away, and they didn't get to see each other very often. Living with her relatives was sometimes a challenge, Rose explained, but her parents wanted her to have a better situation than they could give her on the reservation.

Brad danced with Shelby a few more times, but mostly they sat and listened to the music. Once during a particularly lively number, Shelby tapped her toes in time with the rhythm to let Brad know how much she wanted to be out on the dance floor, and it worked.

He stood up. "Shelby, let's dance."

She looked up in surprise. "I thought you didn't like the fast dances."

"But you do," he stated as he extended his hand.

Brad proved to be a good sport. They learned a few square dances that were fun. But when he asked her to keep dancing while he spoke to someone, Shelby was a little hurt. She knew he had only come onto the dance floor for her. She should have been grateful. But it bothered her how he kept walking off to talk to people.

Shelby was paired up for the next number with an elderly gentleman who had remarkable energy for his age. He told jokes through the entire dance and made everyone laugh. Then the caller had everyone change partners. She ended up with Tyler, the boy who had sat in front of her on the river-rafting trip.

"Hey, what's up?" he asked her.

"Not much."

"Been doing any more swimming lately?" he teased.

"Definitely not!" Shelby laughed. "What about you?"

"I put in enough swim time on the river."

Then couples were switched again. Shelby was laughing when she moved to her next partner.

Then her smile iced over. Cameron stood in front of her.

Each stared in tongue-tied dismay. He recovered first by awkwardly offering Shelby his hand.

"Uh . . . hi. Ready to dance?"

She swallowed. She didn't see Kerri anywhere. "Sure."

The moment Shelby placed her hand in his and felt the warmth of his long fingers close over her own, a stirring sensation swept over her. He began to lead her through an Irish reel. Cameron's fingers laced through hers when they were supposed to make an arch for others to go under.

"You're doing great."

She felt the glow of candlelight within her chest. It burned her.

They were separated several times throughout the song, making her feel more at ease. But each time she returned to him, the awareness was acute. As the number ended, the caller sat down, and another man picked up the microphone to announce a slow song. Shouts of approval filled the room. The song by Alabama that they had listened to in the Hyalite Canyon began to play. Shelby looked up questioningly at Cameron. He scratched at the back of his neck.

"Uh, where's Brad? I saw him earlier."

"He went to talk to someone."

Cameron cleared his throat.

Though there was silence between them, the undercurrent of emotion throbbed loudly. Shelby began to turn away when he suddenly stopped her. "Would you like to dance this one?"

She didn't check the room to see if Brad had come back and forgot about Kerri completely.

"Okay," she said and took a step forward.

Cameron held out his left hand and gently pulled her toward him. She was drawn to the expression on his face as he put one arm around her waist and cradled her hand against his chest. She could smell the clean, masculine scent of his aftershave when she placed her other hand on his broad shoulder. The quiet melody drifted across the room providing a soothing beat for the dancers. At first Shelby felt tense being so close to Cameron. Except for the time he had pinned her beneath him the day of the picnic, this was the closest she had ever been to him. But this was by mutual consent that they stood body to body, swaying to the gentle rhythm of the music.

Making an attempt at lightness, he drew back slightly and asked, "Is 'Pwincess Shebby' having fun tonight?"

"Yes, I am," she smiled, hoping she didn't seem too stiff.

Their brief conversation was interspersed with casual talk and stiff laughter. But gradually they both became quiet.

"You look so pretty tonight." Cameron didn't realize he had spoken aloud until Shelby answered in just more than a whisper, "Thank you, Cam."

Wading in the light of her eyes, he became completely lost for words. But the lyrics of the song became a part of their silent conversation. This time when he pulled her close, Shelby felt her tension melt away. As he felt her body relax against him, Cameron's instant response was to increase the pressure of his fingers at the curve of her back and draw her even closer.

Their bodies moved to the music in complete harmony. Shelby could feel the warmth of his chest through the fabric of his shirt. She felt the rough denim of his pant leg through the thinner material of her own pants. It felt heavenly to move as one.

When Shelby felt Cameron's smooth cheek trail across her hair and move down to her own cheek, she felt her knees weaken. His hand moved up her back slightly in support, and Shelby wondered if he could feel her heart beating madly against his chest. Without realizing it, Shelby let her fingers brush against the thick hair at the back of his neck. She heard his ragged intake of breath and realized that her own breathing was becoming a chore. Though she was listening to the music, her whole being was tuned to an acute awareness of Cameron—the warm pressure of his hands, the clean fragrance of his aftershave, and his comforting nearness.

She felt the muscles of his clean-shaven cheek slide against her own cheek. It sounded like he was whispering something into her hair. Wanting to draw back slightly to see his face, Shelby began to turn her cheek toward him. But Cameron turned his cheek as well, and in doing so, his mouth brushed a fraction of an inch away from her own mouth. The effect was so intense that it left them incapable of dancing. Only a breath away, they faced each other at the edge of the dance floor in silent declaration.

"Shelby," he whispered hoarsely. "I can't do this any more."

Shelby's face expressed her uncertainty, but no words would come. Her heart lurched inside her chest at the way he was looking into her eyes. Never had a man looked at her with such transparent longing.

When a young couple danced right into them and nearly knocked them over, Cameron muttered something unintelligible, turned from Shelby's arms, and walked outside. Watching his long strides, she stood frozen to the spot, wordlessly begging him not to go. Unable to bear the sight of him leaving, she uprooted her feet and followed him.

"Cam, wait! Don't go!" she called into the night, adjusting her eyes to the darkness. When she caught sight of his tall form heading for his truck, she ran to catch up.

"Cam, please—"

He spun around at the sound of her voice. "Don't follow me, Shelby. Go back inside!" His words were harsh and cold, but they didn't stop her from reaching his side.

She was nearly out of breath, but placing a hand on his arm, she asked gently, "What is it, Cam? Why are you upset?"

There was silence. He just shook his head slowly, unable to answer.

"What did I do?" she persisted. "Please tell me. I don't want you to be mad at me."

As her voice broke, her tearful words cut through him with such force that he wrapped her in his arms and cradled her against his chest.

"Oh, Shelby," he moaned, "I'm not mad at you. I could never be mad at you."

He cupped his hands on either side of her cheeks and looked down into her teary eyes. When a single tear slid down her cheek, illuminated by the moonlight, he brushed it away tenderly with his thumb.

"Shelby, I have tried," he began desperately, tracing his fingers over her face. "Heaven help me, I have tried!" Then placing his forehead against hers he whispered, "I've fought the feelings I have for you for so long that I just can't keep them hidden any longer. I am completely and hopelessly in love with you."

A surge of emotion spread through her entire being. "Cam . . ." she whispered, placing a hand against his heart. Not thinking any further, she lifted her mouth in invitation.

All the pent-up feelings of his soul ignited as he pulled her against him and his mouth found hers. His lips evoked passion and tenderness that awoke her completely to the hope of a love she had never known was possible. She felt a sense of belonging to him, a feeling that had evaded her for so long. And now she craved it. As her lips parted under the pressure of his mouth, Shelby felt the intensity of his kisses increase, becoming more demanding. Powerless to do anything else, and only wanting more, Shelby wrapped her arms around Cameron's neck and clung to him for support.

When he drew back slightly, Shelby gasped for air. But his mouth remained against hers as he breathed, "I have no right to love you the way I do . . ." Their lips melted together again. He trailed kisses across the smooth skin at the corner of her mouth and across her soft cheek. As he gently ran his fingers through her hair and down her back, Shelby was lost in the melding of dream and reality into the most magnificent moment of her existence. Never had she kissed anyone like this before. She was alight with an intensity she never would have dreamed she possessed. Her hands slid around his broad shoulders and into the thick, curling hair at the back of his neck. With each kiss she willingly returned, Shelby gave a part of herself to him. She felt replenished in return by Cam's tenderness. In his touch, Shelby knew she would never be the same again.

* * *

Brad had searched the entire area twice. When he finally found his fiancée near the line of parked cars, she was being mauled by his own brother. Shock was immediately replaced by rage.

"What the heck do you think you're doing!" he exploded violently.

Shoving his brother into the truck with surprising strength to get him away from Shelby, Brad then planted a fist into Cameron's face and another into his stomach, doubling him over. Acrid bile formed at the back of Brad's mouth as his muscles convulsed.

"Brad, stop it!" Shelby screamed as she yanked on his arm.

Rubbing his jaw tenderly, Cameron leered at his brother. "I guess I deserved that."

Shelby's eyes shifted frantically between Brad's fuming nostrils and Cameron's marked cheek, feeling completely appalled. *What have I done? How could I have let this happen? No matter what weakness I may have felt, I'm still engaged!*

"What in the world would possess you to do such a thing?" Brad snarled viciously at his brother. "Is this what you've been conniving the whole time I was away from her? To move in for the kill? As if destroying Camille's life wasn't enough, you think you have to destroy mine?"

"Brad, calm down! It wasn't Cam's fault," Shelby countered.

Brad spun around to look at Shelby.

"It was mine," she said.

Cameron instantly came to her defense, his eyes holding hers poignantly as he dabbed at the blood on his lower lip. "No, Shelby. It *is* my fault. I'm so sorry. I didn't mean to—"

"Don't let him confuse you, Shelby!" Brad pointed an accusing finger at her and then at Cameron. "He's responsible, and he'll pay for what he's done. You're just a victim here, honey. That's how he works." Brad's face took on a venomous appearance. "He just takes whatever he wants with no thought for anyone but himself."

Cameron's eyes glinted like steel. "You don't know what you're talking about."

"Oh yeah? I know how you discard what you've taken."

Cameron lunged toward Brad, fists ready to strike. Shelby couldn't take another second.

"Brad, stop! Just take me home now!" she yelled, surprising even herself. It was enough to stun Brad into silence for a moment, but she hardly noticed. By now, tears were streaming down her distraught face. She dragged him by the arm and pleaded, "Please . . . just take me home."

Brad exhaled and dropped his fists. "All right. Let's go." With one scathing look backwards, he spat out, "We'll finish this later."

Touching her wrist, Cameron began to say something to Shelby, but Brad cut him off, roughly elbowed him out of the way, and haughtily escorted his betrothed past the gawking few that had come to investigate the spectacle outside.

* * *

Nothing could be worse than how she felt at this moment. As Brad drove, Shelby cried. She never knew her body could physically produce so many tears. And she had blown her nose so many times that Brad's handkerchief was drenched. Her eyes were swollen, and her head pounded relentlessly. She was embarrassed and humiliated.

But the worst feeling of all was the ache in her heart when she thought about Cameron. She knew how much she cared for him. But did he truly love her or had he callously deceived her? The very thought pierced her, producing a fresh deluge of tears.

Brad glanced over grimly. "Shelby, don't worry any more about this. I don't blame you at all. Cameron imposed himself on you and obviously confused the heck out of you."

"Brad, it's not like that. He seemed . . ." *Wonderful? Tender?* ". . . sincere."

"I know him better than you do. He may have weaseled his way into your affections, but he has nothing honorable to offer. He was just out for a good time—or to prove that he could get to you."

Memories of Cameron's breathy kisses and caressing hands filled her mind. "I think—"

"Don't. Don't think about it any further, or you'll get more confused. Just let me handle this." Brad released the steering wheel with one hand and covered Shelby's fingers. "Trust *me,* Shelby. I love you, and I don't want you hurt. Cameron is a womanizing jerk. His whole life he's had girls succumbing to his charm, falling for him like fish to their bait. But as soon as he's reeled them in, he tosses them all back in the water. I won't have him messing with your life like that!"

"But . . ." Shelby stopped, nearly choking on her words when a sudden thought came to her. Not once since she had started dancing with Cameron had she even thought about Kerri Mullins! Cameron had introduced her as his friend. What if she was really his girlfriend? Had he just abandoned his date to pass some time with Shelby? That would be despicable!

"Brad, do you know who Kerri Mullins is?" Shelby asked between sniffles.

He seemed surprised at the sudden change of subject. "Probably an old girlfriend," he sneered disdainfully. "I saw her there tonight." He drove without saying more for a few minutes, but then curiosity made him ask, "Why?"

"Just wondering," she sniffed. What about the buxom blonde at the visitor's center?

A picture formed in her mind that started to give credibility to what Brad was saying. Could Cameron have just been playing her? He had admitted that he and Brad had competed since they were young. Was this whole thing the result of some kind of male dominance rivalry thing? If that were the case, then why did Cameron bother to say he was in love with her? Why go to the trouble of expressing any feelings if all he wanted was to gratify his physical desires? He'd had plenty of opportunities to take advantage of Shelby before but hadn't.

She shut her eyes as more tears slid down her cheek and dripped onto her jeans. *Maybe it's true. Have I given my heart to a worthless jerk who would trample on my feelings with no regret?* She thought about Cameron's reaction to getting hit. *He said he deserved it.*

Sinking into despair, Shelby cried the rest of the way home, not knowing what to believe anymore. What had she done? Had she been a complete fool? Could she actually marry Brad now? All her hopes were melting away, slipping through her fingers like the tears slipping down her cheeks.

Chapter 21

"Are you ready to go inside yet?" Brad asked cautiously, stealing another peek at his watch.

"I guess so." At least she'd had time to clean up her face a bit, and Shelby desperately wanted to get out of her tear-soaked shirt. "But Brad, please don't say anything to your parents or Laura and Bruce yet. I'm already humiliated. I just couldn't stand upsetting your family right now. I don't know what is going to happen between us, but we really need to talk—"

Brad took Shelby by the shoulders and insisted, "Nothing has changed between us," almost shaking her to get his point across. Then he walked around the car to open her door. When she got out of the car, he stood in front of her.

"Just remember we're still getting married in August! I love you, and you love me. Period. Nothing's going to change that!"

Shelby didn't answer. She had no idea what to say, how she was really feeling or what to do next. All she knew was that she wanted to go straight to bed and cease all conscious thought through sleep. She merely nodded, and they walked together up to the house.

It was late enough that Laura's kids were already in bed and the rest of the adults were watching an old Cary Grant movie in the family room. Shelby excused herself to take a hot bath, and Brad joined the others, sitting on the sofa next to his sister.

"Is everything okay?" Laura whispered, not wanting to disturb the movie watchers.

"Yeah, why?" he whispered back.

"I don't know. You look kind of down."

Brad shifted uncomfortably in his seat. "No, everything's fine."

"Brad, where's Shelby?" Millie asked her son.

"Taking a bath. She's really tired."

Hoping that would satisfy everyone's curiosity for now, Brad cleared his throat and redirected the conversation. "What are we watching? Looks . . . thrilling."

Karl answered, "*Houseboat* with Sophia Loren and Cary Grant."

He sighed and sank back into the cushions as everyone briefed him on the movie details. But the storyline went in one ear and out the other. He had other things to think about.

Laura watched uncertainly as her brother clenched his jaw and stared disinterestedly at the TV screen. Something was not right. It obviously wasn't any of her business, and she shouldn't pry, but she wouldn't be able to relax until she got to the bottom of it!

* * *

Cameron cinched the straps of his pack with another fierce tug and tossed it into the back of his truck. Ignoring the fact that most people like to sleep in on Sunday morning, he started the motor with an angry roar and took off, spewing gravel from the pavement in front of his apartment. The sun hadn't risen yet as he headed south along Highway 191 under the ominous layer of clouds overhead. He soon reached the turnoff and drove over a small bridge to cross the river.

He felt the pressing urgency to reach his destination. Then he would at last be able to think clearly. The events of last night had given his mind an overload, and he needed to get away. There was one place of solitude that he had discovered in the backcountry of this mountain range where the forest could be a healing balm for the soul. Except for last year when there had been fires in the area, he retreated there often. Cameron peered undaunted at the sky's dense gray clouds that were just beginning to surrender their drizzly treasure. It didn't matter a bit if it rained. He was prepared, like always, and the Forest Service's tiny, rustic cabin provided excellent shelter as well as solitude.

Cameron pushed harder on the gas pedal with a growl. How could he have made such a fool of himself last night? Remembering was almost too painful, but images assaulted his memory with a deluge of emotion. *How could I have caved in so easily?*

And some help Kerri had been! What a joke! His friend was supposed to be his moral support so he didn't feel like some lovesick moron at the dance. Taking off early was not part of the plan!

If only he hadn't danced with Shelby for those glorious two dances, his heart would still be intact. If only Brad hadn't been there, if only he had stayed home . . . As it turned out, his life was beginning to seem like one continuous disaster.

But holding her in his arms had been the most incredible moment of his life. Well, almost. Thoughts of the passionate kiss they had shared seeped through his memory, making him feel like he would come apart. Had that kiss meant anything to her, or had he just imagined it because he wanted it to be so? It had seemed that Shelby had returned his kisses without hesitation. But by the way she had left with Brad without even looking back, he wasn't so sure. *If she feels nothing for me, then I've just exposed my feelings for the sole purpose of making an idiot of myself!*

Cameron pulled his truck off onto a seldom-used dirt road, lunging over rocks and potholes as the elevation increased. A distant rumble of thunder echoed his sinister mood. At the end of the road, he turned off the engine and stared unseeing at the expanse of grassy slopes collecting raindrops. Delicate white wildflowers amongst larger yellow ones decorated the base of the pines. A squirrel scampered through a patch of forget-me-nots, bringing more painful memories.

Not wanting to think anymore, he got out, slammed the door shut, and marched to the back of the pickup. Once he had tied his jacket around his waist and put his pack over his shoulders, he locked up his truck. He set off along a narrow trail for about two miles until he reached a tiny one-room cabin surrounded by trees.

The Forest Service wasn't using this rustic cabin much anymore, and Cameron loved it. It had only the bare necessities like firewood, matches, and candles, but he always kept a stash of food there just in case he felt like having a getaway. There was a certain charm about the cozy cabin that appealed to Cameron.

As he set up his things, Cameron listened to the gentle spatter of raindrops beginning to fall more steadily. With physical, as well as mental, exhaustion settling in, he kicked off his boots and stretched out on his sleeping bag and thought about the woman who had changed his life. The last thing he remembered was the steady onslaught of rain and the mounting rumble of thunder.

* * *

Shelby woke up late to the clatter of thunderous skies and hammering rain. Sinking down deeper into the covers, she remembered that it was Sunday. And then the fuzzy traces of sleep dispersed, reminding her of what had happened last night. If there was ever a time in her life that she needed to draw upon the powers of heaven, it was now.

Last night had just about done her in. She wondered where Cameron was right now and what he was thinking about. Was he laughing at his easy conquest or feeling as miserable about things as she was? Did he really love her as he had said? She couldn't stand the thought of being anyone's meaningless diversion, especially when her heart was seriously involved. What was she to do from here? How was she to get up and go to Church with all these people when her heart was aching?

Shelby had to wait her turn for the bathroom, so she offered to help Laura get the kids ready for Church. It would help get her mind off of Cameron—possibly, for a few minutes at least. Laura was beginning to look frazzled as she ironed shirts and pants in the laundry room.

"That's nice of you, Shelby. Tara can't find her white shoes, and I just gave them to her! If they're outside in this rain, we're doomed."

"I'll help her find them. Would you like me to do her hair?"

"If you could, that would be so helpful!" Laura handed her a brush, a rubber band, and a hair bow. "Hey, are you feeling better this morning?"

At that moment, Shelby thought that telling the truth was sometimes overrated. "I'm fine," she said and then quickly set off in search of Tara's white toddler shoes. Tara dashed in front of Shelby to be sure she knew how to play the shoe-finding "game."

"First you look unduh the sofa, Shebby."

The hint of a smile crossed her face. "Okay, let's see if they are under here." Two faces simultaneously peeped under the sofa.

"Not here!" Tara cried jubilantly and then put her little hand in Shelby's. "T'mon, less look s'more!"

"What are you two up to?" Brad asked as he walked in the room.

"Just looking for Tara's Sunday shoes."

"Dey're lost," Tara put in happily as she pulled Shelby along to the laundry room.

"Lost, huh? I bet Shelby can help you find them, Tara."

Showered, shaved, and impeccably dressed, Brad reminded Shelby of the first Sunday she had seen him wearing that suit. Brad watched them go, but before Shelby disappeared he whispered, "You're going to be a great mom someday."

His compliment didn't have quite the effect he had anticipated. Holding Tara's chubby little hand, Shelby felt a rush of pleasure at the thought of holding her very own baby in her arms. She saw a fluffy white bundle in her arms, peering up at her with big, blue eyes. Trying to expand the image to include the embrace of a husband as he kissed their baby's soft cheek, all she saw was a faceless blur.

"Why am I doing this?" she whispered with hands swiping at tears that had suddenly filled her eyes.

"What'sa matter, Shebby?" Tara's voice brought her back.

"Nothing. I'm just being silly."

Shelby patted Tara's cheek and distracted her so they could continue their hunt for the missing shoes. After searching every room of the house in addition to the rain-splattered porch, Shelby felt frustration at not being able to find them. How could one little pair of shoes be so elusive, for heaven's sake?

Five minutes later they found them. In plain sight, where anyone could have seen them, the small white dress shoes rested against the dogs' water dish by the back door. Shelby figured that there was a lesson to be learned here but didn't take the time to think what it could be. Instead, she helped Tara put her shoes on and gave her best effort to fix the bow in Tara's hair. Just as she finished, Shelby heard Karl's agitated voice echo through the house.

"If he's out there in this weather, Millie, then he's not thinking clearly. And if he's not thinking clearly, then he's in trouble! Call Bob at the station and tell him I'm on my way." Something sounded terribly wrong.

"Karl, it isn't safe for you to go," Millie said worriedly.

Karl's answer was unclear as he banged the back door on his way outside. Another clap of thunder bellowed ominously.

"What's going on, Mom?" Laura asked in the hallway.

"The ranger station called about an emergency down near Storm Castle. They need Cam's help, but no one seems to know where he is."

"What kind of emergency?"

"A mudslide that wiped out a section of the canyon. If he went anywhere near that area he could be in serious danger."

"You already checked his apartment?" Laura asked.

"Yes," Millie replied. "We've tried calling around. The Forest Service has tried his pager, but he doesn't respond. That's what worries me the most. He always has his pager turned on."

Laura and Millie turned to the drenching tirade outside the front room window.

"Where's Brad?" Shelby asked them hurriedly. "He could go with Karl."

"I'm right here," said Brad, sauntering up behind them. "What's all the commotion?"

Laura looked at him grimly. "Cam's missing."

Brad snorted angrily and wrapped an arm around Shelby's shoulders. "Is that all?"

Three faces stared at him in astonishment.

"Brad, you know if he gets caught in this storm he could be in serious danger!" Millie looked at the water spewing from the rain gutters, creating puddles of mud under the lilac bushes.

Brad muttered under his breath, "He deserves more trouble than he's likely to get, that's all I can say."

With that, he turned back to the kitchen for breakfast. Shelby watched him leave, dumbfounded by his display of bitterness. She wondered if it stemmed just from last night or from years of accumulated frustrations. She had never seen this side of him and almost felt like she was seeing the transformation of fiancé to stranger happening before her eyes.

Shelby turned back to Millie. "Cameron knows the area inside and out, doesn't he? He wouldn't take any risks."

"I don't know. He's been upset about something lately, and this is the second time he's taken off without letting us know where he's going. I don't know what's going on inside his head these days."

Shelby noticed Laura giving her a peculiar look. "But he wouldn't be out there in it, would he?"

Shelby was racked with anxiety and helplessness. This was her fault. She should have recognized the attraction between them. She shouldn't have kissed him the way she had! With her mind whirling and her heart racing, Shelby wondered if there was anything she could do.

Karl offered a quick family prayer before heading out into the storm. Millie gathered as many umbrellas as she could find and the rest of them dashed to the cars through the pounding rain. In sacrament meeting the Thompson clan ended up taking a whole bench. It seemed strange to Shelby to be part of such a large group. Jared and Brandon sat on either side of Bruce at one end of the bench while Tara sat with Millie at the other end. Laura, Shelby, and Brad sat in the middle. Though wondering where Cam could be, Shelby tried to focus on the meeting.

The bishop gave them all a warm welcome as he conducted the meeting. Brad loosely put his arm around Shelby during the meeting, and she settled back beside him. But there was something different. She couldn't describe it, nor could she stop it from coming, but it was there—an ever-present feeling that things were simply not right.

Life had taken her for a ride so far off the path that she had mapped out for herself, and now she was uncertain there was even a way to return. Where she had ended up was not where she wanted to be.

Brad thought they should still get married. But the peace she needed to know if that was right simply wasn't there. Had it been too much to ask for a temple marriage to a worthy priesthood holder? Had she not been faithful enough? From the beginning, Shelby had never truly felt good enough for Brad. Maybe she really wasn't.

She opened her scriptures. She listened to the testimonies, read, and prayed. *Heavenly Father, where are you? Please help me!* Shelby shifted restlessly in her seat, and Brad gave her an inquisitive look.

When Brad stood and walked up to the pulpit, Shelby felt like a deep-sea diver who could finally gasp for breath upon reaching the surface. Somehow she knew that when he expressed his testimony everything would become clear. She had always loved to hear him bear his testimony at BYU. The answer would come. She sat forward and prepared for his words.

Brad captivated the audience with his charm and spirituality. But when nothing happened to Shelby, she was left bewildered and despondent. When Brad sat back down next to her, he seemed slightly withdrawn. He didn't put his arm around her but, instead, leaned forward to rest his forehead against clasped hands.

Nothing felt comfortable. She wanted to leave. Everything *used* to feel so comfortable this summer . . . before Brad came. I was happy. I was relaxed. I was myself. What happened?

Later in Sunday School, Brother Porter led a class discussion on the power of prayer.

Great, Shelby thought. *Maybe he can tell me what I've been doing wrong.*

Brad sat quietly by her side listening as several members spoke of the blessings they had received through prayer. They were inspiring stories, but Shelby still wondered how to make it work for her. She felt that she had done everything possible to make her prayers truly meaningful, yet she wasn't receiving the answers she sought.

When Brother Porter asked everyone to open to 2 Nephi 9:28, Shelby followed along with the class member who had volunteered to read aloud:

"O the vainness, and the frailties, and the foolishness of men! When they are learned they think they are wise, and they hearken not unto the counsel of God, for they set it aside, supposing they know of themselves, wherefore, their wisdom is foolishness and it profiteth them not. And they shall perish."

Shelby felt an intangible beam piercing her heart. She was struck by what she had just heard. She read the words again: ". . . *they hearken not unto the counsel of God . . . supposing they know of themselves . . .*" Could this be what she had done? When she realized another scripture was being read, she marked the page she was on and quickly flipped to Jacob 4:10. She read along silently: *Wherefore, brethren, seek not to counsel the Lord, but to take counsel from his hand. For behold, ye yourselves know that he counseleth in wisdom, and in justice, and in great mercy, over all his works.*

A picture formed in Shelby's mind with great clarity—Tara's white church shoes leaning against the water dish by the back door. And Shelby realized for the first time that Heavenly Father *had* been listening and trying to guide her. She had been telling *Him* what she wanted instead of allowing him to speak to her. His answers had been in plain sight all along.

Chapter 22

Somehow she had to tell Brad. The thought made her turn as cold as the drizzling rain outside. So many wedding plans were already made. So many people were involved. How could she possibly do it? What would Brad think of her?

Surprisingly, the worst feeling came from the thought of disappointing Karl and Millie. How she hated the thought of hurting them!

This was a total nightmare. But it had to be done. Ever since they had come home from church, Shelby had prayed or had a continuous prayer in her heart to be sure. And now there were no longer any doubts. She *did* love and respect Brad. He was wonderful. But now she knew that she couldn't marry him. She had tried so hard to conform herself into the woman Brad wanted. But she'd been stifled by him. With Cameron, she had always felt safe and accepted enough to be herself.

But what about Cam? He had said that he loved her, but could she believe him? And even more importantly, what were her true feelings for him? Several memories entered her mind: Cameron sharing his feelings with her, Shelby crying in his arms on the hill behind the house, the two of them laughing together and talking in the canyon, the powerful connection when their eyes would meet. And then she thought about being held in his arms as they danced and the intensity of his kiss.

Shelby's heart stirred at the memories, telling her deep down what she had found so difficult to admit. Overwhelming feelings soared through her. Her chest nearly burst as the truth struck deep. She'd never given Brad her whole heart. She had given it freely to Cameron.

I love him! No question. When she was with him, she felt like she had arrived somewhere—somewhere she desperately wanted to be. It was a feeling of true belonging, of coming home.

So where did that leave her? She didn't even know where Cameron was or how he truly felt.

If only she could have met Cameron when he was active and still enthusiastic about the Church and the gospel! There would be fewer complications to this whole mess. As soon as she broke off the engagement, she would have to leave the Thompson home. The thought of having to pack up was unbearable. But the Thompsons would definitely not want her to be here after what she was going to do to Brad. Would there even be an opportunity to talk with Cameron before she left Montana? Everything seemed so up in the air right now.

Well, one thing was certain. She simply couldn't put off talking to Brad any longer. He deserved to know the truth. She said another quick prayer for help and walked into the family room, where Brad was talking to Jared.

"Brad," Shelby began nervously. "I need to talk to you."

Brad stood up and walked over to her. "What's wrong?"

Jared looked up with curiosity.

"Can we talk somewhere?" Shelby whispered.

Brad's face was marked with uncertainty. "Sure. I'll be right back, Jared."

They grabbed their jackets and stepped into the rain outside. Brad quickly led her out to the shed and turned on a dim light overhead. Shelby wondered where to begin.

"What's wrong, Shelby?" Brad asked worriedly.

Shelby thought out her words but found herself asking him something completely different.

"Brad, I need to know how you would go about approaching my mother. I want to communicate with her, but this is such a hard thing to do. How do I go about it without hurting her further?"

Brad thought for a moment as they sat next to each other on the woodpile. A dark cloud rumbled ominously overhead.

"I think that sharing your feelings with sensitivity as well as honesty is the place to start." He looked at the pained look on her face and questioned slowly, "Is this about your mom or something else?"

"Brad," Shelby began with a catch in her throat. "I wouldn't do anything to hurt you, but I'm afraid that no matter what I do you'll be hurt anyway."

Brad took her hand in his and waited in silence as he watched the tears begin to stream down Shelby's face. She choked out her next words.

"Even though I love and respect you, I just don't think we should get married."

"No, Shelby!" he said. "Don't do this because of Cameron!" He stood up and faced her. "It *is* the right thing for us to get married! I know it is! You didn't get messed up by that Sunday School lesson, did you?"

She forced out her reply in between sobs. "No, that lesson helped me see everything clearly for the first time. I'm so sorry, Brad. You are such a good person, a wonderful man . . . You're everything I want in a husband. But I don't think we love each other enough—and it's not because of anything Cameron has said or done. Please try to understand . . . and forgive me for hurting you. I'm so sorry."

Brad sat next to her in devastation. So she didn't love *him* enough, was what it came down to. Under his breath he muttered bitterly, "I loved *you* enough."

What a mistake to have her stay with his family! No matter what she said, he knew this change of heart was because of Cameron. The weasel. Good-for-nothing, revolting excuse of a brother . . . His anger became a scalding fury. Streams of ugly thoughts poisoned his mind and hardened his features into a glowering mask of rage.

Shelby wiped her eyes with the sleeve of her jacket and glanced at Brad's contemptuous expression. "You don't forgive me, do you?"

Brad turned away in a huff but managed to snarl, "Of course I do. But I don't like this! I just can't accept that a few weeks ago you were ready to spend eternity with me and in such a short amount of time you've completely changed your mind!"

Shelby didn't know what to say.

Brad stood up again in frustration. "Shelby, too many . . . *things* here have confused you. Just get away from Montana and then make your decision. Please."

"Brad, I really don't think anything is going to change my mind. I've prayed nonstop about this, and I know Heavenly Father has answered my prayers. For the first time, I feel sure about it."

Brad glowered and asked bitterly, "So what do we do now? Cancel every single arrangement we've made for the wedding?"

"I'll take care of everything. It's my fault."

They sat silently next to each other, wrapped in their own thoughts, for several long, drawn-out minutes. The aspen leaves just outside the window danced in the rain, blissfully ignorant of the solemn mood that hovered around the two figures inside.

* * *

Cameron was jolted awake by the sinister crack of a thundercloud and thrashing rain. A sudden feeling of foreboding enveloped him. He whipped his head around to look out the small cabin window.

Something was wrong. He could feel his heart pounding in alarm. *Is it day or night?* The sky was so dark; it was hard to tell. A glance at his watch told him it was almost 4:30 p.m. Dense gray clouds suffocated the skies while rain poured down relentlessly. He couldn't shake the feeling of danger that made the hair on his neck stand on end.

He stood up and fumbled anxiously through his duffel bag.

"Come on! Where is it?"

Sifting through everything he had brought with him, he realized that it was hopeless. His cell phone simply wasn't there, and he had left his pager behind.

"What have I done?" Cameron muttered to himself, tension knotting his stomach.

Another merciless clap of thunder ripped through the skies and shook the cabin. His eyes jerked to the window, where beads of water fell into streams that raced down the glass in angled paths.

And then he heard it.

The low distant rumbling uphill made him freeze. He listened intently, horrified by the escalating sound.

Mudslide! He had to get out of there now!

Grabbing his pack, he threw on his rain gear and tore outside, leaving his sleeping bag behind. Icy cold rain enveloped him in its damp chill as he rushed to his truck. Then the rumbling became a deafening roar as mud, rocks, and debris exploded through the trees above him.

Too late! There was no time to drive away!

Get out of the path of the debris flow—run!

Fear gripping his every thought, he made his way across the slippery mountain path faster than he had ever done in his life. His boots were becoming caked in heavy mud. He had to make it. If he didn't make it—No! He couldn't think like that!

Keep going! Don't stop!

Those were his last thoughts before he lost his footing. He slipped in the mud, striking his head against a sharp boulder before his body was tossed and battered down the mountainside.

* * *

The moment Brad and Shelby walked through the back door, they knew something was wrong. And it had nothing to do with their own somber mood and circumstances. Shelby sensed a foreboding in the air that put knots in her stomach. It was in Bruce and Laura's eyes when they looked up from where they stood supporting Millie. It was in the hushed words Millie spoke before she hung up the telephone. Even in the background, Jared anxiously whispered something to Brandon.

"What is it?" Brad demanded. "What happened?"

Laura swiped a tear from her cheek as she turned to her brother almost accusingly.

"Dad just called. They found Cameron . . . unconscious near the mudslide."

A sickening dizziness swept over Shelby. Laura continued. "The paramedics took him to the emergency room. He's got a serious head injury and might not make it . . ." Her words were drowned in an anguished sob which made Millie break down even more. Laura's eyes bored into Brad, almost seeming to say, "Is that trouble enough for you?"

Bruce comforted his wife by putting an arm around her. "Honey, why don't you and the kids get in the car, and I'll help Millie."

Neither Brad nor Shelby had moved from their spots. Shelby felt a stomach-turning chill come over her. As Laura gathered the children and headed outside, the seriousness of the situation struck Shelby full force. She felt as if she would faint. *Oh please, not Cameron!*

Millie turned to Brad frantically. "Will you please help your dad give him a blessing?"

Completely shocked, Brad answered, "Yes . . . of course."

"Then let's get over to the hospital."

Within ten minutes, two vehicles sped to Bozeman Deaconess Hospital, the drumbeat of rain and the swish of wipers the only sounds to break the silence of the prayerful, frightened passengers. As they approached the south side of the hospital, they saw Karl waiting just inside the emergency room doors.

When everyone had hurried inside out of the rain, they gathered in the sterile ER waiting room, where Karl updated them on Cameron's condition.

"I don't think he's doing very well," Karl began. His features were haggard, his voice gravelly with emotion. "Right now he is having a CAT scan done. Brad, when he gets back to his room and is allowed visitors, will you come in with me so we can give him a blessing?"

Brad stared blankly as if his father's words hadn't registered. But then his eyes clouded over, and he whispered a shaky "Yes."

He turned and walked away from the group, making his way to a pop machine on the other side of the room. But his tears did not go unnoticed, as he had hoped. Shelby thought about going to him but immediately knew that would be a mistake. Though he looked like a man tormented with guilt, it would only upset him more to have her near him.

Knowing that Cameron's life was precariously hanging in balance, Shelby was assailed by a sense of dread and remorse. She pressed her hand over her face as a suffocating sensation tightened her throat. She felt certain somehow that she was the cause of all this. If she had never entered the picture, Cameron's accident might not have happened. He must have taken off after the dance in a fury. And then with the rain and the mudslide . . .

If only she had never come to Montana! Such heavy thoughts pressed down upon her, making it difficult to remain calm in front of the family. *Please, don't take him, Heavenly Father!*

In such a short time her life had completely changed. Nothing would ever be the same again. But what direction was life going to take? Right now this feeling in the pit of her stomach reminded her of the feelings she used to get right before a move. Life was changing again.

"Excuse me," a young nurse called out to the anxious group gathered to wait for any news. "Mr. and Mrs. Thompson?" Millie and Karl quickly went to the nurse, their faces full of distress.

"How is he?" Millie cried.

The nurse's face clouded over briefly, but she immediately replaced the look with one of hope. "At this moment his condition has stabilized, and he is doing very well for this type of head injury. Mr. and Mrs. Thompson, the two of you are welcome to follow me back to his room and see him for a few minutes. I also have a couple of questions to ask you about his medical history."

"Of course," Millie said eagerly. "We'll give you all the information we know."

The nurse nodded with a smile and extended her arm. "Please follow me." She turned to slide her badge through the badge reader, automatically opening the door that served as the barrier to the waiting room of the ER and the patient rooms.

The remaining group silently watched Karl and Millie disappear behind the heavy automatic doors that slowly closed and locked, wondering if any other family members would have a chance to see Cameron before it was too late.

In the years to come, Shelby would remember this day as a blur. She would think of the white walls and disinfectant, of Laura's children playing quietly with the toys set up in the corner of the waiting room and every so often asking if Uncle Cam was going to die.

She would remember Brad looking like he was in a trance by the pop machine and the horrid smell of someone's microwave chili dinner. She would hear the incessant beeping of medical equipment and snatches of tense conversation coming from behind the doors that would haunt her dreams in the weeks to come.

At one point, someone came to let Karl know that Cameron's truck—partially covered in mud and debris—was being towed down the mountain.

Brad and Laura had been the only others to be allowed back to see Cameron, but he was still unconscious. By the time Brad and his father had administered to him it was getting late. The bishop and home teachers had already come and gone. Most everyone had decided to go back to the house and take shifts at the hospital.

When Karl suggested that Millie return with the others, she emphatically insisted, “No! I don’t want to leave my son. I’m staying right here.”

In the end, Shelby offered to stay with Millie to keep her company. Brad had mutely given her a look so intense it spoke volumes. He left with Karl, still having said nothing, but Shelby could see the torment in his eyes.

Now it felt like hours had passed by as Shelby sat quietly beside Millie. Inside, her thoughts were as scattered as a swarm of bees. Would she get a chance to see Cam? She had been planning to return to Provo next week and wanted the chance to talk to him before leaving. Would he regain consciousness and recover? Worst of all, was this really because of her?

Flooded by all these thoughts, Shelby decided to take a walk. She found some sandwiches and juice in the cafeteria just before it closed. As she returned with the food, she wondered if she should tell Millie what happened last night at the dance. It might shed some light on the situation. Then again, it could be pointless to bring up more trouble now. And she couldn’t stand the thought of losing Millie’s high regard for her.

Shelby awoke with a start, her back hunched and her neck stiff.

“Miss?” The gentle voice was calling to her.

I must have fallen asleep.

“Mrs. Thompson is with Cameron now. He’s been moved to the telemetry unit. Would you like to see him?”

Shelby straightened her back and looked up at the nurse. She didn’t recognize the older woman. She must be with a new shift of nurses. Shelby wiped a hand across her eyes and stood up.

“Thanks. I do want to see him.”

The nurse smiled sympathetically. “Is he your brother?”

“No, he’s . . .” *Well, he was going to be my brother-in-law, but now he isn’t because I broke off the engagement to his brother, and no one even knows about it yet, and to top it all off I fell in love with him, and now who knows what will happen*—Shelby forced her racing thoughts to stop.

"Can I still see him? I mean, even if we aren't related?"

"Well, it's supposed to be family only . . ." she shrugged apologetically. "It looks like you've waited here for a long time. He must mean a great deal to you."

Tears welled within her eyes. "He does."

"I'll show you where to go." The nurse put an arm around her shoulder and led the way.

Chapter 23

Cameron's battered body was connected to a mass of tubes and monitors. There were bandages everywhere. Millie sat at his bedside holding one limp hand, tears streaming down her face. Shelby walked slowly through the wide doorframe and cautiously approached the bed. The two women exchanged worried looks.

"Has there been any change?" Shelby asked hopefully.

She sniffled and smiled. "The last doctor who came in said he was doing a little bit better."

Shelby stood on the opposite side of the bed and looked down at Cameron's pale eyelids. She thought of all the times she had been drawn into the depth of those blue eyes. She gently touched the other hand, taking note of the IV positioning and printout readings from the machines monitoring his vital statistics. It was one thing to attend nursing classes and study textbook situations at BYU. But it was a completely different thing when the patient was someone close to your heart.

"I can't believe this is my own son lying here, hardly recognizable with all these bruises and bandages . . ." Millie's voice trailed off inaudibly.

"He's such a strong person. He'll make it," Shelby said. If only she felt so sure.

"I pray he will."

When another technician bustled in and briskly made a routine check for vital signs, Shelby felt like she was in the way no matter where she stood. Reluctantly, she released Cameron's hand and backed away from the bed. But the very act of moving away produced a very painful reaction. It almost felt like there was an invisible chord in her chest connecting her to Cameron, and by moving back, she was stretching it precariously far.

In spite of herself, she almost laughed through her tears. Wasn't that how Amanda had always described the feelings between Jane Eyre and Mr. Rochester? The image came back with clarity because it was undeniably the way she felt. From the way she had first been drawn to him, there had always been some kind of connection. One that would now be excruciating to sever.

The technician finished his duties, but a nurse came in his place to examine the many dressings on Cameron's body to ensure the bleeding had been reduced. As if by mutual consent, Millie and Shelby left the room and walked back to the waiting room, where they found a welcome sight.

"Karl! Did you just get here?" Millie hurried over to her husband.

Karl walked over to them, holding out a plastic grocery sack. "Yes, I brought you something to eat in case you were hungry."

Millie peeked inside and thanked him but set the bag down on a chair. "They said he's doing a little better."

"Honey, I'm concerned about you. Maybe you should go home and rest for a while. You've been here for five hours."

Millie's face scrunched up in discontent. She looked away for a moment. "I suppose you're right. Will you call me as soon as you hear anything? Anything at all?"

"I promise, sweetheart." Karl proceeded to wrap his wife in a tender embrace.

Shelby felt awed by the sincere love that was clearly manifested between them. She wondered if she would ever have a second chance at love, to marry someone in the temple who she could love as deeply as Millie and Karl loved each other. Her thoughts turned to Cameron, lying nearly lifeless back there. How her heart ached for him. *Please Heavenly Father, bless him that he will recover!*

Later that night, the family gathered together in prayer, fervently pleading for Cameron's life. It was a very tender moment for everyone present. Then, while the family was still kneeling, Brad asked his parents what he should do about work.

"I'm supposed to go back tomorrow, but I'd like to stay here a few more days. I could call my boss and explain the situation."

"Son, I feel very strongly that Cam's going to recover. If you want to stay longer, we'd love to have you, but we'd also understand if you have to get back."

"And there's something else," Brad continued miserably, "I think you all should know."

He looked over at Shelby, and her heart sank like a lead weight. *Here it comes! He's telling them now!* Shelby shook her head as a signal to discourage him, but he continued anyway.

"Shelby and I aren't getting married."

There was a collective gasp as faces turned incredulously from Brad to Shelby. Several emotions were displayed across Laura's face upon hearing the news.

"What happened?" Millie asked brokenheartedly.

Shelby had to speak. "Millie, I'm so sorry. It's just that—"

"We *both* just need some time to think things through," Brad quickly inserted, giving Shelby a sad smile. He was trying to save her from embarrassment! In spite of everything, he was being the perfect gentleman. Shelby smiled back with grateful acceptance, the others speechless.

Early the next morning, Brad called his boss. The man agreed to let Brad stay for an extra two days. Though everyone else was pleased, Shelby felt like it would be harder to be around him for a longer amount of time. It was too uncomfortable. And her biggest worry was that he might try to talk her out of her decision during those two extra days.

For the most part, her fears were unfounded. Shelby mostly watched the children so the others could rotate going back and forth to the hospital. She did house cleaning and even attempted to prepare meals—though they were nothing spectacular. Thankfully, a few meals were brought in by Relief Society sisters.

She called Rose a few times and had some very good conversations with her. She expressed her concern for Rose, which seemed to mean a great deal to the young girl. They even agreed to write to each other after Shelby left Montana. It was one bright moment among the darker ones.

* * *

"Good-bye, Brad." The inaudible whisper upon her lips slipped out as Shelby watched the car disappear down the road.

Part of her couldn't believe she was letting him go, thought that she was completely insane for giving him up. But another part of her felt intense relief. It was over.

Bruce, Laura, and the children had all reluctantly left as well, with the understanding that they were to be kept posted regularly on Cameron's condition. Karl and Millie had been supportive and made it known that they only wanted what was best for Brad and Shelby. They weren't displeased with Shelby at all. In fact, they wanted her to stay as long as she wanted.

"We know you need to go back to Utah." Millie had patted Shelby's hand. "But you're welcome to stay here as long as you want or need to get everything settled."

Shelby had been especially grateful for their sympathy and generosity. What amazing examples they were. Millie had even offered to help Shelby with all the phone calls that would need to be made this week. They had to call the temple, the meetinghouse scheduler, the florist, and a host of other people. It was bound to be laborious and embarrassing.

Shelby sat on the front porch swing, looking down at her bare ring finger. The mark of the band was still there like a gaping symbol of all she had lost. She covered her left hand with her right and rubbed the skin across the mark. *You know that what you did was right.* But what would she do with her life now? Finish her degree? Go on a mission?

The metallic jingle of a dog collar sounded as Wags came up to her. His cheerful face couldn't help but make her smile. He flopped happily at her feet, resting his chin on her toe. Big brown eyes peered up at her in question. Shelby leaned forward to stroke his shaggy hair back and forth. She wondered if Wags had somehow sensed her loneliness and so had come to comfort her.

After a few minutes of sunshine and solitude, and a prayer in Cameron's behalf, Shelby reluctantly went inside the house and pulled out the telephone book. There were a lot of calls to make.

* * *

It was difficult to keep her composure when Shelby hugged Karl and Millie to say good-bye. How she had grown to love this sweet, wonderful couple! Millie had especially accepted her into their home and made her feel like one of the family. It was the closest she had come to experiencing "family" in a very long time. And now it was all coming to an end.

At least she had been able to go to the hospital one last time. She had left Cameron a letter in his room expressing many of the feelings hidden in her heart. It had taken a lot of deliberation to decide if she should leave the letter. She had started to walk away twice—with the letter still in her purse—but finally, she left it beside his bedside and took off before she could change her mind, having no idea if she would hear from him when he recovered.

Giving Wags and Bomber an affectionate pat good-bye was sad. The dogs licked her hands, their tails flailing at a dangerous speed. She would miss them all so much! Swiping at a tear, Shelby unlocked her car door and then turned to Millie.

"Thanks again for everything you've done for me," she managed to say, but her voice constricted in her throat, and it hurt to speak.

"It's been a blessing having you here," Millie said sincerely. "We'd love to have you come back anytime, even if you and Brad aren't getting married. You will always be welcome in our home."

There was no way to keep another tear from sliding down her cheek. The pain in her throat was intense.

"Oh, honey," Millie cried, wrapping her in a motherly embrace, "I'm so sorry it didn't work out." She held Shelby there for a moment, patting her back tenderly. "Everything will be all right."

Shelby attempted a smile through her tears. "Thank you for your kindness, Millie. I'll never forget it."

She got in her car and waved one last time as she drove down the driveway over the rumbling gravel. She would always remember that crunching sound. As she drove away from the Thompson home, the tears were unstoppable. Bozeman was visible in the distance, and the pain she felt inside became a physical ache. Finally unable to drive because of her blinding tears, Shelby pulled off to the side of the road. Down the hill to the right, she heard the roar of the Gallatin River.

Since no one was in sight to see the embarrassment of her red face, she decided to walk down there for a few minutes. She almost felt a need to say good-bye to the river as well. Once she had reached the water's edge, she sat on a large rock and stared into the swift-flowing swirls as they passed her. The water groaned like the depths of her broken heart.

Then, for the first time, she noticed that the river flowed north, back toward Bozeman. She was headed south, in the opposite direction. With this realization, her tears flowed like the Gallatin itself, streaming down her cheeks and dropping into the river to be swept away, never to be seen again.

Alone again in the world, she climbed back up to her car and drove away.

* * *

The metal cane tapped quietly on the carpet as she approached the metal bed rails, a heavy beige purse dangling from Elvira Brown's bony wrist. She dropped a heavy loaf of bread on the wheeled tray and stared down at the weakened body. Then her eyes narrowed into tiny slits.

"You don't deserve my bread," she spat out with thin, tight lips. "You got what you deserved."

She knew it was noble for her to be here, and she knew what her duties were. At least Karl and Millie would know she had visited when they saw the bread.

Elvira studied Cameron in his sleep, pointing the tip of her cane at him. "I know what you've been up to, mister. You ruined one girl's life and then moved on to ruin your brother's . . . with no one in your family suspecting a thing."

Her voice trembled with passion as she shook her cane at him. A frail hand wiped the moisture from her wrinkled cheek. She turned around so as not to have to face him. Gnarled fingers clutched her cane as she inhaled unsteadily.

Elvira stared at the wide hospital door. As she turned back to give him one last glare before leaving, something on the ground caught her eye. Barely visible between the garbage can and the bedside chair was a lavender piece of paper. It must have fallen from the shelf on the wall. She stabbed at it with the end of her cane. After several attempts, she managed to drag the paper along the floor toward her beneath the weight of the cane.

"Hmmm . . ."

Peering down, Elvira read the single word on the envelope: *Cameron*. It was written in a feminine hand, she decided. Her mind churned with questions and possibilities. It was possible this was a letter from his sister or the Relief Society. Millie wouldn't write her son a letter when she was continually at the hospital. But it was definitely from a female . . .

Her heart nearly stopped. It might be from Shelby.

Stooping over with some effort, Elvira stretched down, cornered the lavender envelope, and seized it between two bony knuckles. She flipped it over twice, scrutinizing the envelope in the dim light. She fingered the triangular flap on the back. The seal was not very good. She wondered . . . if she slid her fingernail carefully along the edge . . . There! It opened! Her eyes shifted around the room. Then she slipped the letter out of the envelope and quickly skimmed over the contents.

"I knew it!"

That girl had been up to no good, staying out late and cavorting around with the likes of Cameron Thompson. She should have been faithful to Brad.

She glanced at Cameron's still form. Then she slipped the letter into a pocket in her purse.

"Young people these days need to be taught a lesson," she justified to her image in the small mirror above the sink. Taking one last backward glance, the old woman left the room and made her way home, feeling the burden of having made a difficult, but necessary, decision. She began to hum, "Have I done any good in the world today?"

Chapter 24

Four weeks had passed since Shelby had returned to Provo. And Sara and Amanda *still* couldn't squeeze any information out of her. How could their roommate go to Montana, engaged to the most wanted bachelor on campus, and return miserably *un*engaged? It was unfathomable. How had she decided that "marrying Brad just wasn't the right decision"?

Something pretty drastic must have happened! They speculated over every conceivable scenario in an attempt to understand Shelby's feelings. Sara had even tried to get in touch with Brad but with no success. The role of "roommate" was taken quite seriously in their apartment, ranking as high in importance as a ward calling.

Even their bad-tempered roommate, Jessica, had softened a little. One day, Shelby was alone in the apartment when Jessica walked in and saw her wiping away her tears. Jessica made her a cup of hot chocolate and sat beside her. She didn't really say much and didn't probe Shelby with questions. But her quiet presence was all Shelby needed at the time.

From Shelby's point of view, all the well-intended questioning of Sara and Amanda felt more like a nightmarish interrogation. Right now she just didn't feel like talking about it. She had tried to reassure them that she was fine.

"Really, you don't have to worry about me," Shelby told them one night. "You are the kindest, most thoughtful roommates I could ever ask for, and I appreciate everything you're trying to do. But seriously, I'm fine."

"But you're not happy!" Sara insisted. "And what about Brad?"

"You still love him, don't you?" Amanda exclaimed dramatically.

"I'll always care about him, but . . . no. *I'm* the one that broke off the engagement, remember."

"But we still don't understand why!"

Shelby felt like there was nothing she could tell them right now. It was all just too complicated, too painful. And if they found out anything about Cameron, she could only imagine the fuss that would create.

"Could we just talk about this later, please?"

Sara and Amanda nodded reluctantly. They watched Shelby disappear behind her bedroom door, closing them out of her world at the sound of a click.

* * *

"I don't know what to think, Laura," Millie held the receiver in one hand while vigorously scrubbing the kitchen sink with the other.

"How is he acting, Mom?" Laura's voice asked.

"He's just . . . quiet. I mean, even more than before. He's not his normal self. It's much different than it was after Camille."

"What do you think happened to make Cam take off like he did that night?"

Millie scoured the faucet as she pondered Laura's question. She'd had a suspicion about Cam but hadn't mentioned it to anyone. It's just that he had seemed so much happier while Shelby had been here. It had made her so relieved and grateful to see him laugh again that she had actually planned activities so they could be together—simply to help Cam come out of his shell of hurt and anger. She hadn't meant to do anything else, especially not to hurt Brad!

But perhaps because of her meddling Cam had developed feelings for Shelby. And if such were the case . . . it could destroy him!

"Mom, you still there?" Laura's voice at the other end of the line brought Millie back to the conversation.

"Oh, I'm sorry. I just feel guilty, Laura, like it's my fault."

"Like what's your fault?"

"Laura, I . . . practically pushed them together."

"Cam and . . . ?"

"And Shelby."

"You're kidding!" Rather than sounding shocked, Laura's voice almost sounded amused. It caused Millie even more confusion. "How did you push them together, Mom?"

"I was always suggesting activities where they could be together because I wanted to cheer him up. But what if he started to develop feelings for her? That could have pushed him over the edge after all he's been through. And it would have been all *my* fault—"

"Mom, stop. Nothing is your fault! What happened would have happened no matter what you did. You didn't cause Brad and Shelby to break off their engagement, and you didn't cause Cameron to fall in love with her either."

Millie's scrubbing came to a halt. "You really think he *did* fall in love with her?" she asked warily.

It was Laura's turn to be silent. Finally, she said, "I'd better plead the fifth. I didn't say anything . . . no matter how many thoughts I have on the subject."

"All right Laura, what do you know?"

"Mom, he would kill me if I said anything. You know how he is, expecting absolute silence when it comes to personal matters. Let's just say that I could tell right off that something was going on."

Millie sighed deeply, her heart aching for both sons. One had lost Shelby completely and the other may be silently aching for her at this very moment.

"There's one problem, Laura," Millie said quietly.

"What's that, Mom?"

"I still think that Shelby is the best thing that ever happened this summer, and I still want her as a daughter-in-law! It was so hard to say good-bye."

At the other end of the line, Laura smiled secretively. "You know . . . we'll be in Provo in a few weeks to visit Bruce's family. I was thinking about looking her up—just to see how she is. It wouldn't be meddling or anything, just . . . a friendly hello."

"I think that would be nice." Millie didn't even suspect that her daughter had been plotting and scheming for the last two days. And Laura was a very determined woman.

* * *

Cameron dismissed his students when the afternoon bell rang, gathered up his textbook and lesson plans, and then left the classroom. With a slight limp, he walked down the hallway amid a throng of noisy, rushing students eager to escape scholastic premises. If only he had a touch of the motivation and zeal of these teenagers. Right now it felt like he existed in a haze.

Cameron stopped outside the principal's office. The door was just opening, and a bright-eyed girl waved back to the principal, calling, "Thanks, Mr. Jones! See you tomorrow!"

When she passed by Cameron, she batted her eyelashes and grinned ridiculously.

"Hello, Mr. Thompson!"

"Hello." For the life of him he couldn't remember the girl's name but knew she had been in his class last year.

He was saved from embarrassment when Mr. Jones extended a hand to Cameron's shoulder saying, "Come into my office, Cameron!"

He followed the principal inside a small room filled with binders, books, and several file folders strewn across the desk. Sitting in the more comfortable of two chairs, he leaned his head back against the wall and let out a deep breath.

"That bad?" Mr. Jones grinned, sitting behind his desk.

"No, things have gone fine the last three days. I just get tired a lot."

"That's understandable . . . seeing as how you should be home resting! I told you to take a longer leave."

"I couldn't have stayed home for one more day, Bob. I need to be here. I need to keep busy."

"Just take it easy, then. I worry about you."

Bob Jones was sympathetic to everyone's needs. *It's part of what makes him such a great principal,* Cameron thought. "Thank you. And thanks again for arranging the substitute for me."

"No problem. Mrs. Archer is an excellent sub. But we are definitely glad to have you back with us." His smile made crinkled lines beside his eyes.

"Thanks, Bob. I'm glad to be back."

Mr. Jones observed Cameron for a moment. He had been one of the favorites among the faculty and staff until some unfortunate event that happened last year. But the vague gossip that passed between the other teachers would never hold up in his book. Cameron Thompson was as good as they came.

But in spite of the clean bill of health that was issued him upon his return, there was something different about Cameron. It was in the set of his mouth and the grayness beneath his eyes. It made Bob uneasy.

Cameron stood up slowly and shook the principal's hand. "I'd better get going. I'll see you tomorrow."

"You take good care of yourself, now. We need you around here!"

"Will do."

Walking out to the parking lot in a dull stupor, Cameron tried to ignore the memories that flooded his mind every time he saw his dinged-up truck. Fishing did the same thing to him. Since being discharged from the hospital four weeks ago, every place he went held ghosts of memories that haunted his soul.

She was gone.

Before he had ever regained consciousness, Shelby had left Montana. Besides a small cluster of dried up forget-me-nots in a wood box, there was nothing tangible left to remember her by—only memories and the hollowness that had taken over his world. Where was she now, and what was she doing?

During his recovery in the hospital, snatches of conversation had informed him that the wedding was off, Shelby had returned to Utah, and his brother was planning on moving to San Francisco. He was ridden with guilt, for he knew he was the one to blame for their separation. Another marriage bit the dust. *Good job, Cam. Way to go*, he had thought bitterly.

And yet he was tormented by so many other thoughts. That fateful night at the dance when he had kissed her, he had confessed his feelings, bared his soul. There was just one problem. She had never actually *said* anything about her own feelings. Had he merely imagined that she had kissed him back, that those kisses were as passionate as his own? What was he to believe? Although he had known all along that he could never have Shelby, the thought of never seeing her again was becoming an unbearable torture.

Something had to be done. If he had even the slightest indication that she truly returned his feelings for her, he would be after her in a flash. She had left before he ever had a chance to speak to her. Did she despise him? While he felt that he owed her an apology for ruining things with Brad, he also needed some peace of mind, some kind of closure with her. If he could just find out if she would ever want to see or speak to him again.

But her rejection could be the last straw to break him.

Then the familiar grasp of misery closed in on him. What was he thinking? He wasn't good enough for her. He already knew that. He'd been such a fool wasting all those months of inactivity in the Church. And to what purpose? To soothe his wounded pride? To punish people by not attending?

You have only punished yourself, he thought miserably. *It's your own stupid fault!*

* * *

Shelby pulled several envelopes out of the small mailbox and flipped through them with only a flicker of hope. She let out a defeated sigh. Just a gas bill, two letters for Sara, and some junk mail. She completely ignored the larger white envelope addressed to all four roommates which was obviously another wedding announcement. She didn't even care who it was from. Wedding announcements just kept coming like a cruel mockery to taunt Shelby. Each one had an invisible message marked for Shelby alone: "This might have been you!"

She walked back inside the apartment, tossed the mail on the rickety kitchen table, and crumbled onto a chair.

Four weeks since she had left Montana.

In that time she had emailed Karl and Millie to thank them for their hospitality and to ask about Cameron's health. They had written back to tell her Cam was out of the hospital and recovering well. Surely there had been ample time for Cameron to respond to her letter if he was going to—or wanted to. It was becoming painfully apparent that he was *not* going to call or write. That knowledge sank in heavily, pulling her down into misery.

Thinking about what she had written him was so embarrassing! She had practically offered herself to Cameron if he ever wanted to find her in the future. How utterly stupid and humiliating! *What on earth was I thinking?* Now it was perfectly clear that he didn't want to contact her. The rejection hurt as much as being disowned by her mother, so it was just easier not to even think about it. She was good at locking her feelings away. Avoiding them was much less painful.

For now she had to focus all her energy on school, her job, and just getting through the day. She was also practicing phone calls to her mother with rehearsed scripts and speeches. But nothing ever felt right. The one time she actually tried calling her mother, she never got past dialing the area code. It was something she was determined to accomplish, though.

Someday. Perhaps the time still wasn't right.

Right now Heavenly Father's ways seemed far more than mysterious. She was downright baffled. What purpose had there been in being engaged to Brad or in staying in Montana? What purpose had there been in getting to know Cameron? And why did she have to hurt so much inside? Did Heavenly Father truly have a plan for her, or was she senselessly wandering through life? In her mind, she knew the answer, but the knowledge still hadn't made its way to her heart.

Shelby sat in the kitchen, staring at the telephone and thinking about her mother. She was startled when it suddenly rang.

"Hello?"

"Hi, is this Shelby? This is Laura, Cam's—er, Brad's sister."

"Laura! How are you?" Shelby asked eagerly.

"Great. We're in town visiting Bruce's family, and I just thought I'd call—to say hi. How are you doing?"

For a moment Shelby felt like pouring out her feelings to Laura. She had really liked Laura, and it would be such a relief to confide in her. But she couldn't tell Laura how awful life was right now, how confused and downhearted she felt. Laura couldn't change the fact that she was not marrying Brad, and she certainly wouldn't know what to do about Shelby's mother. So Shelby answered the indeterminate, age-old standard, "I'm fine." *Ha!*

Laura asked her about school and then told her about Tara's latest escapades, which made Shelby smile. "I miss your kids. They're so great."

"I don't know about that all the time, but they miss you too. We *all* do, Shelby."

Shelby felt her throat constrict and couldn't answer. Laura continued, "I was wondering if we could get together to visit before we leave."

"Sure, I'd love to see you." Shelby managed to say.

They agreed to get together that Saturday before Laura and Bruce headed home to Idaho Falls, and Laura gave her the address of Bruce's parents where her family was staying. When Shelby hung up the phone, she wondered if seeing them all again would be good for her or if it would only make things worse.

Chapter 25

Sara and Amanda popped their heads around the corner of Shelby's bedroom door, a mischievous gleam in their eyes. "What are you two up to?" she asked warily.

"We're going to kidnap you!" They sprang over to clasp Shelby's arms while she eyed them in exhausted disbelief.

"You've got to be kidding."

"Nope," Amanda answered firmly. "We've decided that you need some cheering up—"

"—so we're taking you shopping!" Sara finished enthusiastically.

Shelby looked at them pathetically. "I can't go today. I'm sorry."

"Come on! It'll be fun!"

"I have to go somewhere."

"No you don't; it's Saturday."

"Actually, I'm meeting with . . . Brad's sister and her family."

"What?" they asked simultaneously, each face a study of disbelief.

"Are you and Brad getting back together?" Sara whispered, slightly alarmed.

Amanda gasped before Shelby pronounced emphatically, "No!"

"Then what's going on, Shelby? Why won't you talk to us?"

"Look, Brad's sister, Laura, is in town with her husband and kids. She called to say hi and asked to see me before they head back to Idaho. That's all."

"Why does she want to see you? Do you think she wants to get you and Brad together again?"

"No, it's not that. When I met her in Montana we got along really well. She's just being friendly. There's no harm in that, is there?"

Sara frowned. "Not unless it hurts you to be around her. What if it just makes you feel lonely to be near someone who was about to become your sister-in-law?"

"I'll be fine," Shelby reassured them, appreciative of their intense loyalty. "Thank you for worrying about me. It shows how much you care." Then her roommates wrapped her in a double embrace.

Later, Shelby drove to the address Laura had given her. It was a lovely older home on the east bench with tall, stately trees in the front yard and an expensive sedan in the driveway. Shelby sat in the car for a moment and wondered if this was a good idea after all. She could just back up and leave. But she'd have to call Laura with an excuse, and she didn't want to lie. She thought about how much she really did want to see her and the children. Then Brandon shot out of the front door, pushing in front of Tara.

"Hi, Shelby!" he shouted and waved.

Tara glowered at her brother and whined, "*I* was going to tell Shebby 'hi' first!"

Shelby got out of her car, knelt down, and wrapped her arms around Tara, and then ruffled Brandon's hair. "Hey, you guys! How are you doing?"

Brandon said "Fine," while Tara answered, "Sad."

"Why are you sad, Tara?"

"Cuz you're not detting meh-weed to be my aunt anymore." Her lower lip hung down.

"Oh, honey, that doesn't mean I can't still be your friend."

"Weally?" Tara smiled.

"Really," Shelby grinned.

"Oh tay!"

The three of them headed inside the house, where Laura and Bruce warmly greeted Shelby. They introduced her to Bruce's parents, who welcomed her graciously to their home. Shelby wondered how much Bruce's parents knew about the situation, but no one mentioned Brad.

Though she didn't want anyone to bring up uncomfortable subjects, she secretly wanted to learn something new about Cameron. Any tidbit of information that might give her an indication of what he was doing or thinking would be nice. But they only mentioned his recovery and return to teaching. *So he's moved on with his life.*

Lunch was served, and Shelby found herself enjoying her visit more than she had thought would be possible. Soft music drifted from the family room into the dining area. Tara poked her fingers into the butter like she had in Montana. Shelby watched her, a grin on her face. It took a minute for Shelby to register why the melody in the background seemed familiar. Her toes quietly tapped under the table as she listened to the friendly conversation around her. But when she finally made the connection, her heart jolted within her chest. This was the song! From the CD in Cameron's truck. The same one they had danced to just before he—

Shelby felt ill. She could almost feel the blood drain from her face, leaving her skin white. Every word reminded her of pleasures that shouldn't be remembered. The music played on and on.

Bruce suddenly commented, "Hey, I love this song."

Laura nodded. "I think it's one of Cameron's favorites too. He always listens to Alabama."

Shelby was about to excuse herself to go to the bathroom when Laura asked her, "Did you ever hear Cam play this in Montana?"

Shelby forced a casual look on her face as she answered, "Yeah." She looked away, hoping no one saw anything unusual in her demeanor.

Laura didn't stop there, unfortunately. "Speaking of Cameron, I heard there was a possibility that he might be down here in a few weeks. We should have him give you a call. I'm sure he'd like to see you."

Bruce gave his wife a subtle what-are-you-doing look, but Laura didn't acknowledge it. Shelby had no idea what to say.

Trust me, he doesn't want to see me, Laura. If he did he would have already tried to call or write. She nodded, but her words came out barely more than a whisper. "Sure. I'd like to see him again."

* * *

Sister Brown pulled to a noisy stop in front of the Thompsons' home, where their two dogs were barking madly at her.

"Hush, you foolish mongrels!" she commanded.

Yes, she was doing the right thing. It wasn't easy being the bearer of bad tidings, but it had to be done, she thought stoically. Someone had to let this poor family know what had been going on.

She patted the side of her purse where a certain lavender envelope was concealed. Donning her gloves and straightening her crocheted sweater, she ignored the steam rising from the hood of her car and opened the car door.

"Stop that racket at once, you silly dogs!" came the imperial order. "I am here on very important business." She swung her cane in the air, and the dogs fled with a whimper.

Millie opened the door just then with questions in her eyes. "Why do you want to have a meeting with us, Elvira? Is something wrong?"

Making her way to the front door, the elderly woman answered, "First, get Karl. Then I'll tell you everything." A feeble hand dramatically lifted to her heart.

Karl was summoned, and though he was rolling his eyes, he sat down directly across from his tiresome neighbor. "What can we do for you?"

Sister Brown placed one hand over the other in her lap and struck a saintly pose. "I have come under very unpleasant circumstances, but this needs to be done. You see, I have been concerned lately about your family's welfare. I don't wish to upset you," she shook her head tragically, "but I have something to say that you will not like one bit."

Karl and Millie waited somewhat tolerantly, eyebrows raised. Their neighbor continued.

"You see, I saw something a while ago that upset me greatly, and I feel strongly that I should inform you."

"What did you see," Karl prodded. "Another fire?"

Millie's lips twitched humorously, but she gave her full attention to Sister Brown.

"No, no. It was while Brad's fiancée was here. She was outside one night and . . ." her voice trailed off with a quiver. Pressing a hanky to her mouth, she carried on. "That Cameron of yours must have found her, and . . . well, he made improper advances toward her, his own dear brother's future wife!"

Silence. Two pairs of eyes stared wide.

Millie recovered first. "What do you mean?"

"I drove up here that night—I thought your barn was on fire. When I got out of my car, I saw Cameron trying to force himself on Shelby—to take advantage of her!"

"What?!" Karl spluttered in anger and disbelief.

Sister Brown proceeded defensively. "He was trying to kiss her. Fortunately, I arrived in time to stop him. But just imagine what this type of behavior could do, what damage to Brad and his forthcoming marriage . . ."

"Sister Brown, Brad isn't getting married," said Millie. "The wedding is off."

"What?" she shrieked. "Then it's true!"

Karl exclaimed, "What are you talking about?"

"I was right all along! Cameron was plotting to destroy his brother's future!"

Karl had heard enough. He stood up, walked over to Sister Brown, and stated, "This conversation is finished!" Opening the front door for her, he said, "I don't appreciate what you're trying to do here. No matter what you have heard or may mistakenly have against my son, he has done nothing wrong!"

Elvira Brown stood also, her back as straight as it would allow. She held her head high and said, "All I'm trying to do is to save your family from embarrassment. I don't know why I even bother."

"Now look," Karl said crossly. "You don't know what—"

"But I do know. I have proof, right here in my purse." Producing the lavender envelope, she shook it in front of Karl and Millie. "See if this doesn't make you think twice about what I said."

With a toss of her wrist, she passed the letter to Millie and then huffed out of the house, with murmured grumbling, all the way to her car. As soon as she was gone, Karl muttered furiously, "I don't know why she bothers either!" Then he stormed into the family room, leaving Millie to stare at the letter in her hand.

* * *

Alone in her room, Shelby curled back against the oversized pillow on her bed, thinking about her day with Laura, Bruce, and the kids. *At least I managed to get through it.* It had been wonderful and painful at the same time.

Turning to one side, she reached inside her nightstand drawer and pulled out a photo from beneath a stack of books. It was the first photo she had ever seen of Cameron. Memories came sweeping through her troubled mind. She pictured Cameron driving her through the Hyalite Canyon, sitting at his favorite spot on the mountain where they had talked. She remembered how it had felt to be wrapped in his arms as he stood behind her teaching her how to fish. She missed him so much that it hurt. It was as real as a physical ache that had no relief. How could he just put her out of his mind and move on with his life? Why hadn't he responded to her letter? Was she just another conquest, like Brad had said? Maybe the accident had changed his feelings.

A tear ran down her cheek as she realized her feelings for Cameron simply wouldn't go away. She thought about her dream of having a home and family, of all she had lost because she and Brad weren't right for each other. It was hard not to be engaged anymore, to not belong somewhere . . . with someone.

Shelby also mulled over the situation with her mother and how desperately she wanted to be close to her. Cameron had suggested that she write her mother a letter expressing her feelings.

Shelby immediately sat up, swiping the tear away. She'd do it! She would write to her mother. It was time to do this. With a prayer in her heart, Shelby reached for pen and paper. She would tell her mother how much she loved and missed her, how much she needed her.

Pouring her whole heart into the words she wrote, Shelby was amazed at the inspiration she received. Heavenly Father knew what she needed and was freely blessing her with the words that might touch her mother. She expressed her love, grief, and hope for reconciliation. Like a healing ritual, her deepest feelings were finally being released, flowing from within all the way out to her fingertips as they formed the words on paper. When she finished writing, Shelby read her letter once before sealing it in the envelope. Before she could change her mind, she stamped the letter and drove to the post office in town.

It took a lot of courage to actually drop the letter in the narrow slot and walk away, but she did it. Shelby sent a prayer with that letter, hoping it would touch her mother's heart and break down the walls that separated her from her daughter. As she pulled out of the post office parking lot and drove through town, Shelby finally felt a measure of peace.

On Sunday she fasted and asked Heavenly Father to bless her mother when she received the letter. She prayed that her mother would feel touched with a desire to accept Shelby back into her life.

* * *

Cameron stared at the mysterious, small envelope for a moment. His name was the only writing on the outside. Hoping it wasn't some kind of hate mail from another one of Camille's friends, he opened it. It began "Dear Cameron," but he quickly flipped over to the back side to see who wrote it. His heart nearly stopped. He had to force himself to breathe as he sat down.

Shelby had written to him? When? All this time he had wished for a chance to see her again, to know what her feelings were. Now here he sat with something in his hands that could change his life. If she had written anything that could give him the slightest hope . . . but what if she never wanted to see him again because of what had happened? Could he take the rejection?

> Dear Cameron,
>
> If you only knew how I feel as I sit helplessly at your bedside, willing you to wake, yet knowing I have to leave before you open your eyes. I pray for you every day and ask Heavenly Father to spare your life. I know he is answering all our prayers. Your parents were told just today that you are showing signs of improvement. As I touch your pale cheek and hold your limp hand, I wish I could somehow share my thoughts so you would know what I'm feeling.
>
> I'm so sorry I left you at the dance. I'm sorry you were hurt because of me. I don't understand what has happened to me since I came to Montana, but I know that I love you. You have done so much for me. You've given me a part of yourself that I will treasure forever. I'll never forget that.
>
> If you regret what happened between us once you have recovered, I'll understand. I think that none of this horrible

accident and resulting pain you are in would have happened if it weren't for me. But if you want to see me again, I'll be here.

I want so much to know you are well and happy, but I have to leave in the morning. When you have recovered, I'd love to hear from you. No matter what you decide, I'll always cherish the memories you have given me.

Love,
Shelby

Cameron dropped his head into the sheet of feminine handwriting, squeezing his eyes shut in a failed attempt to hold back his emotion. "Oh, Shelby . . ."

Chapter 26

August heat faded as autumn leaves emerged until summer was a fading memory. Like the puff of breath on a dandelion, summer and all its memories blew away. October's beauty abounded on campus with autumn leaves cascading in masses and the hint of winter's chill in the air. The cloudless blue skies draped like a curtain along the edges of the snow-capped peaks of Mount Timpanogos. And still no word from Cameron.

Shelby knew the time had come to move on. With no further reluctance, she began to fill out her mission papers. She wanted to be endowed and serve the Lord. Her bishop had even helped her see how it could be financially possible to serve a mission.

Her days were busier than ever before, which helped a great deal. To be completely absorbed with school, work, and the thought of a mission made getting up in the morning much less painful. There was always something to do, someplace to be. It was actually quite fulfilling in many ways.

Then the unthinkable happened. Shelby's mother wrote back. It was an enormous shock to have Sara run inside like a whirlwind and hand over the small pale pink envelope with the thinly scrawled words *Grace Hamlin* in the upper left-hand corner. The return address indicated that she was still living at the same address. That alone was a miracle—that she hadn't moved. But the greatest miracle of all was that her mother had finally acknowledged Shelby's existence.

The letter sitting reverently in her hands, she decided not to open it until she had the chance to be alone, somewhere quiet. She tucked it away in her purse and thought about it constantly throughout the rest of the day. What kind of letter would it be? She dreaded opening a nasty letter full of angry accusations or denunciations. If only there could be some suggestion of kindness in what her mother had to say, it would mean everything in the world to Shelby.

Late that evening, after she had taken her turn washing the dishes, she took a drive. Without really thinking about it, she found herself at the Provo Temple, which she decided to drive around several times. Then she found a private spot on the west side of the parking lot that faced the lit-up temple spire and turned off the engine. *Here goes.*

She carefully tore open the pale pink envelope and removed the letter.

Shelby,

I've been badly hurt by your joining the Mormons and leaving home. If you only knew how much I cried, what you put me through. You were all I had left, you know. After your father died, I needed you, and you weren't there for me. I still don't understand why you did it.

I said that I never want to see you again. Even though you're my daughter, I'm still angry. I don't know if I can ever forgive you. It isn't fair to expect me to forgive you and act like nothing ever happened. If you want your mother back in your life again, you'll have to leave the Mormon church. I'm sorry, but that's the choice you have to make.

Grace Hamlin

The letter slipped through Shelby's fingers as she sank forward, overcome. Her forehead rested against the steering wheel and the tears fell. Great sobs racked her body as she cried from pent-up years of acute pain.

"Mom . . . oh, mom, why . . . ?"

Shelby wrapped her arms around her torso, rocking back and forth as she cried all the tears she had held so long inside her. A flood of emotions that had accumulated over all these years was unleashed. Anger and grief knifed through her, while rejection and confusion smothered her. *How can she be so selfish! She didn't even sign the letter as my mother!*

An hour later the immense release left her feeling completely drained and very weak. She turned on the heater and began to pray as she had never prayed before. She focused on the light emanating from the temple and never stopped praying until she felt the strength to go back to her apartment.

* * *

Brad closed his scriptures and exhaled forcefully. From the cement bench he sat on, he looked out across the Marriott Center lawns and patches of flowers getting covered by fall leaves. It was a glorious autumn day, but he still felt miserable. With all that he had been through, the Lord surely had something in mind for him. But what?

It would be so much easier just to know right now. Hadn't he felt a confirmation that he should marry Shelby? He had been so sure at the time. So why was he going through this trial? For what purpose had all this happened? He had loved her so much!

Shelby's words echoed through his mind. *I just don't think we love each other enough . . .*

He *had* loved her! He was sure of it!

Then the prickling seeds of doubt crept into his heart. Did he really know what eternal love was supposed to feel like? Maybe it felt more powerful than the comfortable, good feelings he'd had for Shelby.

A twinge of guilt came over Brad as he thought about his brother. He knew that he'd been kind of a jerk to Cameron and really should apologize. He just wasn't sure how to go about it. It was so uncomfortable to contemplate, especially the thought of having to do it over the phone. He could email him, but it would be better to ask someone's forgiveness in person. Brad shuddered. He just wasn't ready. He was still upset with Cameron.

Brad said a quick silent prayer for strength to do what was right. Then he packed his scriptures back in their case, picked up his briefcase, and walked to his car. Driving north, he was grateful he had at least been able to sign a contract for another apartment on the other side of campus. He didn't know if Shelby had moved as well, but he wanted to be sure that they wouldn't be running into each other all the time. At least he'd be moving to San Francisco soon.

Thus absorbed in his thoughts, Brad didn't even notice the red truck with light blue Montana license plates parked along the curb in front of his apartment complex.

* * *

"Let me get this straight. You're trying to tell me that not only do you want me to forgive you for what you did in Montana, but you also want me to give you my blessing so you can steal her away? I don't think so!"

Brad shot off the sofa. His voice had become so loud that he knew the downstairs apartment could probably hear him, not to mention the one next door. But he couldn't seem to stop himself. Only thirty minutes ago he was trying to think of a way to apologize to Cameron, and now his brother was here in Provo, and all Brad could think of was attacking him again.

From the faded, brown plaid chair he sat in, Cameron looked unwaveringly at his brother. Brad stood in the middle of the family room, nostrils flared and lips pursed. Cameron felt a tremendous sense of regret that he and his brother couldn't have better feelings between them.

"Brad," Cameron finally said, his voice considerably calm. "I love her."

"How dare you!" Brad fumed.

"Look, I'm just telling you the truth. I'm being honest here."

"You make me sick."

"Why? You've had plenty of opportunity to get her back."

Brad's mouth contorted into an ugly smirk. "Oh please. You ruined everything before I had a chance. You ruin lives, Cameron."

"Let's get one thing straight, once and for all! I never did anything to Camille!"

"How can you say that?" Brad asked abhorrently.

"She was pregnant with someone else's baby, not mine! How can my own brother believe the worst of me?"

Brad's head whipped back like he had been struck. "Your silence confirmed the accusations."

Cameron clenched his teeth and looked away. "Well, I was wrong.

I should have refuted all the lies she spread. But I didn't. I just can't believe you accepted the lies instead of trusting in me."

Brad tapped his hand against the wall in agitation, contemplating his brother's words. Then, with one final whack, he spat out, "Fine. Go look for Shelby. I'm not going to stop you."

He started to pace the room, looking in any direction other than his brother's. Then he stopped at the window, a thought having popped into his mind like a lightbulb turning on.

"But I think you've forgotten one thing," Brad said smugly. "Shelby wants a temple marriage. She'll never give that up. Not even for you."

* * *

It was a chilly Saturday outside, but inside the apartment, Shelby was working up a sweat by scrubbing the kitchen floor. Pausing for a moment to wipe a hand across her forehead, she asked, "Amanda, can you toss me that rag over there?" Then she opened a window a couple inches to let in some cold air.

Three of the four roommates had chosen to clean the apartment this weekend. Jessica had claimed to have a study group at the library and wasn't around. So Amanda chose fridge duty, Sara got the bathrooms, and Shelby took the kitchen floor.

Shelby was certain that the ugly industrial vinyl floor could never have looked good, even the day it was installed (which was probably twenty years ago). It had little depressions that collected every ounce of dirt and grime into little brown-pocked circles. Shelby was sick of trying to get it clean. Her right arm was sore, and her jeans were getting wet at the knees.

"Here it comes!"

Like a missile, the wet rag was launched across the kitchen and landed on Shelby's head.

"Thanks a lot!"

Amanda giggled as her head popped around the lower half of the refrigerator door. "Come on, it cooled you off."

"I can think of better ways to get cooled off," Shelby countered.

Sara called from the bathroom, "What's going on out there? Am I the only one doing any work around here?"

"Watch it," Shelby laughed back, "or Amanda will throw a wet rag at you too! She's dangerous to have around on cleaning day."

Amanda's retaliation was spraying Shelby from the sink faucet. She had deadly aim. Now Shelby felt more wet than dry. It only took a few seconds for Sara to join in the fray. Sopping rags began to fly around the apartment as a full-fledged battle broke out, shrieks of laughter filling the apartment.

No one heard the knock at the door.

When the doorbell rang a minute later, the three stopped to look at each other in merry guilt. Nearly soaked from head to toe, Shelby made her way across the slippery kitchen floor. Her face alight with mirth, Shelby opened the door.

She nearly collapsed from shock.

It wasn't possible. It couldn't be him! Yet there he stood, with his gorgeous tossed brown hair, broad shoulders, and penetrating blue eyes. Aside from a thin scar on his forehead from the accident, he looked fantastic. In fact, he looked more desirable today than ever before. Shelby gaped, and his name escaped as a whisper on her lips. *Cameron!*

"Hello, Shelby."

His voice was like an icy river that coursed through her body and made her shiver. The slow, questioning smile on his face immediately brought back the recollection of her wet shirt and jeans, not to mention her dripping hair. She could have died.

A deluge of thoughts surged madly through Shelby's mind. *Why is he here? How did he find me? Why didn't he ever answer my letter?* Frozen in her stare, she couldn't seem to find the words.

But how wonderful it was to see him!

"Hey, Shelby, who is it?" Sara and Amanda were close behind her.

Cameron briefly glanced at the two other dripping girls but quickly returned his gaze to Shelby's stunned face. His eyes communicated the uncertainty he felt.

"Come in," she managed to say amid the crowding roommates. Cameron stepped inside.

In a state of disbelief and anticipation, Shelby showed him into the family room. Sara and Amanda were quick to follow right behind him, making searing backward glances at Shelby, glances that could mean anything from "Holy cow, who is *he*?" to "Hurry up and introduce us!"

Cameron sat on the sofa and looked up hopefully at Shelby, but Amanda practically jumped over the furniture to secure the spot beside him. That left Sara and Shelby the ugly green-and-brown-plaid loveseat that creaked with the slightest movement under their weight.

"Cameron, these are my roommates, Sara and Amanda. Sara and Amanda, this is Cameron Thompson . . ." She wanted to leave the introduction at that, but hurriedly inserted, ". . . Brad's brother."

"Brad's brother?" Amanda threw a scrutinizing look toward Cameron, who nodded apprehensively.

"Ahhhh . . ." Sara said meaningfully, making Shelby want to cringe. *Please, I'm begging you—don't say anything!* Both of them had the potential to utterly mortify both her and Cameron.

"Uhh . . ." he began somewhat uneasily, before anyone else spoke, "what are you girls . . . up to?"

Accompanied by her roommate's giggles, Shelby swallowed her pride and answered. "We were cleaning the kitchen and sort of had a . . ."

"Water fight!" her roommates chimed together.

"I see." His lips twitched upward.

Shelby quickly asked, "What brings you to Provo, Cameron?"

How could her voice sound so calm when she was exploding inside at the very sight of him? It was torture. The very man she had dreamed of night and day for the last two months was actually sitting here in her living room. The one person she longed for but hadn't known if she would ever see again. *What do I say? How do I act?* She had no idea what his purpose in coming was. If he were here just to drop by to say hello, then she couldn't reveal the way her heart ached for him.

"I'm in town for . . . uh, business." He fidgeted slightly and glanced at Shelby.

Opting for sincerity, Shelby said, "It's good to see you, Cameron."

His eyes locked with hers, trying to communicate the words he couldn't speak. "It's good to see you too." He paused and then added, "I've missed you."

For a moment the roommates were forgotten. All that existed was that intangible cord tautly holding one to the other. Unspoken thoughts sparked across the room like an electric current, jolting the heart and senses. Breathing became difficult.

"I've missed you too, Cam." Shelby gulped, ignoring the ridiculous, gaping expressions on her roommates' faces. "You look great," she found herself saying. "Have you recovered completely?"

"Recovered from what?" the roommates asked noisily, bringing attention to the fact that they were still in the room.

Cam said, "I had a little run-in with a mountain while Shelby was up in Montana." He laughed sheepishly, and the electric blue of his eyes caused more currents to race through Shelby's frame. "But I'm fine now," he finished, still looking directly at her.

Shelby smiled tenderly. "I'm so glad to see you're better."

Suddenly, Sara stood up and asked if Cameron would like some pop. As if on cue, Amanda stood up too, adding that they had some cookies in the kitchen.

"No thanks," Cam responded politely, but Sara and Amanda had already made it into the kitchen. "Actually, I really should be going."

When he stood, Shelby came to her feet. Feeling an intense panic, she couldn't keep her eyes off of him. *Going? You just got here! Please don't go!*

"Shelby," he said seriously, "I was wondering if . . ." His gaze shifted from the kitchen back to Shelby as he rubbed his chin hesitantly. "Could I talk to you outside for a minute?"

Her heart flip-flopped. "Yes, of course."

She led the way outside, where she found his red truck parked in front of the apartment complex. Just seeing his truck there brought back a flood of pleasurable memories. It was a reminder of Montana, a tangible connection, just as much so as the man walking beside her so quietly. An ache grew in Shelby's chest when she saw the dent and scratches on the truck, but she turned to face him.

Both hearts raced as they gazed at each other, completely spellbound. Then Cameron raised a hand to her cheek. "I've wanted to see you for so long . . ."

Shelby could hardly believe what she was hearing. A surge of emotion swelled within, and her eyes filled with tears. "Oh, Cam," she sniffled, "I was so worried about you."

Then she was in his arms breathing in the heavenly pine scent of his shirt collar. He held her as if he would never let her go. With his lips against her hair, he choked out the words, "We need to talk."

When Shelby pulled back slightly, she saw the emotion in his face. "When?"

"Are you busy this evening?" he asked, almost pleading. She shook her head to say no. "Would it be okay if I picked you up around four o'clock?"

"That would be great." She impulsively smiled through a tear.

"Really?" His mouth curved upward.

She nodded. *Oh yeah, this is more than great!*

"Is four too early?"

"No, I'll be ready." Conscious of her soggy state, she said, "I'm sorry I'm getting you all wet."

"I don't care." He still held her, not wanting to leave. But finally he released her and took a step backwards. "I'll see you in a couple hours, then."

He walked to his truck, climbed in, and rolled down the window to say good-bye.

Shelby waved. "See you then."

He lifted his hand to wave back and then drove away, leaving Shelby to stare after him in joyful wonder until long after he was out of sight.

Chapter 27

"What did he want?" Amanda squealed like an overly excited poodle.

"What is going on, Shelby?" was Sara's slowly-enunciated response. "A *lot* more must have happened in Montana than you told us!"

Shelby had barely stepped foot in the door when her roommates had launched their attack for answers. Amanda, of course, wanted to know every juicy detail, while Sara pressed for facts.

Shelby clutched her hands together and pressed them to her face. She was speechless. And yet her heart felt like it would burst into joyful arias. She wasn't sure what had just happened or what would happen this afternoon. All she knew was that her world had turned from hopelessness to thrilling anticipation.

"Shelby Hamlin, talk to us!" Sara's voice cut into her thoughts. "Is *he* the reason you're not engaged?"

Shelby breathed deeply and then peeked around her hands. "Not entirely . . ."

"What's that supposed to mean?" Sara laughed.

"We became good friends in Montana . . ."

Amanda said dreamily, "He's in love with you, Shelby. Did you see the way he looked at you?"

Extremely interested, Shelby grinned and asked, "How did he look at me?"

"Like he could eat you up!"

Shelby's cheeks warmed to a rosy glow.

"Why won't you tell us what really happened?" Sara asked with as much concern as hurt. "We're your friends. We care about you. Please tell us!"

Shelby wandered over to the sofa and sat down where Cameron had sat. "I don't really know where to begin. It's all so complicated. I had convinced myself that marrying Brad was what I needed. You know—find Mr. Right, temple marriage, family, everything! But even before Montana I'd been having these feelings that something wasn't right. That really scared me."

"You never said anything!"

"I know. I was just confused. I didn't want anything to get in the way of my goal for a temple marriage . . ."

"But you started to like Brad's brother," Amanda filled in.

"As a friend. Well, maybe more than a friend. There was just something always there between us. It grew into more and more until one night—" Shelby dropped her head in her open palms and sighed heavily.

Amanda couldn't take it. "One night, *what*?"

"We were dancing at a Church dance and things were getting—well, he suddenly left me on the dance floor. I shouldn't have followed him outside . . ."

Sara and Amanda waited expectantly, their eyes wide open.

"Brad found us when Cameron was kissing me."

Two jaws dropped.

"Yeah, it was pretty bad. Brad went crazy and punched Cameron. It was awful."

"The kiss was awful? Or the fight?" Amanda asked.

Shelby laughed aloud. "No, the kiss was . . ." She could only shake her head. "There are no words. It was heaven. So I'm completely at a loss. Here's Brad," she said, holding up her left hand, "who seems perfect, but I don't love him like I should." Now holding up her right hand, she continued, "Then there's a brother who knocks my socks off but isn't very eligible."

"Why isn't he eligible?" they asked together.

"There are a few issues, but the main one is that he isn't active in the Church." Shelby put her head back in her hands again, and her roommates wrapped her on either side into caring arms. They knew exactly how important that was to Shelby. "But I'm crazy about him . . ."

* * *

Later, as Shelby showered, the adrenaline began setting in. This evening she'd be with Cam! While getting ready, she wondered if this was a date or if they would just talk. A few doubts began seeping their way into her mind. It was completely possible that he only wanted to apologize about the night at the dance, given that they hadn't seen each other since then. Not while he was conscious, anyway.

But what if his intentions were more serious? She thought about the way he had said, "We need to talk." Her stomach fluttered at the idea of being with Cameron in a romantic setting. But how would she stay true to her ideals? She couldn't settle for anything less than—*Never mind all that; he's probably not here for anything more than a friendly visit, so don't get worked up!*

With her hair wrapped in a towel, Shelby hurried through her makeup routine. Then she started blow-drying her hair, examining herself critically in the bathroom mirror. Sara popped her head inside the door to offer her nicest sterling silver bracelet, which Shelby accepted gratefully. In her bedroom, she tried on three outfits but still couldn't decide what to wear. Within minutes Amanda walked up, her hands extended, holding out two sweaters. Shelby knew they were Amanda's prized wardrobe items.

"Would either of these work for you? Just pick, and it's yours for the day."

One was black with a zip-up front. The other was peach-colored with lettuce-edge ruffles on the sleeves. Shelby opted for the peach one with a fretful "Thank you."

When she was finally finished doing her hair, having slightly curled the ends, Shelby put on the denim jeans she had worn with Cam a few times in Montana. *Now for shoes.* She didn't know if they would be going somewhere nice, out for a walk, or just a drive. First she tried on a pair of pretty, thin-strapped sandals, then her sneakers, and finally chose a pair of loafers.

Feeling like a nervous wreck, she stood fanning herself with a manila file folder left on the kitchen table and tried to convince herself to calm down. *I'm making more out of this than I should! He might only say he's sorry about everything that happened and then leave for Montana, never to see me again.*

But if that happened, Shelby knew her heart would break all over again. She had to see him after today. But how could she justify such desires when he wasn't the faith-centered, unshakable, testimony-bearing kind of guy?

"What am I going to do?" she moaned out loud as she sank into a chair.

Amanda, overhearing her from the back room, called out, "You're gonna have a blast, that's what you're going to do! Man, Shelby, I wish I were in your shoes. I thought Brad was something, but this Cameron is gorgeous!"

"Yeah, he's definitely that. He's also a very nice person." She checked the clock. "Oh no, I only have ten minutes!" Shelby leapt out of the chair and ran to look in the mirror. Mascara not streaked, lipstick on, teeth cleaned . . . "I'm so nervous!"

When the doorbell rang, Shelby's heart felt like it slammed up to the ceiling before it made a dead drop to the floor. Trying to breathe evenly, she gripped the edge of the bathroom counter and stared into the porcelain sink as if fascinated by the little scratches near the drain. She was vaguely aware of Sara saying something in a nervous whisper to Amanda and footsteps slowly approaching the front door.

Then his voice.

"Hi. Is Shelby home?"

"Umm, I think she is. Come on in, and I'll see where she is."

I think she is? Why is Amanda acting so nonchalant? As if she didn't know I was having a panic attack back here!

Muffled footsteps were followed by a whisper at her side. "Shelby?"

She flinched back at the tap on her shoulder and looked up at her roommates.

They mouthed the words, "He's here," while pointing their fingers in exaggerated movements toward the front room.

This is ridiculous! Just stay calm! Remembering she had said those same words the first night she had run into Cameron didn't seem to help.

Amanda left with a wink and walked back to the front room. "She'll be out in a minute."

Even Cameron's deep-voiced "thanks" could set the butterflies off inside. She inhaled deeply, grabbed her purse from her bedroom, and walked out to meet him.

"Hi, Cameron," she managed to say.

He stood instantly when he heard her voice. "Hi." He stared back, the azure light in his eyes flickering. "You look . . . beautiful."

"Thank you." She blushed.

Entranced, he forgot to say "You're welcome." Shelby caught Sara and Amanda rolling their eyes. *Okay, so we're not having a profound conversation.* But more things passed between them than mere words. Cameron's eyes swept over her appreciatively, taking in the tantalizing gold of her hair sweeping over the peach sweater. And she observed how stylish his khaki pants and blue flannel shirt looked together. She realized that no matter what he wore, he always exuded an air of ruggedness as well as dignity.

He broke the silence. "Ready to go?"

She nodded with a grin. He extended his hand, his eyes never leaving her face. Shelby slipped her hand into his warm grasp, and they headed outside. As he helped her into the truck, a flood of memories washed over her. It was so strange to be repeating things here in Provo that they had done together in Montana.

"I packed us a picnic dinner," Cameron said after climbing in on his side. "I hope that's okay with you."

"It's perfect."

"Nothing like my mom's cooking, of course."

She smiled. "Anything you brought will be great, Cam."

He drove away from campus and headed north. Shelby thought he seemed very comfortable driving around town.

She asked, "Where are we going?"

"If I can find my way, I wanted to go up Provo Canyon to a spot Brad told me about."

Shelby nearly choked as her heart slammed against her rib cage. "You've seen Brad?"

"Yep," he smiled with a twinkle in his eye. "Yesterday."

She could only stare back incredulously. Did they fight again? What happened? Did they make peace? There were no apparent battle wounds.

"Don't worry, no black eyes this time."

He was grinning roguishly, making her heart skip a beat. If there had been a fight he wouldn't be grinning like that. Something was going on.

"Shelby . . . ?"

"Yes?"

"I have wanted to tell you something for a long time." The tone in his voice made her skin tingle. "I never had the chance before you left . . . I mean, I was in the hospital, so I couldn't really tell you . . . but ever since I came home from the hospital I've wanted to say that . . ."

Shelby leaned forward slightly, waiting anxiously for his next words.

"I truly am sorry for what happened the night of the dance. I should never have kissed you like that, and I am so sorry about the fight with Brad. I know it was embarrassing for you, and I would do anything to be able to erase the terrible memories of that whole night."

"Cameron, wait. It wasn't your fault. And besides," she trailed off, adding rather daringly, "the memories aren't all bad."

His head spun to look at her hopefully. "They aren't?"

"No." She blushed as he comprehended the implication.

She wanted to know what he was thinking and feeling and had to force herself not to turn away like she tended to. Not that she knew exactly what she would do once she found out. All she knew was that powerful feelings were surging through her in the presence of the man who had kissed her one night a couple months ago.

Cameron became quiet as he pulled off the right side of the road where there was a small gravel parking area overlooking the Provo River. He turned off the engine, draped one arm over the steering wheel, and turned to face Shelby. There was only a small space separating them.

"Shelby," he began. "Are you sure you're not mad at me?"

"No, of course not."

"What about Brad?"

"What *about* him?"

"Do you still love him? You must want to get back together with him."

Shelby answered quietly, "Brad isn't the one I want to marry."

A sudden shadow passed over his eyes. "Is there . . . someone else now?"

How should she answer a question like that? *Yes, you dummy, it's you!* Shelby merely shook her head.

Cameron thought for a moment. "So there aren't any nice little return missionaries ready to hunt me down with flying fists if you spend the day with me?"

She chuckled. "No, I don't think so."

"That's good."

He jumped out of the truck and hurried around to get Shelby's door. She watched him through the front windshield in wonder. He was a feast for her hungry eyes. How she had missed him! And here he was, wanting to spend the day with her. She wanted to savor this time with the one man who had possessed her every thought for so long. It was like a tremendous offering had been presented to a starving soul who could only relish in the moment and not think beyond it.

The canyon was ablaze with vivid fall colors intensified by the late afternoon sun. They walked over a carpet of leaves to the edge of the river, where they found a large fallen tree trunk to sit on. There were a few other sightseers around the area, but where they sat it was completely secluded. Bright yellow leaves silently floated down to the water's surface and drifted away. The only sound they heard came from the river wandering leisurely down its path of rocks and moss. A fiery, salmon-red maple tree covered them in speckles of sunlight and shade.

Cameron scooped up a handful of small rocks. "So . . . how have you been, Shelby?" He plucked a few rocks out of his hand and tossed them into the meandering current.

She smiled halfheartedly. "I've been all right."

He threw the rest of the rocks into the river and then turned toward her. "I mean how have you *really* been?"

It was difficult to look him in the eye. She was sure he could see right through her. "I guess I've been sort of . . . lonely."

He nodded but let her continue.

"I tried writing to my mom like you suggested."

"What happened?" he asked hopefully. "Did she write back?"

Shelby nodded, hiding the lump in her throat. "She did. She wrote back to tell me that she doesn't think she can forgive me and that I have to leave the Church if I want to see her again."

Cameron's voice conveyed his dismay. "Shelby, I'm so sorry. I know how much that must have crushed you."

Seeing the tenderness and compassion in his eyes, she looked away and blinked several times, hoping she wouldn't fall apart. When her emotions were back under control, she turned back to him and shrugged. "I tried, right?"

Cameron wanted to wrap her in his arms, to take away all her pain. He also felt undeniable fury toward Shelby's mother for inflicting such wounds on someone he loved. "She has no idea what she's missing, what happiness she denies herself by not being with you. You are a treasure, Shelby. And someday she will comprehend what she has tossed aside and lost."

Shelby surprised him by laughing slightly. "You're like a knight in shining armor, here to rescue me and make me feel better with all those flattering words."

"I meant everything I said. You *are* a treasure, Shelby, and I'm so sorry you've been hurting. I wish I could do something."

"You know, that's how I felt when you told me about Camille. It made me so mad I could have punched her in the nose."

Suddenly, Cameron laughed too. "Ah, yes, my fierce little warrior." He wrapped an arm around her, remembering. Shelby leaned against him, feeling that he knew her better than anyone ever had or ever would. Being with him felt so natural, so . . . right.

"And what about you?" she asked. "How have you been?"

Cameron didn't want to move too fast. But he wanted to be completely honest. "I've been wondering if I would ever get to see you again."

She smiled. "I wondered the same about you."

"You know," he said, his voice now gravelly, "there's something else I wanted to tell you."

Shelby instantly found it difficult to draw breath. "What?"

He tossed a few more rocks in the water before he spoke. "I just wanted you to know how much I enjoyed the time we spent together in Montana. I felt like we became . . . close friends." He looked at her intently. "I wondered if . . . we could still be friends?"

Taking a deep breath, she said, "I hope we'll always be friends, Cam. But there's something I need to understand." Shelby paused to take courage. There was so much she needed to find out, needed to ask him, that it was hard to know where to begin.

"What is it?" Cameron's voice held a note of worry.

"First of all, who is Kerri?"

His eyes opened wide. "Kerri Mullins?"

Shelby nodded.

He rubbed a hand along his jaw. "She's just an old friend."

"But wasn't she your date at the barn dance?"

Cameron hung his head down. "No, not exactly." Shelby waited for him to explain. "I asked her to come with me." He raked one hand through his hair and shifted uncomfortably on the tree trunk. "She was . . . She was just my defense against you."

"I don't get it."

He took in a deep breath. "Kerri's engaged to a friend of mine. We were all buddies growing up. I was never interested in her. But I begged her to come with me to the dance so it would look like I was—happy or something, instead of wishing I was in Brad's place with you."

Cameron looked at her sheepishly, and Shelby's mouth curved into a small smile. "I saw the picture of you and Kerri in your room."

He almost laughed. "A juvenile move on my part. I knew you'd be using my room and found that picture to make it look like I was interested in her. I was trying so hard not to give myself away."

"But . . . why didn't you ever call me after I left Montana? You never answered my letter to at least tell me you were all right."

"I thought of nothing else but you! But as far as your letter goes . . . Unfortunately, I didn't get it until last week."

"What?" Shelby cried out incredulously. "I left it right there—"

"Old Lady Brown found it in the hospital and decided to take it—out of the kindness of her heart, her Christian duty, and all that."

"You've got to be kidding!" she fumed.

"I suspect she was trying to protect *you* . . . from *me*."

"Aughhhh!" she bolted up and turned away from him, angrily crossing her arms against her chest. An onslaught of emotions came over her. *How dare she interfere like that! All this time wondering why he never called, thinking he didn't want to see me—and* she *had it!*

Cameron stood and came up behind her. He slipped his hands up her forearms and gently pulled her against him. "Shelby . . ." he whispered against her ear. "Do you have any idea what your letter meant to me? More than anything, I want you in my life." He turned her around to face him, and her eyes filled with moisture. Cupping her cheeks with his warm hands, he said, "I love you, Shelby Hamlin."

A tear slid down her cheek. But she smiled. "I love *you*, Cameron."

Then he was kissing her, over and over until she trembled weakly against him. She felt the warmth of his breath on her mouth, her cheek, and the soft curve of her jaw. His hands wove into her hair as his lips claimed hers again. His heart spoke to hers, healing all the loneliness she had endured. She answered with an intensity that made him feel whole.

Then he wrapped her in the warmth of his arms and held her snugly against his chest, where she could feel the steady beat of his heart.

"I'm so sorry for all you've been through," he whispered into her hair.

"Cameron, it's *you* that's been through too much." She pressed her face against the soft blue flannel, listening to the steady beat of his heart. "But leaving you in the hospital was pretty awful. Having no idea if you were going to live or die, wondering if I'd ever see you again." Her voice became more impassioned. "Then finding you were well and never hearing from you . . . I waited and waited for an email or a phone call . . ." Choked up, she was unable to continue.

"Oh, Shelby . . ." he murmured tenderly. "I'm sorry." His warm hands stroked her hair as he pressed a kiss against the curve of her cheek. She lifted her head slightly to receive his lips upon her other cheek and then her forehead. With each kiss came the whispered breath of his love.

"It hurt so much to leave you . . ." she said in a ragged whisper.

He continued to rock her. "I'm here now."

"And I don't want you to leave. Ever!"

Cam groaned. "I don't know how I can leave you now." He held her to him so closely that she could hardly breathe.

"But you will. You have to go back to Montana, and I have to stay here. Where does that leave us? How can anything work if we aren't even near each other?"

Cameron said, "We'll figure things out."

She sighed. "There are some definite issues we need to resolve."

"I know. I'm not here to make any demands on you either. I just had to see you, to be sure how you feel, and to let you know that I love you. It's obvious I'm not all that Brad is—"

Shelby put her fingers over his lips to stop his words.

"No, it needs to be said." He kissed her fingertips but took her hand away. "I haven't been doing all that I should, I haven't been what I know I should be. And you deserve much better."

"Cam—"

"It's the truth. And if I don't get my life back in order, then I don't deserve your love."

Shelby lowered her head as fresh tears filled her eyes. There was truth in what he said. She could not give up what she knew was right—being married in the temple was the only way she would choose. A love like they felt for each other deserved to be sealed for eternity. If there was no hope for that, then they truly had no future. But Shelby was still fairly new to the gospel and didn't really know what was involved in becoming worthy again. Would it be a matter of weeks or a year-long repentance process? What if she wasn't worth all it would take?

"What are we going to do?" she asked.

Cam reached for her right hand and held it between his own. "It wouldn't be fair to ask you to wait—"

"I will!" Shelby cried. "I would do anything to have you."

She was instantly crushed in his embrace. "Do you know how much I love you?"

His words echoed Shelby's own longings. Her lips found their way instinctively to his. But this time his mouth covered hers hungrily, like a soldering heat that sent a spiral of sensations through her. His arms encircled her, pressing her closer. Through her sweater she could feel the heat of his hand against her back. His kisses became desperate, for he knew this moment couldn't last. Their time together would soon end, and they would be separated again.

Shelby clung to him, unable to bring him close enough. "I love you, Cam."

His answer was drowned by the groan that escaped his lips as he buried his face against the hollow of her neck. He thought about all the times in the past he had wanted to touch her, hold her in his arms, and kiss her. Not wanting to ever release her, yet knowing he must, Cameron drew back.

But Shelby held fast to him, unaware of his concern. She kissed his cheek where she knew his dimple was hiding; she kissed the cleft in his chin. He couldn't resist taking her lips again, unable to get enough of her sweet taste.

Finally, he pulled away, raking his fingers frantically through his hair. "I wasn't going to do this, I really wasn't . . . I know it's too soon, and you deserve so much more."

Cameron suddenly knelt on the grass in front of her, taking her hands between his own. "I have loved you from the moment I met you, Shelby Hamlin. You are my dream of forever. I'll do whatever it takes to share those eternal blessings with you. Will you marry me?"

Choking on her words through a mist of tears, Shelby answered, "Yes, Cam. Yes!"

Lowering his head to her lap, he let her knees dry his own tears as she wrapped her arms about him. Here at this moment, she knew that she had arrived at that haven she had been searching for all her life. She had more love now than she had ever dreamed of. This was home.

Epilogue

Lanterns lit the walkway that led to the front door of the cozy log bed and breakfast. Pine trees on either side glistened in the soft light. Potted pink and yellow tulips, mingled with purple pansies, nodded in the chilled nighttime breeze, welcoming the newcomers.

"I hope you like it here, Mrs. Thompson."

Relishing in the sound of her new name, Shelby kissed her husband boldly. Their suitcases clattered to the ground with a thud as Cameron returned the kisses of his new bride. Locked in an embrace, the newlyweds were startled when the heavy door suddenly opened. A short, plump woman in her late seventies greeted them with a twinkle in her eye.

"You must be the Thompsons."

Cameron grinned at the woman and, with arms still around his wife, announced proudly, "Yes, Cameron and Shelby Thompson."

"It's nice to meet you. I'm Doris Hopkins. Come on in, and make yourselves at home. You'll love it here. April is a lovely time for a honeymoon."

Cameron retrieved the fallen suitcases, and they followed the talkative woman inside. The pungent smells of pinewood and cinnamon wafted through the entryway. Around the corner was an inviting family room where brown leather sofas surrounded a fire that crackled in a large river-rock fireplace. A plate of home-baked cookies had been set out on the pine coffee table. A partially finished puzzle was spread out on a table beside a tall window that was sure to provide a spectacular view of the mountains in the daytime.

"There are always cookies set out, so eat all you like. Hot chocolate too. There's a hot tub with towels on the deck outside, and over here is the dining room. Tomorrow we'll be serving stuffed raspberry French toast with bacon and sausages. Now, if you'll follow me upstairs, I'll show you where your room is."

Following closely behind Mrs. Hopkins, Cameron sent Shelby loving messages in every glance, causing her heart to turn over in response. From the moment they arrived at the temple this morning, through the end of the small reception, she had felt this day was like a piece of heaven on earth. They had been showered with love and affection, and their joy was full.

"Here's the honeymoon suite," Mrs. Hopkins was saying as she held the door open for the two of them to pass through. "You have a private bathroom right through here, and this is the door to your own deck."

"Thank you," they said at the same time.

"It's a beautiful room," Shelby added, noticing the handmade patchwork quilt on the bed and lace curtains in the windows. A vase of delicate spring wildflowers rested on the dresser beside a pitcher of water and a dish of gourmet chocolates.

"If there's anything you need, just let us know. Breakfast will be served around nine in the morning, but come down whenever you're ready." Mrs. Hopkins turned to leave. "Oh, by the way, we leave the front door unlocked so our guests can come and go whenever it's convenient."

"Thanks again, Mrs. Hopkins." Cameron held the door open as she left their room and then closed the door softly behind her.

When he turned to look at Shelby on the other side of the room, she swallowed, suddenly feeling very much the innocent bride that she was. Sensing her uneasy thoughts, he opened the door to their private deck.

"Would you like to sit under the stars for a few minutes?" he asked with tenderness.

Shelby let out her breath, not realizing that she'd been holding it in. "I'd love to."

She walked onto the deck with Cameron, where they found a porch swing to sit on. Snuggling up against him, Shelby rested her head against his shoulder and marveled at the love she felt for this man, her husband.

"Did you enjoy your wedding day, love?" Cameron asked, his chin resting on top of her head, his fingers stroking the hair she had curled.

"It was the best day of my life."

"I've never seen anything so beautiful in *my* life than the way you looked today."

Shelby kissed him tenderly. "And I about melted when I saw you in your tux."

"You know what? My sister will finally be able to breathe again," Cameron chuckled.

Shelby closed her eyes for a moment, thinking about the day. Laura had definitely not been able to wipe the grin off her face; she was so happy for them. So were Millie and Karl. Cameron's grandparents, aunts and uncles, had all been there as well, welcoming her into the family. She thought about Tara, Jared, and Brandon running around rambunctiously with their cousins. *I love my new family!* There had been several ward members from Bozeman that Shelby had come to know, including Rose Blackburn, which had made her very happy. And even though Brad couldn't make it—since he was getting settled in San Francisco—he'd been considerably forgiving after all that had happened. Shelby knew it had hurt him to tell her she'd be a wonderful sister-in-law. *Always the gentleman to the end.*

Altogether, it had been a perfect day. Well, almost perfect. If only her mother could have been there. But Shelby had a peaceful feeling that someday Grace Hamlin would come around.

Cameron laughingly asked, "Did you notice what Tara was doing all night?"

"Yeah, she kept snitching the mints out of her basket and wouldn't let anyone else have any!"

"Until Bruce chewed her out for not doing her job." When their laughter subsided, Cameron kissed the smooth skin of her cheek, filling her with warmth she could melt into.

"Cam?" she sighed.

"Hmm . . . ?" he asked distractedly, his lips tracing the contours of her face.

"Thank you for the small reception. It was exactly what I wanted."

"I'm glad." His kisses trailed lower along her jaw. "I hope you'll like going into Yellowstone for our honeymoon. I can hardly wait to show you everything."

Shelby sighed contentedly. "I know I'll love it. I feel like I'm living in a beautiful dream. I'm so excited to finish nursing school at MSU and to live in Bozeman. I've loved it here from the very first, you know. It's always felt like home."

Brushing her curls over her shoulders, he placed one kiss at the back of her neck. "Shelby . . . there's something that I'd like to do together as soon as we get back."

"What's that?"

"I'd like to start looking for our first home. A small, white house with a big front porch. We'll plant lilacs and roses and anything else that reminds you of your Grandma Hamlin."

She turned in Cameron's arms to face him. "Oh, Cam, thank you! I love you so much. Grandma would have loved you too!"

"I love you, Shelby Thompson. Forever."

All inhibitions vanished in their kiss. Heaven's light shone down as Shelby was lifted into the cradle of his arms and carried inside, never to be alone again.

About the Author

Jeanette Miller was born in northern California but spent most of her childhood in Guatemala, Puerto Rico, and Costa Rica, where her father worked. She cherishes her experiences of living in Latin America. In her teenage years, she dreamed of becoming a teacher and a published author. Jeanette attended Brigham Young University, where she earned a degree in Elementary Education. After graduating, she taught third grade for four years in the Spanish Immersion program. There, she enjoyed writing and directing plays for her students.

As a young mother, Jeanette started writing in moments snatched between changing diapers and making peanut butter sandwiches—or whenever her nose wasn't in a book. She loves all things Jane Austen and Charlotte Brontë's Jane Eyre. When Jeanette isn't reading a novel in this genre, she's watching their movie equivalents. She also loves scapbooking, designing jewelry, and eating chocolate. She would love to travel all over the world someday. Jeanette and her husband, Michael, have six children. They live in Pleasant Grove, Utah.